D0174343

"Did you have a nice ... Daddy?"

Finn grimaced.

"He did," Kendall reassured his daughter. She reached up and patted Finn's cheek—his scars. "He can be a bear sometimes, can't he, Lizzie? But we find cranky old bears cuddly."

Cranky old bears? Cuddly?

Lizzie giggled.

Finn thought he should look in the mirror, if only to see for himself what Kendall saw, because his self-image didn't jibe with cuddly old bears.

Kendall disappeared into the tack room. Finn was tempted to follow her and ask her to take another good, long look at him. His wasn't a face that inspired women to cuddle. And if his disfigurement didn't scare her off...

I'd what?

Finn shook himself. This was trouble. Plain and simple. *She* was trouble. The Monroe princess was only looking to brush up on her cowgirl skills. She wasn't looking for a broken man like him...

Dear Reader,

Life is never a straight road, is it? Adulting comes with hard trade-offs. Nurturing a family and other relationships takes time. Earning that paycheck and planning for the future take time. And just when you think you've got it all figured out, life throws you a curveball and all your plans go out the window.

Finn McAfee assumed his life was on track. Marriage, children, running the family ranch with the support of his parents and sister. But now his wife is gone, his parents and sister have moved away, and the weight of keeping the family ranching legacy alive is on his shoulders alone. As for media manager and public relations whiz Kendall Monroe, she loved her big city, corporate life. Until she was let go. She's finally figured out what she wants to do next, but now life has thrown her another wrinkle. Both Finn and Kendall need to pivot. But what choices will they make, and how will those decisions impact their chance at a future together?

I enjoyed writing Finn and Kendall's romance, balancing the serious with lighthearted moments and a lot of foster animals (such cuteness!). I hope you come to love The Mountain Monroes as much as I do. Each book is connected but also stands alone. Happy reading!

Melinda

HEARTWARMING

Healing the Rancher

—

Melinda Curtis

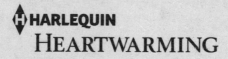

If you purchased this book without a cover you should be aware that this book is stolen property. It was reported as "unsold and destroyed" to the publisher, and neither the author nor the publisher has received any payment for this "stripped book."

HARLEQUIN®
HEARTWARMING™

Recycling programs
for this product may
not exist in your area.

ISBN-13: 978-1-335-42675-8

Healing the Rancher

Copyright © 2022 by Melinda Wooten

All rights reserved. No part of this book may be used or reproduced in any manner whatsoever without written permission except in the case of brief quotations embodied in critical articles and reviews.

This is a work of fiction. Names, characters, places and incidents are either the product of the author's imagination or are used fictitiously. Any resemblance to actual persons, living or dead, businesses, companies, events or locales is entirely coincidental.

For questions and comments about the quality of this book, please contact us at CustomerService@Harlequin.com.

Harlequin Enterprises ULC
22 Adelaide St. West, 41st Floor
Toronto, Ontario M5H 4E3, Canada
www.Harlequin.com

Printed in U.S.A.

Award-winning *USA TODAY* bestselling author **Melinda Curtis**, when not writing romance, can be found working on a fixer-upper she and her husband purchased in Oregon's Willamette Valley. Although this is the third home they've lived in and renovated (in three different states), it's not a job for the faint of heart. But it's been a good metaphor for book writing, as sometimes you have to tear things down to the bare bones to find the core beauty and potential. In between, and during, renovations, Melinda has written over thirty books for Harlequin, including her Heartwarming book *Dandelion Wishes*, which is now a TV movie, *Love in Harmony Valley*, starring Amber Marshall.

Brenda Novak says *Season of Change* "found a place on my keeper shelf."

Jayne Ann Krentz says of *Can't Hurry Love*, "Nobody does emotional, heartwarming small-town romance like Melinda Curtis."

Sheila Roberts says *Can't Hurry Love* is "a page turner filled with wit and charm."

Books by Melinda Curtis

The Mountain Monroes

Charmed by the Cook's Kids
The Littlest Cowgirls
A Cowgirl's Secret
Caught by the Cowboy Dad

Return of the Blackwell Brothers

The Rancher's Redemption

The Blackwell Sisters

Montana Welcome

Visit the Author Profile page at Harlequin.com for more titles.

THE MOUNTAIN MONROES FAMILY TREE

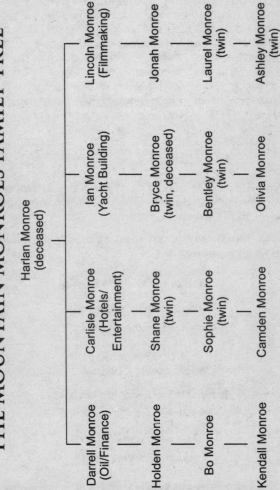

Harlan Monroe
(deceased)

Darrell Monroe
(Oil/Finance)

- Holden Monroe
- Bo Monroe
- Kendall Monroe

Carlisle Monroe
(Hotels/
Entertainment)

- Shane Monroe
  (twin)
- Sophie Monroe
  (twin)
- Camden Monroe

Ian Monroe
(Yacht Building)

- Bryce Monroe
  (twin, deceased)
- Bentley Monroe
  (twin)
- Olivia Monroe

Lincoln Monroe
(Filmmaking)

- Jonah Monroe
- Laurel Monroe
  (twin)
- Ashley Monroe
  (twin)

PROLOGUE

I CAN RIDE the creek trail faster than you!

Nine-year-old Kendall Monroe had told her two older brothers that last night after they'd boasted about their race times at dinner. This summer, she'd decided she wasn't going to be left behind or counted out because she was little. And she wasn't going to stick to horses who were nags. Monroes were tough. She wanted to prove it.

I can ride the creek trail faster than you!

She was eating those words now.

Kendall trudged toward the pasture gate, where her father's runaway horse stood waiting for her, reins dangling to the ground, hooves caked in mud. Kendall didn't look much better. Her shirt was untucked, one sleeve torn and her boots muddy. The closer Kendall got to the gate, the more the tears threatened to return.

Do not cry.

Holden and Bo would never let her forget it. As if on cue, her two older brothers came out of the barn on the other side of the fence, spotted her and started to laugh. Their laughter undercut her pride until she felt small and useless and wanted to go home.

Home was thousands of miles away in Philadelphia in a grand mansion that made the ranch in Texas seem shabby.

Ginger, the old ranch hand who was in charge of the Monroe kids this summer, strode out of the barn with that bowlegged gait of hers and a scowl. "What in the world…"

Chin thrust in the air, Kendall snatched Brandy's reins and stifled a groan of pain.

Her backside hurt where she'd fallen. And that wasn't all. Her body ached all over. It hurt just to reach for the reins. Plus, her forearm was scraped and it stung, along with a welt on her palm where a fire ant had bitten her. She'd lost her cowboy hat and her nose felt like it was getting sunburned, despite it being early in the morning. The Texas summer sun was as cruel as the creek trail.

"That horse better not be injured." Ginger opened the gate and took Brandy's reins. "I can tell from the way you look that you did something foolish. I don't care if you do something foolish on foot but leave the horses out of it." She led the mare away.

Kendall shut the gate.

That's when her older brothers closed in.

"Where did you fall? Jumping the creek, I bet." Holden laughed. He was fifteen and a stick-in-the-mud, practically perfect in the eyes of the family and, unlike Kendall, was transitioning easily from life in Philadelphia to summers in Texas. "You can't just *look* like you're a good rider, Ken. You have to work at it."

She sucked her lips into her mouth, trying not to say a word. Or worse, sob, because tears backed up in her throat thicker than too much peanut butter on a dry cracker.

"I bet you got dumped at Rattlesnake Bend." Bo was thirteen and found everything Kendall did amusing. He grinned at her. "Wow, Ken. Were you dragged through the creek bed?"

She had been, although thankfully not far before her boot slipped free of the stirrup. Still, Kendall refused to answer Bo. She needed a shower, a clean set of clothes and a hug, not teasing or laughter at her expense.

Mom appeared on the front porch, looking like she was headed into town, what with her high heels and high hair.

"Don't tell Mom you fell," Holden whispered, leaning closer. "We're supposed to be watching out for you."

"And don't you dare cry." Bo turned, facing

Kendall as he walked backward toward the house. "You were warned. Ginger told you to practice more in the arena before gallivanting around."

Kendall hated practicing, if only because she was the youngest and everyone was quick to point out how unskilled she was.

"I can't wait to tell the Monroe cousins." Bo was absolutely gleeful. "They're coming tonight."

Nine more kids to tease me? Ugh.

Mom caught sight of them and gasped. "Kendall! Are you okay?"

"Ye-e-es." Kendall plodded forward, trying once more not to cry.

When she reached the front porch, her mother did a quick examination—feeling Kendall's head for bumps, holding out her arms to check for wounds and bruises, gently prodding her ant bite. "You're showing some wear and tear," Mom said finally and with a sigh. "But I think you'll live." Mom drew Kendall into a make-it-better hug that didn't judge.

The tears came then.

"What's this?" Grandpa Harlan opened the screen door, a concerned expression on his tanned, wrinkled face.

"This…" Mom stood, placing one hand on Kendall's shoulder. "This is a strong young woman. Someday, she'll be one of the most important Monroes. She'll do important things. I can't wait."

Kendall nearly burst with pride. She scrubbed away her tears.

Grandpa Harlan nodded. "She's tough, that one. Full of potential."

"That she is." Taking Kendall's hand, Mom led the way to the bathroom, where she ran a hot bath and brought Kendall clean clothes. She didn't lecture. She didn't hover. But she was there in case Kendall needed another hug, which she did.

Later that morning, Kendall stood inside the living room, watching her brothers riding in the arena.

Grandpa Harlan came to stand next to her, smelling like he'd just finished smoking a cigar. He looked into Kendall's eyes. His gentle smile was framed by bushy gray sideburns that ended halfway down his chin. "Are you still mad at the boys for teasing you?"

Kendall shrugged because even at nine she knew the teasing was just the half of it, but she wasn't quite sure what the other half that upset her was.

"You know, being family involves a little sacrifice and a little forgiving, and that includes forgiving yourself." Her grandfather spoke in a low voice meant just for her.

And she knew… She knew there was more to what he was telling her. But she didn't get it. Her body hurt and her feelings hurt—all because of the horse and her brothers. What had she done that she needed to forgive herself?

"Give yourself time," Grandpa Harlan said, further complicating his message as he added, "Do you know the secret to my success?"

Kendall shook her head, taking note of her grandfather's faded checked shirt and his worn blue jeans. "Is it because you don't buy fast cars?" She'd heard her father say that once.

His smile spread. "No."

Kendall peeked out to where the boys were riding in circles with Ginger shouting instructions from the center of the arena. She sighed. Circles were boring, Ginger was too strict and Kendall had no idea how her grandfather had become a gazillionaire. "Is it because you bought a lot of houses?" She'd heard her uncle say that once.

"No." Grandpa Harlan chuckled. "My secret is knowing how to pick myself up after things don't work out…with a smile. I don't let my pride get in the way." He bent until his face was level with hers, placing his hands on his knees. "I've never done anything perfect the first time around." He gave the ends of Kendall's long black hair a gentle tug, before turning his head and glancing outside.

He's gonna make me get back on a horse!

Kendall grabbed hold of her grandfather's bushy sideburns and brought him back to face her. "I'm not going riding again." Because she may only be nine, but she knew what talks alone with Grandpa Harlan meant—you had to forget about whatever bad had just happened and try again. "I'm done with horses and mud and—" her throat nearly closed "—being laughed at."

He covered her hands with his, still smiling. "Being good at something takes practice. And if you stumble—"

"*Or fall*, they'll laugh at me." Kendall slid her hands free and leaned on the windowsill. "I don't like being teased."

That was it. From now on, she was going to be perfect.

CHAPTER ONE

OF ALL HER adult female Monroe cousins, Kendall Monroe was the woman who most dearly loved a good pair of high heels. Sandals, preferably. Six inches, ideally. This year's latest release, for sure.

Oh, her cousin Laurel might have argued that as a fashion designer, she was in the running for the Monroe Most Likely to Keep Up Appearances. But since Laurel had taken up residence in a small, rural town in Idaho and had twins, and since Kendall still lived in downtown Philadelphia, she was going to assume the coveted title was now officially hers. Whoever held the title could opt out of nonholiday events held at the Monroe family ranch in Texas.

For the record, Kendall loathed the family ranch in Texas.

And dirt.

And creepy-crawlies.

Not to mention snakes, scorpions, larger-than-life fire ants, ornery horses who thought they knew more than she did and superior-minded relatives in cowboy hats who made perfection on horseback seem easy.

Seriously. Texas wasn't for Kendall, which meant ranching wasn't for Kendall. And on the whole, her Monroe siblings and cousins were fine with that.

So it was a surprise when she got a call from an unknown Texas number on her cell phone and heard the distinct South Texas twang on the other end of the line. "Did y'all know you're harder to track down than a fox on his nightly visit to the henhouse?"

"Uh… Who is this?" Kendall was walking in downtown Philadelphia as she'd tapped her earbud to answer, carrying two shopping bags filled with five pairs of shoes because there had been a sample sale at her favorite fashion designer's showroom.

Who could resist a boutique shoe sale? Not Kendall.

"This is Carol Connelly of the East Texas Connellys. You may have heard of us out at the C-Bar-C. We've got the largest herd of Gelbvieh in the West, which means our product has more demand than those computer chips people are so short of and—"

"Carol."

"—we've got a challenge ahead of us. We've

been presented with the opportunity to be the exclusive southern supplier of beef to—"

"Excuse me." Kendall paused at an intersection, waiting for the light to change. "Are you sure you have the right person? This is Kendall Monroe."

"Oh, darlin'." Carol chuckled. "You're the sweetest thing. Haven't you heard that women need to be more assertive? Of course, I was lookin' to connect with you, *Miss Kendall Monroe*. You're the one who posted all those fun photos and videos on social media with that boat-captain cousin of yours. Daddy thinks your campaign looked staged, but I told him no woman plans to take photos like that with bags under her eyes and lipstick smudged on her teeth." Another chuckle interrupted Carol's diatribe.

Slightly annoyed, Kendall ran her tongue over her front teeth as she crossed the street, moving from the shade of one high-rise into the muggy, September-afternoon sunshine.

She had indeed recently gone on a road trip with her cousin Olivia, a now-retired, sailboat-racing captain. She'd also taken photos and video of their girl trip and posted them online. But she'd done so to celebrate life with her cousin, not as any promotional campaign. And she'd had to be talked into lowering her guard when it came to polished appearances, not to mention reluctantly participating in activities she'd never have done otherwise, like mountain biking and jet-pack rides across the water. "Thanks for reaching out, Carol, but that doesn't explain why you've called me about Gilbert."

"Gelbvieh." Carol huffed a little. "I was under the impression that you knew about ranchin' and that I wouldn't need to be educatin' you."

"Gelbvieh. I assure you that I am educated." Kendall had a degree from Brown in communications and had spent the last ten years working in public relations for her family. She reached her car and stowed her purchases in the trunk, ready to escape the muggy heat and the blazing sunshine on this side of the street. "And I'm experienced."

"Good, because Daddy says we aren't hirin' no city slicker. He wants a real country girl to handle our biz-ness."

Across the street, a man in a truck slowed down, opened the vehicle's door and dropped a good-sized box at the curb, before driving off.

"Hey, don't do that!" Kendall shouted at the guy before sliding behind the wheel of her brand-new, leased coupe. The car had heated and air-conditioned seats, knew how to parallel-park itself and was quicker on the brake than she was.

"Are you talkin' to me?" Carol asked, all high on her horse.

"No. There was a guy littering." And Kendall was a Philly girl, after all. Folks from Philly weren't shy about calling out jerks. "You haven't said what your business is. And frankly, Carol, I'm not sure you can afford my retainer." Although Kendall wasn't sure what that should be. She hadn't worked for anyone except family. Ever.

But things had changed in the last year. Her Grandpa Harlan, the family patriarch and founder of many successful companies, had died and left his businesses to his four sons, the only condition being that they could no longer employ or financially support any of his grandchildren. Hello, unemployment and eviction. Goodbye, professional swagger. On a positive note, rumor in the family had it that the condition was only going to be for a year.

Hoping the rumor was true, Kendall had been living on savings and doing some unpaid social-media and public-relations work for her siblings and cousins. But now, her funds were running precariously low. She'd been think-ing it was time to branch out on her own and find a job elsewhere—hence the leased luxury car, recently updated wardrobe and new designer shoes. She'd wanted to live the leader look as she pitched her services to celebrities and companies on the East Coast.

A flap on the dropped box on the sidewalk moved.

Kendall kept her eye on it as she put her car into the mode to pull out of the space parallel to the curb between two delivery vans. The dashboard lit up and played a short musical interlude, reminiscent of a spa experience rather than the stress she associated with parallel parking and unparking.

Carol had been talking nonstop the entire time. "…and I don't think you understand how huge this opportunity is. Burger by the Layer is one of the fastest growin' gourmetburger chains in the country, and they credit that growth to their fun, grass-roots, socialmedia campaign. We need us one of those."

The box flap moved again. A white kitten cautiously inched its way out of the box.

Kendall hit the brakes and put the car in Park, front end jutting into the street. "Carol, there's a kitten. Hold that thought, will you?"

"A kitten? I thought some guy was litterin'."

"The jerk dumped the kitten." Kendall got out, crossed the street to the opposite sidewalk and picked up the little ball of fluff, who immediately clawed her way up Kendall's pink sweater and rooted her way to the hair behind Kendall's neck, trembling.

Farther up the road, someone honked, which for downtown Philly wasn't unusual.

Kendall paid the horn no mind and checked the box for more kittens, relieved to find it was empty. It was hot and she was ready to get back in her air-conditioned car, where she could figure out what to do with the kitten.

The horn blared again. This time closer. A city bus was approaching from one direction and…

Kendall turned around just as a huge semi-truck avoided the oncoming bus and sideswiped Kendall's front fender and continued on its way.

"My car!"

The kitten applied its claws to Kendall's neck as if afraid the truck was coming for it next.

People came out of buildings up and down the block. Someone was already on the phone with the police, and said, "Yes, I'd like to report a car accident."

"Kendall, are you okay? Was that crunching noise what I think it was?"

"Hit-and-run?" Kendall hadn't even taken

the license plate number. She wanted to cry. "I put less than a hundred miles on that car." She had hoped it would be her inner sanctum. And she hadn't taken that extra insurance in case the car was totaled. She was going to be out several thousand dollars, practically the last of her savings.

Kendall gently brought the kitten from behind her neck to beneath her chin, instinctively giving it a snuggle. "I'm sorry, Carol, you were saying?"

"Net-net, darlin', we trust a Texan with our business. Daddy knew your granddaddy and has been to your family's spread in these parts. He wants you to come out to the old homestead and stay a while. Not that he doesn't trust a Monroe." Carol tittered. "But he wants to make sure you know the front end of a steer from the back end."

"Are you…? Are you offering to hire me?" The kitten purred. "My fee is—"

"Daddy already talked to your cousin Shane Monroe, who gave him a ballpark retainer figure." Carol named a sum that was ridiculously high, ridiculously tempting and ridiculously needed, given the state of Kendall's car. "You just have to get on out here and ride the range with Daddy. He may be seventy, but he works the ranch like a young'un and he'll only do business with someone who'll do the same. He's having a little procedure done next week, but in two weeks or so he's gonna be back to managin' cattle and ridin' fence."

Work a ranch?

There'd be dirt and horses.

And paychecks.

Kendall glanced down at her expensive, black, six-inch heeled, cutaway pumps. "Can I get back to you?"

"Of course, honey. You were just in an accident. I'll get those chairs ready to put in the wagon and send you the particulars."

Kendall thanked her and hung up, not even trying to decipher the meaning of Carol's words. She lifted the kitten so she could look it in the eyes. "Well, Boo, after calls to a tow service and my insurance agent, it looks like the third person I need to call is my cousin Shane."

He had some explaining to do.

"START EXPLAINING, SHANE." Despite her opening, Kendall didn't give her cousin time to answer. "I don't need you interfering in my professional life. I'm a grown woman with a good business reputation." In some places. In others, she was known as being hard to work with, a stickler about standards, procedures and, above all, appearances. "I can handle my own career and find my own business opportunities. I'm more than just a pretty face, you know."

"I know."

Nearly two hours after her accident, Kendall was sitting in the back seat of a rideshare, along with her bags of recently purchased shoes (nonrefundable) and the white kitten (nonreturnable). Her beloved car was on its way to a scrapyard (nonsalvageable). And, if she was being honest with herself, her career was going there, as well.

She heaved a sigh of defeat. "Tell me everything about Carol Connelly and the C-Bar-C."

It didn't matter that she didn't want to work for the Connellys. Kendall needed this job, now more than ever. If only she could pass the old rancher's criteria.

"Did Carol reach out? I'm glad." Shane's voice crackled in her ear, cutting out slightly. "I meant to call earlier, but things have been busy here."

She didn't want to hear more of Shane's idyllic life in bucolic Second Chance, Idaho, where he'd found love with Franny Clark, owner of the Bucking Bull Ranch. All her cousins who lived there went on and on about it at every opportunity. "About Carol…"

"The only way the C-Bar-C is getting to supply Burger by the Layer with beef is if they create a fun social-media presence and add to the experience and reputation of the burger chain, hence their need for you. I know you can brush up on your cowboy skills and charm Mr. Connelly."

Sweat broke out on Kendall's forehead. Visions of being thrown from the saddle when she was nine came to mind, playing in slow motion and on a loop.

"With a little ranching refresher, you can bluff your way to a payday," Shane told her. "Buy some cowboy boots. Pick up a pair of leather work gloves. And then—"

"What? Scuff them up and make them look used?" Kendall huffed. "I don't need a crash course in ranching. I'm good at what I do." Capturing pictures and editing video into can't-take-your-eyes-off-it content. Writing post headers and blurbs to convey the right note of quality and heart. Creating press releases that made reporters and bloggers interested in featuring the companies and people she represented. "And I am who I am." A city girl through and through.

"They're not asking you to move in. They just want you to show up and—"

"Pretend to be a bona fide cowgirl. You

know I hate the Wild West." Heck, she wasn't even fond of Second Chance, the small town in Idaho she and her siblings had inherited. "Who's going to tutor me on ranching? You?" He'd gotten engaged to a rancher last spring, but Shane was far from a true cowboy.

"If I ask nice, Franny can help, although fall is a busy time at the Bucking Bull and—"

There was a loud bang. Some static. And then the line went dead.

"Shane? *Shane? Shane!*"

Boo stopped purring.

"Is everything all right?" her driver asked.

"No." Kendall tried calling her cousin back, stomach filled with dread when he didn't answer.

Because that bang sounded eerily like the moment earlier this afternoon when her car had been hit.

CHAPTER TWO

"DID YOU MAKE an appointment with the doctor, Finn?"

"No." Findlay McAfee grabbed a hay bale by its binding and carried it from the stack in the ranch yard into the barn. "Dr. Carlisle said the follow-up was optional."

His mother made a derisive sound. "That's not what she said." Her voice trembled through his phone's earbuds. "Dr. Carlisle said *recommended*. Don't gamble with your health."

"I'm not. They got everything during surgery a month ago, Mom." Finn hefted the hay bale onto the stack on the barn's lift platform.

"You, your father and me." Mom sounded like she'd choked back a sob. "That's all the reliable family Lizzie's got left since Jenny died." Lizzie being his daughter and Jenny his wife.

Finn leaned on the hay bale, hating that he was upsetting his mother, hating that the follow-up treatment was energy sapping and body-function changing, hating that he was a one-man show on the McAfee Ranch. If he was sidelined, or experienced long-lasting side effects, he'd fall behind…on everything, including his plans for the future.

He'd had the procedure to cut out the melanoma. They'd said they'd gotten it all. He'd missed half a day of work for the surgery, had two weeks of limited physical exertion and missed half a day to get his stitches removed. For a single dad who ran a cattle ranch by himself, he'd missed all the work he could afford.

"Promise me you'll think about it," Mom said quietly. "You have to be thinking about it or you wouldn't have asked me to find you a single woman to date, one who's willing to live in Second Chance."

Finn promised nothing if it meant thinking about cancer. He stood and wiped the sweat from his brow, glancing around. The barn was unusually quiet. Lizzie, his four-year-old, was nowhere in sight. "Mom, I'll call you later."

"Finn—"

He hung up on her, turning back to the daunting stack of hay. It had been delivered while he was moving the herd earlier. If he'd been here, he would have paid extra to have the hay transferred to his loft. He glanced up at the gathering rain clouds and sent up a prayer: "Don't rain yet." Not until he was done.

But he couldn't finish moving hay until he had eyes on Lizzie.

Lizzie had a habit of disappearing on him when his back was turned. And since they lived alone on a large cattle ranch in the remote mountains of Idaho, there was no safe place for her to wander off to.

"Lizzie!" He tilted his cowboy hat back, scanning the ranch yard for her bouncy blond curls and pink boots, listening for a reply.

The only answer came from the chicken coop, and the soft clucking of hens.

Finn tried a different approach. "Peanut! Come here, boy!"

And bring your charge with you.

Peanut was their golden retriever. He was usually good about sounding off if Lizzie was getting in trouble, or running to Finn when he was called if Lizzie was nearby.

Nothing.

Finn's worry meter ratcheted up a notch. "Lizzie! Peanut!"

Not for the first time today, Finn railed at the universe for taking his wife two years ago. Being both a father and a rancher hadn't been hard when Jenny had been alive. Now, everything was difficult, and the future was at risk.

He poked his head in the barn, saw nothing and jogged around to the back, where the misfits were corralled. He counted four heads—Larry the llama, Doug the donkey, Evie the emu, Gary the goat. They all stared at him. No Lizzie or Peanut.

Finn completed the circuit around the barn, stopping at the attached henhouse. No little girl sat inside petting Chickie Chicken, their Rhode Island Red hen. No dog stood watch outside the gate.

Worry increased to fear. Finn jogged across the ranch yard to the house, continuing to call their names.

Still no answer.

He opened the door and charged in, about to bellow the names of the missing when he noticed a muddy trail of tiny footsteps on the hardwood entwined with large, canine paw prints. They wound their way toward the living room.

Finn came around the corner.

His daughter was asleep on the couch, muddy cowboy boots discarded at her feet. Peanut was snuggled against her, watching Finn with a calm gaze that seemed to say *"Shh. I've got this."*

Relief flooded Finn's veins. He sank onto a chair and washed his hands over his face, pressing one palm over the scar tissue on his left cheek, running his right hand around to the scar on the back of his neck, where they'd cut out the melanoma.

Relief gave way to melancholy. The old house was quiet. Bedrooms that had been filled with family for decades were barren. No dishes or pans clattered with life in the kitchen. There were no voices, was no laughter, in the hall.

You didn't prepare me for this, Jenny.

His childhood sweetheart hadn't prepared him for the void she left after succumbing to lung disease. For the breath-stealing moments of joy and heart-pounding moments of fear he faced alone. Him. A heavily decorated, heavily scarred former marine who looked anything but ready for the role of single father to a toddler girl. And now…cancer.

They got it all.

That's what Dr. Carlisle said. That's what he wanted to believe.

Peanut thumped his tail without moving another muscle, a habit he'd developed because Lizzie was sometimes a light sleeper. That was telling. Even the dog knew not to wake Finn's little dynamo.

Finn made the stop gesture with his hand and snuck back outside, where it was just beginning to sprinkle. If he hurried, he could get the rest of the hay into the barn before any significant harm came to his feed order, or Lizzie woke up from her nap.

But the rest of his to-do list was going to have to wait until Lizzie was awake, fed and gently lectured—*again*—about the need to stay out of trouble and stick with him.

He just hoped that one day his lecture would sink in.

"WHAT ARE YOU doing in town this late?" Mackenzie greeted Finn and Lizzie after dinner that night as they entered Second Chance's general store. Mack looked like she'd had a long day. Her green grocery apron was stained, and her brown gaze seemed weary. Like him, Mack ran her own business. Like him, she was a hard worker. On paper, she'd be a good candidate to date. Truth be told, he'd like to have more kids, a large family to fill the big, old house on the ranch. But when he looked at Mack, there was no spark of attraction, no curiosity about what made her tick.

"I'm closing soon," Mack told them.

"Won't be long. We're out of bubble bath." Finn led Lizzie to the small selection of soaps and shampoos a few aisles back. "And someone is determined to have a bath tonight."

"Ducks need baths, Daddy." Lizzie pretended to be a duck, flopping her bent arms and occasionally quacking as she followed him.

A crate of ducklings had been left on their doorstep when they were behind the barn feeding the misfits after dinner. It was a mystery how people knew the McAfee Ranch was a haven for unwanted or injured animals. Jenny had started taking in broken stock when they'd gotten married five years ago. But she'd been gone two years now.

"Quack, quack, quack."

"Nice, ducky," Finn told her, grabbing the bubble bath just as Lizzie grabbed a yellow shower puff. "You've got one like that at home, love."

His daughter held up the yellow puff to him, a plea in her big blue eyes. "But it's not the color of baby ducks." She smiled like the well-behaved angel he hoped she'd one day become, melting his heart.

"All right. Come on." He led Lizzie to the sales counter, glancing at the bulletin board behind Mackenzie. "No one's asked about my job posting? The one that said, 'Ranch hand wanted. Room and board plus pay.'"

"Had a guy in earlier look at it, but he didn't seem interested." Mackenzie shook her head.

"Have you tried advertising down in Ketchum or Boise?"

"Yeah." Somehow, in the course of him helming the family property, he'd developed a reputation as a hard boss. Him. Savior of orphaned ducklings. Go figure.

Movement outside caught Finn's eye. Two trucks pulled in. The first was a shiny, new gray pickup he didn't recognize that parked in front of the store. The second was a beat-up, blue-and-white pickup pulling a stock trailer that stopped next to a gas pump. A familiar, run-down-looking cowboy got out from the old truck. His cowboy hat brim was smashed in front, as if he'd walked into a wall. The broken straw ends poked out, as prickly as the man's drunken personality.

Finn glanced down at Lizzie, who was oblivious to the traffic outside. She clung to the checkout counter as she watched Mackenzie punch buttons on the cash register. Maybe she wouldn't see her maternal grandfather.

Maybe I won't feel guilty for keeping them apart for a year.

A man and a woman entered, having arrived in that newer truck. Instinctively, Finn turned his face away as they passed, lowering the left brim of his cowboy hat to cover his scars.

"How can you have blown your savings?" the tall cowboy grumbled, scowling at the woman as he stood in front of a display of wine. "You're my sister."

Sister? That was surprising. The woman was dressed for the city—fancy high-heeled, half boots, jeans that clung to every outline of her body, a flowery, flouncy blouse and dangly earrings. Her thick, long black hair was straight, and fell smoothly over her shoulders. She was a rare bird up here, a looker, and if it hadn't been for Lizzie and his scars, Finn might have looked his fill.

Mack rang up Finn's purchases while he sent covert glances toward the other customers.

"Money management is my thing, Kendall," the tall cowboy continued with obvious disdain. "I could have helped you months ago. You'll be broke by years' end. 'Broke, broke, broke,' as little Adam would say."

"'Broke, broke, broke,'" the woman named Kendall said, mimicking the man as she propped a hand on her hip. "I didn't plan on being laid off, totaling my car, or spending a fortune repeatedly visiting my family in Second Chance this year." She shook herself a little, like a duck shedding excess water. And suddenly, she didn't look nearly as annoyed. "Stop worrying. I've got this. I have prospects."

"You have one prospect and it's a long shot." Still scowling, the cowboy glanced down at his sister's feet and her black, shiny half boots, the ones no self-respecting rancher would wear to work in. "You shouldn't gamble with the roof over your head. At the very least, you could have cut back on your clothing budget."

"Leave it, Holden. If I wanted a lecture, I'd go see Dad." Kendall's gray-eyed gaze bounced from her brother to the front door. "I'm worried about Shane. He looked awful in the hospital. And the doctor said he needed surgery to stop the internal bleeding."

Holden. Shane. Names started to click. These were Monroes. The Monroes had inherited the town of Second Chance last winter, and although they'd gotten a rocky start in town, they were now making good things happen. New jobs were opening up—new businesses, too. Things in the sleepy town were changing as they headed into another winter.

Now if only some cowboys in need of work would move to town...

Mack recited the total of Finn's purchases. He pulled out his wallet, noticing Lizzie's attention shift to the Monroe woman and stay there. Finn could relate. Even now, his eyes kept moving in her direction.

"Two black eyes. A punctured lung. Internal bleeding." Kendall hugged herself. "He could have died."

"It could be worse," Holden said quietly. "Shane was lucky you were talking to him when he ran off the road and crashed. After you called me, Bernadette and I found him quickly. Since she's Dr. Carlisle to everybody else she had him airlifted to Boise straight away." The tall cowboy turned his attention to the wine selection, rubbing a hand over his chest as if the episode had been upsetting. "But now Franny and everyone at the Bucking Bull are going to be focused on his recuperation. You'd just be in the way over there."

This time, it was Kendall who frowned. "I spent summers on our Texas ranch, same as you, Holden. I can help Franny feed and water stock, muck out stalls, even saddle a horse."

Even saddle a horse.

She sounded like a greenhorn. Finn almost laughed.

"All I need," Kendall continued, "is to brush up on my ranching skills and lingo so Old Man Connelly approves me to promote his ranch on social media. I'll give it a few days and then ask if Franny could use my help at the Bucking Bull."

"Finn is looking for a ranch hand." Mackenzie slid Finn's purchases across the counter, nodding at him. "He's got a big spread, a large herd of cattle and he's always in need of help. I bet you could work something out."

The two Monroes turned to stare at Finn. He knew what they'd see right off—the stained blue jeans, his dusty brown cowboy hat and scuffed cowboy boots. The things that said he was no hobby rancher. What they couldn't see, because his face was averted and whiskers partially covered his jawline, were his scars. He didn't want to show them, didn't want to see their reaction or hear their hastily made excuses about how his ranch—*his knowledge*—wasn't right for Kendall.

Grrr.

He was simultaneously angry at the world and sickened with himself for this weakness. He was a former marine, a ranch owner and a dad. He should hold his head high and set a good example for Lizzie.

Self-chastised, Finn faced the pair head-on, letting them see his left cheek and his scars. "Sorry, but I'm not running a dude ranch."

Kendall didn't flinch. Her gaze didn't fall from his. Her expression didn't turn pitying.

Nor did she gasp in horrified surprise. She was a class act. But on the other hand, she didn't admit she was far from qualified to be his ranch hand. She. Just. Stared.

"Finn put up a flyer." Mack ripped down the flyer and held it toward the Monroes. "Advertising for help. Ranching is hard up here. Hands are hard to come by."

"That's enough, Mack," Finn said as kindly as he was able to.

She paid him no mind. "But it's harder when you're a single dad."

Finn handed Lizzie her puff and took the bottle of bubble bath. "I need capable ranch hands, not…" He left the sentence incomplete, having been raised not to disrespect others, especially women.

"But she's broke, Daddy." Lizzie swung her puff by its string. "That's what the cowboy said. And we take in broken things."

Finn smiled at the Monroes, but when he spoke it was only for his daughter. "Look at the nice lady, honey. She's not broken."

I am.

THE STORE DOOR closed behind Finn and Kendall was able to breathe again.

Finn's gaze had been intense, so focused on her. There'd been no escape, no shrinking back. She felt flushed, as if she'd had her breath stolen by a hot summer wind on a dry Texas day.

And yet, she felt the urge to run after Finn and tell him she could help. Like he was the one in need of rescuing, not her.

Holden took Finn's flyer from Mackenzie and glanced over it. "Room and board plus salary." He looked down at Kendall. "You could waive the salary."

Kendall huffed. Or at least, she tried to. It came out more like a shaky breath. "You just said I needed money."

"You won't need money if you land the C-Bar-C account in a few weeks. You said so yourself." Holden set a bottle of wine on the counter. "This could be your chance to find someone to teach you the inner workings of a large cattle operation."

Kendall shook her head. She'd rather wait and see if Shane's fiancée, Franny, would need her at the Bucking Bull. Finn was just so very…unlike her. Finn reminded her of that summer she was nine in Texas, of struggling and eating dirt, of jokes made at her expense, of failure and embarrassment.

She smoothed her hair over one shoulder.

Outside the store, Finn put his purchases in his truck, patted a big yellow dog and then headed toward the Bent Nickel Diner, delicate little daughter in tow, her blond curls bouncing. Kendall was mesmerized by him. Finn was broad and muscular. He walked with his shoulders square and head high, as if he hadn't been hiding his disfigured, whisker-trimmed cheek most of the time they'd been in the store.

What a contradiction.

Kendall watched him through the front store windows, taking in his chiseled profile, the fringe of dark brown hair coming out of his worn hat brim, remembering the shockingly blue eyes that dared her to look away. His words, his posture, his attitude… It all said, "I don't need anyone."

Except he did need someone, or he wouldn't have put up that flyer.

But he doesn't need me.

That much was clear.

"Getting hired as a ranch hand is a long shot." Holden paid for his wine. "Maybe Finn could use a babysitter or a housekeeper. He could give you a ranch refresher over the dinner you make him." He gave a wry laugh, knowing full well that Kendall couldn't cook.

That poked her pride. "I can help around a ranch." She lifted her chin, much the way

Finn had done. "I'm stronger than I look. I've taken Pilates for years."

The store clerk was trying hard not to smile.

Kendall's pride moved aside to let anger chop out her words. "I can do hard things, Holden. Just watch me." She stomped out.

Holden and the store clerk laughed as the door swung closed behind her.

It began to sprinkle as Kendall marched over to the Bent Nickel.

Raining on my parade!

Her arms swung and her boots struck the pavement with confidence. She flung open the diner door and stormed inside, not even pausing to collect herself. Instead, she headed right for the rancher and his daughter, taking the stool to Finn's left, and waved to her cousin Camden behind the counter. "I'll have a tea, please."

I'll have a tea?

She gritted her teeth. She should have asked for a beer, which the diner had recently obtained a license for, if only to prove she was tough enough to work on a ranch.

Kendall spun the stool sideways to face the dismissive cowboy. "I can help you."

"I already have a babysitter. She drives up from Boise twice a week." Finn raised a hand, catching Cam's eye. "Can you make those milk-shake orders to go?"

"I'm a hard worker," Kendall said with her head held high.

Finn stared straight ahead, mouth closed. The scars across his cheek were pink with raised, jagged lines.

She wanted to trace those lines with her finger and find out if they were as hard as Finn seemed to be. She wanted to look her fill without feeling like her attention was unwanted, like *she* was unwanted.

Kendall tossed her hair over her shoulder.

"I can vouch for Kendall being a hard worker," Cam said over the roar of the milk-shake machine. "She's always on her computer or phone."

Although Kendall appreciated her cousin's intentions, his comment wasn't helping her case.

Finn's mouth thinned. He looked like he hadn't been kissed in a long time and he was never going to admit that it bothered him.

I haven't been kissed in a long time and it bothers me!

She bet Finn was a good kisser. She bet when he took a woman in his arms that he held her close and didn't let go until she was breathless.

Kendall sucked in a breath. There was something about this man that got under her skin and wouldn't go away. She didn't understand it, but she didn't back away from it either. She put her forearms on the counter, leaned toward him and practically shouted, "Test me. Go on. I'll surprise you."

His little girl stared at her with wide blue eyes, seemingly already surprised.

Finn drew a deep, deliberate breath, and then released it just as slowly as he reached for his wallet and drew out two twenties. "I forgot to buy dog food. Mackenzie knows which brand it is. You load it in my truck and you've got the job on a trial basis."

Dog food? Piece of cake! "Thank you. You won't regret it."

"I already do." Finn turned to face her, holding the money between them. Every nuance of his expression conveyed disappointment with life or karma or the human race. It was heartbreaking. "Or I will regret it, if you can lift and load the dog food. If you can't get it in my truck by yourself, the deal is off."

It felt like all her life someone had been doubting Kendall, trying to tell her what she could and couldn't do. Or worse, how to do what she wanted to do.

She was done with it.

"No problem." Kendall took his twenties and hurried back to the store.

"HEY, FINN." DR. CARLISLE entered the Bent Nickel, baby bump first. She adjusted her thick glasses as she set her sights on Finn, coming to stand next to him at the counter. She placed a hand on his shoulder and angled her head, presumably to look at the surgery scar on the back of his neck. "How are you feeling?"

Cam delivered their milk shakes in paper cups with plastic lids.

"Fine. Never better." Finn put a straw in Lizzie's shake. "Hey, love. Why don't you go sit by the window while I talk to Dr. Carlisle?"

Lizzie slid off the stool, carrying her chocolate milk shake with both hands as she headed toward a front booth.

Meanwhile, Dr. Carlisle paid for her takeout order, accepting two large boxes of the dinner special from Cam. "Finn, it's been a month. You haven't scheduled the adjuvant therapy."

"You said you got everything." That came out surlier than he'd meant it to.

"I did." The doctor gave Finn a reassuring smile. "The additional treatment is precautionary but recommended in patients with lesions the size of yours."

Lesions. Cancerous growths, she meant. Why didn't doctors say what they meant?

"Doc...five days a week for four weeks..." Finn's right hand came up to the fresh, bumpy scar on the back of his neck. It was still tender to the touch, kind of like his emotions when discussing the Big C. "I can't afford any more lost time at the ranch. Fall is a busy season." *Life* was a busy season.

And you said you got it all.

Dr. Carlisle's expression didn't change. "But winter is coming."

"Sure. I'm less stretched after the first snowfall." He'd give her that. But when things slowed down, he was going to have to put some effort toward finding someone new to share his life with—apologies to his angel, Jenny. And that someone needed to be committed to raising kids on the McAfee Ranch. "But that doesn't mean—"

"It's a date, then." And just like that, Dr. Carlisle assumed she'd won. She made a hasty retreat. "You made the right decision."

"Hang on." He stood, grabbing hold of his milk shake. "I didn't agree to anything."

She paused at the door, looking back at him

before nodding toward Lizzie. "But you will."
And then she left.

Grrr.

A helpless sort of anger shuddered through
his veins, similar to the emotion he'd felt when
he was first diagnosed. Similar to the emotion he'd felt after his injury in the service. He
hated not being in control. He hated being off-
schedule. He hated this feeling of brokenness.

Finn moved to the booth near the front
window and put Lizzie in his lap. They both
slurped their chocolate shakes and waited for
Kendall to come out of the store with the dog
food.

The fifty-pound bag of dog food.

There was no way that slip of a city woman
was going to heft that bag out to his truck and
toss it in the truck bed.

"Mommy always said misfits need a home."
Lizzie leaned against him, reciting the words
he'd told her because she'd barely been two
when Jenny had died. "Mommy always said
our hearts are big enough to make room for
one more."

Why had he told her those things?

"Kendall Monroe isn't a misfit." She looked
like she'd fit in anywhere in the world, except
at the McAfee Ranch.

"You heard what the cowboy said, Daddy.

She's broke, broke, broke." Lizzie sucked on her milk shake.

Broke? Despite what Kendall said, Finn didn't believe that for a minute. Monroes had money. Everybody knew that.

Kendall appeared on the sidewalk in front of their truck, large dog-food bag on her shoulder.

Finn set down his cup. Lizzie leaned forward. In his truck, Peanut stopped panting and stared at Kendall from the front passenger seat. It had stopped raining. Everyone and everything was on pause.

Kendall wobbled on her way to the back of the truck, as if struggling under the weight of the bag, but she got there. And once there, she bent her knees and then rocketed to her toes, throwing the bag off her shoulder. If she hadn't staggered back and nearly fallen, he might have thought he'd completely misjudged her.

Cam, who'd been drinking Kendall's tea and watching over Finn's shoulder, chuckled. "I guess you've got yourself a ranch hand."

"A ranch hand! I can't wait." Lizzie excitedly clapped her hands. "Can we take our misfit home now, Daddy? She can sleep in my room. She's gonna love the ducklings and Peanut and Chickie Chicken. She's gonna love—"

"No." Finn didn't want his new ranch hand to love anyone. He set Lizzie on the floor as Kendall marched back in the diner, triumph in her big gray eyes. "I'll expect you tomorrow morning at dawn, Miss Monroe."

"My name's Kendall." She handed him his change, smiling with just the right note of triumph and geniality, as if he should be happy about her winning that challenge. "Your flyer said room and board. I'll get my things at the Lodgepole Inn. That way, I can start in the morning."

Finn bit back a groan.

CHAPTER THREE

"OH, GABBY, YOU'RE HERE. Good." Kendall hurried through the lobby of the Lodgepole Inn telling herself she was excited to have found a way to brush up on her ranch skills. Working for a sexy, cantankerous cowboy had nothing to do with the anticipation she was feeling. "Can you kitten-sit a little longer?"

"Sure." The preteen sat behind the check-in counter with Boo sleeping in her lap. She was wearing a pink tank top that said, Don't Miss Out on Second Chance, and had her strawberry blond hair in two messy buns high on her head.

Kendall stopped to scratch Boo behind the ears. "Boo's a sweetheart, isn't she?"

In the manager's apartment behind Gabby, Kendall's cousin Laurel was pacing the kitchen while holding three-month-old baby girls in cach arm.

"Boo's mostly a sweetie, but she keeps trying to climb the drapes," Gabby said in a low voice, glancing over her shoulder toward Laurel, her stepmother. "How much longer do you need me to watch her?"

"A few days maybe?" Kendall turned toward the stairs, explaining about the opportunity with Finn.

"Not so fast." Laurel and the babies entered the lobby. The girls were identical twins, down to their gummy smiles and tufts of fine red hair. They were adorable but looked as if they'd done a number on Laurel. Her bright red hair had fallen out of her ponytail on one side and her cheeks were flushed. "Gabby can't kitten-sit. Summer is over and classes have resumed. Plus, Gabby has two little sisters to help care for. We can't have the twins bothering guests."

It was a weekday in mid-September. The only guests were Monroes, who'd make allowances for crying babies. Kendall opened her mouth to say so.

Behind Laurel and the babies, Gabby sent the high sign to Kendall, warning her not to argue.

Heeding that alert, Kendall changed tactics. She walked over to Laurel and took one of the twins before proceeding upstairs to her room. "Look how cute Hope is."

"That's Hazel." Laurel climbed the stairs right behind Kendall, feet pounding more than was necessary on the creaky treads. "And don't think I don't know what you're doing. You're trying to butter me up. It won't work."

"I have no idea what you're talking about." Kendall entered her room. She smoothed Hazel's red eyebrows, earning a wiggle of happiness in return. "I'm just trying to give you a little break, Laurel." Kendall lay Hazel down in the middle of the bed, took her sister Hope from Laurel and put her down, too. Then she took Laurel's hand and drew her to the bathroom doorway, pointing at the mirror. "You need a minute for yourself."

Catching her reflection, Laurel made a little mewing noise, much like Boo when she'd been in her carrier too long. Laurel removed her worn scrunchie and vigorously finger-combed her hair. "I love being a mom."

Ooh, that sounded defensive.

"You're a great mom." Kendall went around the room, gathering her things together for the move, keeping an eye on the babies on the bed. There wasn't much to pick up since she'd just dropped off her luggage less than two hours ago. After having flown into Boise this morning, she'd spent most of the day at the hospital, and the last hour or so taking photos of some refurbished kiddie carnival rides her cousin Bentley was restoring. "But even great moms need a break now and then."

Laurel faced Kendall, looking more like herself. She arched her thin red eyebrows.

"Let's make a deal. You keep Boo for a few days, and I promise to take you to dinner, just you and me. No babies." Kendall tickled Hazel's toes. "No offense, sweet cheeks."

"I can't leave them." Laurel placed a hand on each baby's belly and gave them a playful shake, eliciting more gooey smiles. "I'm breastfeeding."

Kendall slid her laptop into its bag. "Didn't cousin Sophie have a pump or something when she was breastfeeding her twins?"

"If I pump, it goes in a bottle. Bottle to breast creates nipple confusion. And confusion of any type in babies isn't fun." Laurel's gaze turned distant. "Not fun at all."

"I take it you've tried this."

Laurel nodded.

Impulsively, Kendall hugged her cousin. "You're going to be okay. Someday soon, you'll regain the Monroe Most Likely to Keep Up Appearances crown. How about this? I'll come into town tomorrow for dinner. We'll sit at one table in the Bent Nickel and your darling husband, Mitch, can sit with the babies at another table." She held Laurel at arm's length. "You'll feel like an adult, I promise."

"Even wearing a nursing bra?" Laurel's lower lip thrust out. "It's like wearing body armor."

Kendall nodded reassuringly. "Even if you wore a girdle. Are you up for it?"

"Yes." Laurel's gaze drifted toward the bed. She sighed and stepped free. "But I was serious about the kitten. She can't stay here. Gabby's got school, Mitch is working on the renovation, and I can't watch the twins plus Boo." Laurel faced Kendall, crossing her arms over her chest. "You can, and will, take *your* kitten with you."

"All right," Kendall said, relenting. "Boo is going to be a ranch cat, at least for a few days." She'd be extra careful with the little scamp so that she wouldn't run off into the woods.

"What's gotten into you with this kitten?" Laurel demanded. "You've never had a pet before. Not so much as a hamster."

Kendall shrugged. "I just saw her get dumped and that was that. I realized the moment she looked at me that she was my boo. You know, my sweetheart?" Kindred souls understood each other. Kind of like the way she'd felt when Finn's eyes locked on hers. Kendall scrunched her nose.

That wasn't it at all.

There had been no immediate kinship or affection when she and Finn had done the staredown. It was attraction. A simple chemical reaction.

"What's wrong?" Laurel ran her thumb over Kendall's forehead. "You're making frown lines."

Kendall forced herself to relax. "There's no single thing bothering me." There were several—her bank account, the car situation, the job opportunity she desperately needed and a widowed cowboy's cautious gaze. But she didn't want Laurel to worry. She had enough on her plate. "I'll be fine." She'd milk Finn for all his ranching knowledge and be back at the Lodgepole Inn within a few days. A week, tops.

Laurel tried to send her off with a smile, but her confidence in Kendall was about as solid as Kendall's confidence in herself.

Still, Kendall wasn't a quitter. "I'll be fine," she said again.

It took Kendall three trips to help ferry the twins downstairs and then lug her things to Finn's truck. On the last trip, she spotted her luggage exactly where she'd left it next to the cab and realized that Finn was going to treat her like the ranch hand she was pretending to be, even if it was only temporary.

Kendall opened the back door to load her purse, laptop bag and kitten.

"Hi." Lizzie looked half-asleep. Her blue eyes were droopy and her blond curls were askew.

"Hi." Kendall set the cat carrier on the seat and her purse and laptop bag on the floor.

Boo meowed.

In the front seat, the dog stopped panting and cocked its ears.

"What's that noise?" Finn sat behind the wheel. He turned off what sounded like a lullaby on his phone.

Boo meowed again.

The dog hopped in the back, batting Lizzie with its tail, whining as it stuck its nose against Boo's carrier, making her hiss.

"Peanut, stop!" Lizzie hollered, wide-awake now as she swatted at the dog's tail.

"Peanut!" Finn commanded. He slapped the front seat with his palm. "Come."

The dog—who was a gazillion times bigger than a peanut—returned to the front, circled and then rested his muzzle on the seat back, watching the cat carrier as if he couldn't wait to make friends with Boo.

"The kitten isn't coming with us." Finn stared at Kendall, eyes nearly as narrow as the scars making a wishbone on his cheek.

Kendall wasn't in the mood to cater to cantankerous cowboys. "I rescued Boo from the streets of Philly and brought her out here. There's no way I'm leaving her behind." Forgetting the argument with Laurel, Kendall gave Finn the smile she'd perfected with two older brothers before tossing her suitcase, the bag of cat litter and the litter box in the truck bed.

"They're misfits, Daddy." Lizzie gestured for Kendall to get in and hurry up about it. "We have room. Miss Kendall can sleep in my room."

"Princess Kendall is staying in the bunk room," Finn muttered.

"That's Cowgirl Kendall to you, mister." Kendall took her seat, sliding the cat carrier to the middle, a motion Peanut watched carefully.

Finn scowled. "I'm your boss, remember?"

"That's Cowgirl Kendall to you, *boss*." Kendall buckled in.

Lizzie grinned at her. "She's funny, Daddy. Can we keep her?"

"No." Finn backed out of the inn's parking lot.

Kendall found the little girl adorable and Finn too rigid. "Do you always talk about people as if they aren't within spitting distance?"

"Yes." He had big hands. They moved effortlessly around the steering wheel. "Lizzie, don't get attached to the cowgirl princess or her cat. They're both temporary."

"Daddy."

Since Kendall agreed, she didn't retort. But really...*princess*?

It was clear after just a few minutes that Finn wasn't going to converse with Kendall, so she turned her attention to his sweet little daughter. "Do you have a cat at home?"

Lizzie shook her head solemnly. "We have enough trouble keeping our chickens from being eaten by the coyotes or Peanut. Daddy says kittens would be coyote snacks."

Kendall drew Boo's carrier closer to her side. "I guess that's why you have a big dog. To keep the coyotes away."

"Yup." Lizzie glanced at Boo. "Everyone should have a ranch dog. Do you have one?"

"Nope. Do you have other ranch hands?" Kendall tried to catch Finn's eye in the rearview mirror. She'd had more success catching a cabbie's attention during rush hour in downtown Philly.

"I'm Daddy's only helper," Lizzie told her.

"Grandpa Oscar used to be his helper but he moved on. And Mommy used to be his helper, but she's in heaven."

"I'm sorry for your loss," Kendall said automatically, thinking his widower status explained why Finn was grumpy.

And grumpy isn't sexy.

She'd keep telling herself that until it sunk in.

"Daddy, I want Miss Kendall to sleep in my room." Lizzie kicked the back of Finn's seat half-heartedly with her little pink cowboy boots.

"Ranch hands stay in the barn," Finn said woodenly.

The barn? *Shades of Texas summers past.*

Kendall contained a little shiver. "Do you have a horse, Lizzie?" Was it too much to hope this was a working ranch without horses?

The little girl gave a big nod, dashing Kendall's hopes. "My pony's name is Pete."

"Pete the pony." Finn might have smiled. He certainly sounded like he found this amusing. "Pete has a smooth gait, doesn't he, Lizzie?"

"Pete is pokey." Lizzie stuck out her lower lip as if this was a point of contention. "He never runs."

"But he has a smooth gait," Finn said staunchly. "And he loves you."

Kendall felt the need to stick up for poor, pokey Pete. "I bet Pete is the nicest pony on the planet."

"I love Pete," Lizzie said, sighing contentedly as she twisted a blond curl. "Even if he's slow. He likes alfalfa and apples."

"In case you can't tell, cowgirl princess, we've been studying our alphabet," Finn said, definitely letting a proud smile creep onto his face. "Which has led us to alliteration."

Pride in his daughter was darn attractive. Kendall bit her lip to keep from smiling back.

"*A* is for apple. And alfalfa. And ant." Lizzie looked to Kendall with the most charming of gazes, blinking those big blue eyes. "Do you know words that start with *A*?"

"Aardvark." Kendall went with a classic.

"We don't have one of those at the ranch." Lizzie kicked her feet a little. "Daddy, I want a andvarkle."

"*Aardvark,*" Finn corrected. "Sorry, love. They don't live around here."

"They're in one of my books." Lizzie was going to make a wonderful lawyer someday. She knew just how to present a statement that had no immediate, logical argument.

"That doesn't mean they live around here," Finn said with good-natured cheer.

Lizzie held up her hands. "Then why is a andvarkle in my book?"

"It's *aardvark*," Finn said, still using that warm voice he had yet to employ with Kendall. "And kids around the world learn their letters. They need examples of things they can find near or far."

"Where is the kid with the andvarkle? I want to see him."

"Aardvark." Finn's amused gaze finally connected with Kendall's in the rearview mirror, nearly making her blush. "And whoever that aardvark-owning kid is, he probably lives on the other side of the world. Not everyone has as many misfits as we have."

"That's because we're lucky!" Lizzie kicked her feet again, but this time with more enthusiasm.

Their good cheer reassured Kendall that this was going to work out. Maybe Finn was only grumpy with new hires. They'd find their footing and get along better tomorrow.

They came around a curve in the narrow highway and a small, green valley revealed itself, colors soft and welcoming in the fading light.

"That valley is gorgeous. Can we stop and take a picture?" Kendall dug in her purse for her phone. "Can you believe how that ranch down there looks? Now that's Americana. White-clapboard farmhouse with a tilting cupola on the roof. That's a fixer-upper, for sure." She chuckled. "Even the barn looks like it's withstood the test of time, but won't last much longer."

Instead of stopping so she could take a picture, Finn turned in the sparsely graveled driveway. And kept going.

Uh-oh. "This is… This is your ranch?"

"This is home." Lizzie sighed contentedly, unaware that Kendall had just cast shade on that very thing.

CHAPTER FOUR

LIZZIE WAS ENAMORED with a woman who thought their ranch was decrepit.

Grrr.

Finn's fingers fumbled as he tried releasing the latch on Lizzie's car seat.

"Daddy, Miss Kendall is my friend and needs to sleep in my room." Lizzie may have whispered, but he had no doubt that Kendall heard every word from the other side of the truck, where she was slinging several bags over her shoulders. From the looks of things, she was trying hard not to smile as she picked up the carrier with the kitten.

She'd learn soon enough that she had little to smile about. Ranching was bone-weary work, if only because it was never-ending.

"Ranch hands sleep in the barn." In the bunk room that was narrower than a jail cell. The multipoint latch on Lizzie's seat finally released. He lifted her into his arms and hurried on. "The barn is this way."

Motion-sensor floodlights illuminated the ranch yard as he led Kendall to the barn.

Nose to the ground, Peanut lost interest in the kitten in favor of a new scent and criss-crossed their path.

"I want Miss Kendall to meet Pete." Lizzie eyes were glazed, the result of being up way past her bedtime no doubt. "And Larry, and Doug, and Evie, and Gary."

"She'll meet everyone tomorrow, love." When he gave Kendall tasks only a capable ranch hand could accomplish. "Right now, I need to show Kendall where she's going to sleep because after that you're going right to bed." No bath.

"That's not fair." But Lizzie yawned.

"What's rule number one of ranching, love?"

"Get a good night's sleep." Lizzie laid her head on his shoulder.

Finn had the main barn door open, and the lights inside turned on just as Kendall reached them, juggling all her luggage, and sounding winded. Horses poked their heads over stall doors at the intrusion. Peanut ran back and forth in the breezeway without finding a scent to intrigue him. He trotted back outside.

Finn set Lizzie on a bench outside the bunk room before he opened the door. It had a musty, stale smell to it. He almost went to open the window to air it out but thought better of it. The condition of her quarters was bound to scare off the city gal. He removed his cowboy hat and beat it against the mattress on the bottom bunk, nearly chuckling at the amount of dust that rose in the air. No one had slept here since he'd kicked out his father-in-law a year ago. This was no five-star hotel. It wasn't even the Lodgepole Inn.

Kendall stood in the doorway, poker-faced and regally magnificent, as if she was above dust and dinge. As if nothing he could do would scare her away.

A woman like that...

He suspected she had the power to worm her way past his defenses.

She's gotta go.

"Home sweet home." Finn took a plastic zipped bag from a cupboard. It contained a rolled sleeping bag and pillow. He unfurled the sleeping bag on the mattress, half-hoping that a mouse would leap out. Or at the very least, a big, scurrying spider.

Nada.

"You had no expectation that anyone would take this job, did you?" Kendall carefully set down her collection of items in the small room. Her expression was just as well-modulated as her movements, so neutral he couldn't tell what she was thinking. Still, he waited to see if she wanted a ride back into town.

She faced him, a pretty smile on her delicate face.

Here it comes.

"What time do we start in the morning?"

Finn frowned, staring at her fancy boots. She wanted to stay? Impossible.

He tried again. "The coffee machine at the house kicks on at five. Breakfast is feed yourself. We tend the stock by six, if not sooner. And then, after Lizzie's been fed, we'll saddle up and move the herd."

"And…"

Finn gave her a sharp look.

"My family owns a ranch in Texas. There's always a list a mile long of things needing doing." Kendall arched her eyebrows. "And…"

He crossed his arms over his chest. "I've been meaning to fix the crooked cupola." He arched *his* eyebrows, hoping to convey he was going to send her up on the roof.

"I swing a mean hammer." Her smile warmed, inviting him to find humor in this situation.

It would be easy to succumb to her kind eyes and her polished ways, to submit to this fascination he had for her. But it would be unfair to both of them. He had no time for anything that wasn't long-term love, and she didn't seem like the type to fall for a broken cowboy. So he pursed his lips and closed himself off.

Her smile faded. She cleared her throat. "I'm having dinner with my cousin in Second Chance tomorrow night."

Grrr. "I'm not a cabbie service."

"I'll get a ride." She reached into the pet carrier and brought out her kitten. Small, white and fluffy, it was as adorable as Kendall was. Lizzie was bound to fall in love with them both if he didn't do something about it.

He set his jaw.

Kendall chuckled. "I can tell from the look on your face that you think I won't come back tomorrow night."

"Not only do I think it, I hope it." Why not be honest? He hadn't wanted to take her on.

Kendall nodded, not giving away if his lack of faith in her abilities and commitment hurt her feelings. "Do you mind my asking—"

"IED. Six years ago. Afghanistan. I was a marine." He'd been wondering when she'd get around to his visible scars. Finn pointed at his cheek.

"Oh, I..." Kendall blushed, shifting the kitten in her arms. "I was going to ask where you wanted me to wash up."

She wanted to know where the bathroom was, not about his life-altering accident? Finn suppressed a groan. He led her past Lizzie, who was asleep on the bench, to the other side of the barn. "It's here. Next to the tack room. It's a wet room, which means—"

"There's a central shower drain with no enclosed shower." Kendall didn't turn up her elegant nose. Her expression gave nothing away. It was just a feeling he had that she wasn't thrilled with the way things were working out. "How very worldly of you."

"It's convenient." For washing dogs and kids, if need be, without tracking mud in the house. Finn noticed there was a layer of grime on the floor. He refused to apologize for it. He had his hands full running the ranch.

"My Grandpa Harlan used to say that you should leave a place cleaner than when you found it." Kendall gave him a wry smile, white kitten tucked beneath her chin.

For a modern-day princess, she showed a lot of gumption.

"I'm sorry about the IED and your wife." Kendall walked back toward the bunk room, murmuring to the kitten and being magnetic just by breathing. At the door, she turned and smiled down at his sleeping daughter. "And I'm sorry about the fixer-upper comment. I'm not here to slow you down. I'm not looking to hire on. In fact, you don't have to pay me. Just put up with a few questions while I help you get things done."

Did she expect him to be happy about a few questions and no salary? He wanted her and those kissable lips gone.

Grrr.

Finn scooped up Lizzie and showed Kendall where the lights were, then closed the door behind him to a chorus of coyote yips, hoping his new hire wouldn't last until lunch tomorrow.

"WE'RE NOT IN Kansas anymore, Boo." Or Philadelphia, for that matter. There was no large fancy bed, no shiny new lighting, no reassuring sounds of the city.

Coyote cries weren't reassuring, especially when she'd been told that small creatures were coyote snacks.

Fear found a place in her chest. Kendall checked every door to make sure they were firmly closed before putting the kitten on the floor. Only then did she take in her surroundings more carefully in a way she hadn't been able to when Finn was around.

The barn was divided evenly into four sections by two breezeways. The planked floor was dusty with a sprinkling of straw and in need of a good sweeping. The outer walls and main support beams were thick and looked hand-hewn. But the stall walls were made of modern materials—smooth, even planks topped with metal railings and metal stall doors. There were six stalls down the length of one side, two stalls next to her bunk room and no stalls near the bathroom and tack room. Horses of every color and size peered at her. Some leaned their chests against their stall doors to extend their head and neck into the breezeway, unabashedly curious.

Boo scampered around, kicking up dust as she went.

Almost automatically, Kendall reached for her phone and snapped a picture. Capturing photo opportunities was second nature to her, as was cleaning.

"Grandpa Harlan wouldn't have allowed his barn to be this dirty," she said to Boo as the kitten zipped by. Granted, Kendall's grandfather hadn't been a single dad running a working ranch. And granted, he'd employed a slew of people to keep all the outbuildings and the ranch house properly clean.

Kendall entered the grimy bathroom. It didn't improve upon the second viewing.

There was a mop inside, plus some bottles with cleaning solution, not that it appeared any of it had been utilized recently. There was no way she was using that room until it'd been scrubbed from one end to the other. A quick perusal of the tack room and she found other helpful supplies. She wouldn't be able to sleep until she gave the bathroom and bunk room a good cleaning.

Boo ran past. A horse nickered. Several horses still had their heads poked over their stall doors, watching her and Boo.

"I suppose I should introduce myself." Petting the horses and feeding them treats had been one thing she'd enjoyed about the family ranch, more so than riding. She found a covered bucket with alfalfa cubes, removed the lid and brought it to the first stall, which had a small wooden nameplate. "Hello, Pete." She snapped his picture with her phone.

Lizzie's small black pony stretched his velvety nose toward the top rail of his stall door.

"You're adorable, Pokey Pete." She handed him an alfalfa cube and gave him several friendly pats before moving to the next horse, a dapple gray, identifying him by his nameplate. "Hello, Romeo."

Boo stared up at the gray horse from outside his stall. Also adorable. Also deserving of a picture.

Romeo nudged her shoulder when she didn't offer an alfalfa cube fast enough. Farther down the line, a buckskin whinnied impatiently.

"I'll get to everyone," Kendall promised. And then she'd tidy up, spend a bit of time studying ranch practices online so her handsome new boss would be impressed and possibly play around with the pictures she'd taken. Because she'd need a portfolio of ranching posts to show the Connellys, which meant she was going to have to create a social-media page. What better place to practice than the McAfee Ranch?

Finn would have a meltdown if he found out.

That just meant she'd call the ranch something completely different. Something her grumpy cowboy boss would never find out about.

FINN SAT UP in bed, chest heaving and skin damp with sweat.

The dreams...

They'd been coming more frequently since his cancer diagnosis.

They were like the worst clips of bad movies stitched together. Except they weren't movies. They were scenes from his life—the IED blast and resulting chaos, the car accident he'd been in, the stroke his dad had suffered a year after Finn returned, the snowy night Jenny had died, the cold feel of the hospital bed under his chest as Dr. Carlisle cut out the melanoma. Flashes of the moments in his life when he'd felt his mortality and that of those around him.

He got up and went to the bathroom to splash water on his face, then had a drink of water and listened to the light patter of rain on the roof overhead. Letting all that water wash away the bad.

He moved to the window and looked out at the ranch, imagining his father, his grandfather, his great-great grandfather and the original McAfee, Gregory, staring out the same window at the same shadowy night. This was home. They'd all loved this ranch as much as he did, putting in hard work to create something to pass down to the next generation. He didn't want all that responsibility to fall solely on Lizzie. It was part of the reason he wanted more kids. But not the only reason. He'd loved the stories of their family history and seeing old photographs of large families gathered in front of the ranch house or the barn. Families said permanence.

"I feel like a part of this place," Jenny had told him when she'd painted the old kitchen cabinets a cheerful white. "Someday, our children will roll their eyes at how much their mother appreciated these ancient things. But because of them, I feel closer to those who came before me in this kitchen and I'd never agree to rip them out."

Finn's throat threatened to close. That was yet another thing he had to make sure Lizzie knew about her mother.

The wind blew raindrops against the windowpane, rattling the frame, tapping the glass, drawing Finn out of his reverie.

Light from the barn caught his eye, glinting through the small bunk-room window. It was close to midnight and his new ranch hand was still awake. Or perhaps trying to sleep with the lights on because she'd been spooked by the creaking of barn wood, or the call of passing coyotes.

He squelched the urge to check on her and offer reassurance, instead he returned to bed, spirits lifted.

Five o'clock rolled around early when you'd

had little or no sleep. The cowgirl princess was in for a very rude awakening, one that might lead her to give up on their bargain.

CHAPTER FIVE

FOUR FORTY-FIVE A.M. came too soon.

Kendall sat up, shivering in the cold barn and forcing herself to stay awake.

After Finn left the barn last night, she'd spent an hour sweeping the breezeway, cleaning the bunk room and the bathroom, during which time Boo had dashed to every corner, stopping occasionally to arch her back and hiss if a horse startled her.

Kendall had spent another hour falling down a rabbit hole of recommended ranching practices, making notes in her phone. And a third hour creating a profile for the Second Chance Ranch on social media. Her first post had featured Boo kicking up dust as she tore through the barn, and the caption *Make way!*

But when Kendall finally turned out the lights to sleep, Boo was too wound up to snooze. The kitten had climbed the wooden bunks, as she'd undoubtedly done to the Lodgepole Inn's draperies. She'd pounced on

Kendall's feet in the sleeping bag. She'd flung kitty litter around the room.

And now, in the gray light of dawn, Boo was finally asleep on Kendall's pillow and Kendall was blinking bleary eyes.

She wasn't feeling much better when she stood at the front door of the ranch house shivering in her jean-patterned leggings and a hoodie with creases, wondering if she should knock or just barge right in. She wanted caffeine like nobody's business.

The door swung open. Finn stood inside wearing a blue T-shirt, blue jeans, gray socks and a look that said, "You aren't welcome here."

If only his gruffness were a turnoff.

Kendall sighed, resisting the urge to snap his picture, knowing it would never capture his rugged character.

He held a big mug of coffee. After a moment, he handed it to her. "I don't normally give ranch hands my coffee, but you look like you need it." He frowned at her sneakers. "No shoes inside."

"Understood." Despite not being a coffee lover, Kendall took a moment to drink deeply from the mug, and another to kick off her sneakers before following him, letting the smell of freshly brewed coffee guide her.

The farmhouse was a classic, two-story American foursquare. The hall branched to a living room in the front corner, which contained antiques mixed with a comfortable brown couch draped in a brown log-cabin quilt. There was space for a Christmas tree in the far corner and the wood mantel had small holes, as if from hooks for stockings. The living room opened to the dining room in the back corner with an antique table large enough for a big family to gather. She followed the hall past a bathroom and laundry room, past a steep staircase with an intricately carved newel post, and to a kitchen in the rear of the house. It was classic Americana in there, too. The cabinets were dated, but had been painted a bright white. The Formica counters were a soft cream with a midcentury starburst pattern and matched the faded, cracked linoleum. Everything in the house spoke of family, tradition, hand-me-downs and love. For just a moment, she imagined herself as part of the fabric of such a place.

"Sleep well last night?" Finn interrupted her musings with a question that almost sounded smug. He slid a good-looking omelet onto a plate. It smelled delicious. He brought the plate over to the kitchen table, sat down and began to dig in, having already poured himself another cup of coffee.

Welcome? She wasn't. But she was determined to win him over, the same way she was going to win over the Connellys by not giving up. "I slept like a baby last night. The mattress was like a cloud." A hard, lumpy cloud.

He paused from eating. His gaze flew to her face, as if he was familiar with the quality of the bunk-room mattress and testing her sincerity.

Kendall infused her smile with nothing but gratitude.

He made a sound that might have been surprise or doubt. "You're welcome to anything in the fridge."

Feed yourself. That's essentially what he'd told her about breakfast last night.

Kendall set her coffee mug on the counter and explored the contents of his refrigerator. There were lots of eggs, plenty of greens, yogurt and juice. Her stomach growled.

Finn glanced at her over his shoulder.

"Yes, I'm starved." She usually grazed through her day with six or more minimeals. She doubted she'd have time for more than a cheese stick between breakfast and lunch. If they had cheese sticks, which they didn't.

She took two eggs, the milk and a bag of

shredded cheese, and combined them all in the frying pan he'd used, turning it to medium-high heat. She was in a hurry, wanting to get food out of the way so she could grill him about his day, about ranching practices, about his life working with cattle.

Finn turned his chair and studied her. "I take it cooking isn't a strength of yours?"

"You can't tell that just by watching me make eggs." She hated cooking. Didn't most single people? She stirred the ingredients in the frying pan, wondering what might have given her away.

"You have a hole in your sock," he said instead of arguing about her cooking skills.

She curled her toes self-consciously. "I was in a hurry when I packed." Sheesh, he was really on her case. She hoped he wasn't going to be like this all day.

"Riding while wearing sneakers is dangerous."

He was. Criminy.

"I can wear my boots. They have heels. And when we fix the cupola, I'll put my sneakers back on."

"Cupola," he murmured, a scowl passing over his face as quickly as a dark rain cloud moved across the plains. "You're burning your...whatever that is." In a flash, Finn was up and had turned down her burner, then snatched the spatula from her hand and turned her eggs. "You do know that you let the eggs start to cook before you add anything, like cheese? And that eggs like to be cooked gently? Slowly?" His gaze skimmed her lips. "They don't like to be mishandled."

Neither do I.

Kendall frowned at the frying pan and the blackened side of her eggs, although her annoyance was directed at herself and the way her feminine radar pinged every time he looked at her.

Or my lips.

Kendall gave herself a mental shake. "I suppose I've been given egg-frying advice once or twice." Not that she'd listened. Not that she wanted to listen now. She had other things on her mind, namely…

He looked at my lips!

"Once or twice?" Finn scoffed. "Once or twice being the number of times you've cooked breakfast?" He returned to his plate and that really good-looking omelet.

"I'm not a domestic goddess."

"Or a tried-and-true rancher."

Kendall might have retorted but her eggs were smoking again. She turned off the burner and opened cabinet doors, looking for a plate.

"Above the dishwasher." Finn held his coffee mug above his plate with both hands, as if it was precious to him. He was a paradox. Grumpy. Witty. Standoffish. Scrumptious. Prickly.

Scarred. No, not scarred.

She didn't think of him that way. She barely noticed his scars this morning. It was as if her brain smoothed them away.

After finding a plate, Kendall had to pry her eggs from the frying pan.

"A little butter or oil will take care of that next time."

Kendall didn't want to subject herself to cooking in front of him again.

Maybe I can learn everything I need to about ranching today.

The thought pleased her enough that she was able to choke down her burned eggs, aided by drinking copious amounts of hot black coffee. Not that she was going to complain.

"You know, you don't have to drink your coffee black. There's creamer in the fridge," Finn told her in a rare moment of kindness. "And you could have tried to make another batch of eggs. I wouldn't have docked your pay."

"Thank you for offering, but my coffee and eggs were fine."

"Sure." He rinsed out his coffee cup. "That's why you've been heaving those weary sighs."

"Those weary sighs are just part of my morning routine." She carried her empty dish and mug to the dishwasher. "I sigh. Often. All through the day and probably through the night, as well. Get over it."

He looked suitably horrified.

She was, too, when she realized what her statement implied. She was usually circumspect with her statements. That's why she was so good at public relations. She didn't put her foot in her mouth. And yet, here she had.

Because even with those scars—or perhaps because of them—I want him to like me.

The thought shocked her.

"Let's get the stock fed." She glanced around, making sure she'd cleaned up whatever she'd touched. "And you can teach me some buzz words."

"*A* is for alfalfa," he said woodenly, striding toward the front door. "*B* is for barn."

"Not funny." She hurried after him.

FINN HAD NEVER fed and watered the stock without giving some love and attention to them.

Not that they weren't receiving love and attention aplenty from Kendall. She had a kind word for each animal and knew just where to touch them to make them happy—under the forelock, behind the cheek and ears. By the time they'd worked their way through the barn, Finn was ready for a kind word and her gentle touch, preferably her fingers running through his hair.

I've been alone too long.

No good would come of acknowledging this attraction he had for her. He used the alphabet vocabulary lesson to keep a wedge between them.

"*L* is for gate latch," he told her as he clicked the last stall door closed. He led Kendall toward the back barn door and the misfits, pushing a wheelbarrow with different kinds of feed.

They were behind schedule and Gary the goat knew it. He could be heard bleating all the way from the back pasture.

As Finn passed the bunk room, a small white paw jutted beneath the closed door, a playful attempt at attention.

Kendall drummed her fingers on the wood as she passed. "I'll be with you in a minute, Boo."

Finn didn't look, but he heard more scratching. He led Kendall outside. "These are what

Lizzie calls our misfits." That wasn't exactly right. Jenny had labeled them misfits and Finn had kept up the practice. He gestured to each animal in turn. "A llama who's battling arthritis—Larry. A goat who came to us with a broken leg—Gary. An emu who'd been overly stressed and had completely molted when someone dropped her off—Evie. A donkey that was bullied by a herd of horses. You can see the scars on his withers and flanks, where he was bit so hard the skin had broken. He's Doug."

"You take in broken things," Kendall murmured, as if remembering what Lizzie had said last night in town. "And you name them using alliteration." She moved past Finn to greet his four-legged charges, who stood at the fence ready to be fed.

Evie stood apart from the others, nearer to the place Finn put her feed bucket twice a day. But it was Kendall who kept drawing Finn's attention. She'd drawn her long black hair into a braid over one shoulder. Her long legs were covered in denim, but it was the thin, stretchy kind that offered little protection from sharp objects or inquisitive animal teeth. She was wearing a green Eagles sweatshirt that looked like she'd folded it precisely when she was packing. Not that she apologized for it or complained that there was no ironing board in the barn.

On the whole, things could be worse. He'd trade a little worse for a lot less attraction.

"What do they eat?" She stroked Doug's neck.

"Mostly hay and alfalfa pellets for the four-legged creatures." He dropped hay flakes in their feed trough. "Evie needs a special bucket of food."

"How on earth did you figure out what to feed an emu?"

"It's called the internet," he replied, deadpan. "But seriously, you need to watch out around her. Emus like shiny objects—those earrings you're wearing—"

Kendall covered her ears.

"—cell phones, belt buckles, your eyes when they catch the light," he continued with his litany of warnings. "Be careful around her."

"Noted." She slipped her earrings into her sweatshirt pocket. "How is she around Lizzie?"

"She's fine as long as Lizzie doesn't move too fast." Finn realized he'd gone too long without dropping the alphabet. Their banter was beginning to sound chummy. "*R* is for ranch hand, by the way. You should be taking notes. Tomorrow, I'll expect you to feed all the animals yourself." Which would free him up to put out calls to sell some stock and get a head start on his quarterly ranch paperwork, which was due next week to his accountant.

"I've got this." Kendall grasped the wheelbarrow handles and pushed it back toward the barn.

"You've got this the way you had the eggs this morning?" He caught up to her easily.

"I ate them, didn't I?" She slid him a sly smile. "*C* is for complaints, of which there were none."

He liked her. This wouldn't do. And neither would the direction she was taking.

Finn placed a hand on her arm, halting her. "We need to go around the back. The chickens are next." He'd placed a bucket of chicken feed in the wheelbarrow.

"The chickens and the ducklings." Kendall pivoted without dumping the feed and pushed on. "Lizzie wouldn't want you to forget the ducklings."

In addition to a good pair of cowboy boots, she needed a decent pair of gloves. Neither of which were his problem.

"You've gone silent, boss, just when I was getting used to instructions by alphabet." She didn't just sneak a glance at him this time. She paused and let that tender smile of hers sink into the pores of his being.

She was pretty, kind, sophisticated and a complication he didn't need.

"Are you criticizing my management style?" He tried to infuse his question with a barricade of gruffness, but he knew he'd failed.

She laughed and pushed on. "The cowgirl princess would never criticize her rancher boss. Wouldn't want to be fired my first day."

She wasn't exactly his employee, not when she didn't expect to be paid. He took the opening anyway. "You can quit anytime. I won't judge."

"You judged me the moment you saw me." She scoffed, but good-naturedly so. "Don't be fooled by my manicure, boss. You should know. Everybody wears their armor differently."

"I don't know what you mean."

"Don't you?" Kendall parked the wheelbarrow in front of the chicken coop. "You've kept your right side to me as much as possible all morning. You even tilt your hat to the left."

Grrr.

Finn resisted the urge to bring his hat brim down. "Women and children have been known to run screaming from my scars."

"If that were true, folks in town would

have warned me about you long ago." Kendall reached for the bucket of chicken feed and headed toward the coop door.

The chickens were already strutting about the enclosure, clucking excitedly, eager for breakfast. The orphaned ducklings followed every move Chickie made. Lizzie was going to love that.

Finn came up behind Kendall in case she left the gate open too long and a hen or duckling tried to escape. He shouldn't have worried. She kept the bucket low and latched the gate firmly behind her. And then she spread the chicken feed in sweeping strokes, just as he would have done.

"This isn't your first chicken-coop experience." What else was she going to surprise him with?

"Right you are." She laid a thin line of feed for the ducklings before tossing more food for the flock. "We summered at the family ranch, and I hated almost everything about it."

"Too dirty for you." His fingers clung to the chicken wire the same way he clung to her words.

"I didn't fit in." She kneeled to stroke Chickie, who was pecking near her feet. "Not on horseback anyway. And not when it came to controlling cattle. Or when it came to fixing fence, driving tractors, chopping firewood. My attempts were laughable." Kendall got to her feet, her expression pained, and wasn't looking at him. "And so, I stopped trying to be something I'm not."

"And yet, here you are." The words fell from his lips without thought.

Kendall did look at him then—looked at him and frowned. "That's right. Here I am." She moved closer to him, closer to the gate.

Finn waited to hear what she had to say next, eager despite their differences, or maybe because of them, to know more about her.

He waited. And waited…

She smiled in that way of hers that said she was made of sterner stuff than most people gave her credit for. "You're blocking my path, boss."

He was. And because he didn't want her to know it embarrassed him, he didn't step aside to let her through. "You aren't going to quit by lunchtime, are you?"

She shook her head. "Not even by supper."

CHAPTER SIX

"Okay, Rebel. How about a little patience? It's been a long time since I've put a bridle on a horse." If Kendall had to guess, it'd been fifteen years.

She held the bridle to the brown mare's nose. Her hands were shaking.

Kendall glanced over her shoulder to make sure Finn hadn't returned from checking on Lizzie and feeding her breakfast. She'd been bluffing her way through ranch chores since they'd started working at dawn. Mostly, she'd been a success, she might add, not that Finn was vocal in his appreciation.

Who was she kidding? He hadn't given her a word of praise or thanks.

But she'd surprised him in a good way. She knew she had. It was there in his wide blue eyes and how his lips twitched when she said or did something unexpected. She'd ignore the sizzle between them and earn his respect before she was through here. But first, Kendall had more hoops to jump through, starting with saddling their mounts.

She shook the leather bridle, making it jingle softly, causing Rebel's ears to swivel. "I know you know what this is."

The mare looked away.

"Don't make me use my stern voice, Rebel." Kendall put the bridle in front of the mare's nose again.

Rebel pivoted, turning her back on Kendall and moving to the corner of the stall, as if that was the end of the conversation.

Lizzie flung open the barn door and skipped inside with Peanut at her heels. Boo scampered into the bunk room, managing to escape Peanut's notice.

Lizzie's curls bounced. The dog's tail wagged. The sunshine caught dancing dust motes.

Inside Rebel's stall, Kendall had no bounce, no wag, no dance moves. But somehow, she was going to have to get Rebel saddled before Finn came back.

"Can you close the bunk-room door, honey?" Kendall didn't want to press her luck. Peanut seemed like he'd love on Boo in a way the kitten wasn't ready for.

Lizzie dutifully closed the door and then skipped to Rebel's stall. She peered through the rails and proclaimed, "Rebel isn't a bit horse."

"You're right. She's a full horse, honey." Kendall tried once more to approach Rebel with the bridle, but the horse only turned her back once more, swishing her tail as if Kendall was a pesky fly. "Mares are horses, no bit about it."

"I know that." Lizzie climbed up on the stall door railings, hooking her skinny arms over the top. "Rebel don't use a bit."

Peanut sat below Lizzie and to one side, watching his beloved little charge worshipfully.

"Oh." Kendall unlatched the stall door, giving Lizzie a ride on the open and close. "I thought I got her bridle where your dad told me to." She went into the tack room, followed by the girl and the dog, and glanced around. Sure enough, Rebel's name was written on a piece of wood over a peg that had a hackamore hanging from it. Kendall had taken the bridle for Monty, which was on the next peg over. "This is what only one breakfast does for a body." Not to mention lack of sleep. She returned Monty's bridle to its peg.

Lizzie skipped back into the breezeway. "Can we play with Boo?"

"You can play with Boo, but until she gets

bigger, I don't think Boo should play with Peanut. Okay?"

"Peanut is going to be sad." Lizzie skipped over to the bunk room, placing her hand on the knob. "Daddy said you'd saddle Pete for me."

"And I will, just as soon as I saddle Rebel." Now that she recognized the system, she'd be able to locate Pete's gear. Kendall entered the mare's stall. "Well, girlie. Second time's a charm, I hope."

Rebel took one look at Kendall and what she was holding, and ambled over, sweet as you please.

Kendall slipped on the hackamore without any more issues. She led the mare over to the tack room and looped her reins on a hook outside the door. "Now I need brushes and a hoof pick." The activities involved in taking a ride were coming back to her. She was worried about putting on the girth strap though. She couldn't remember how to fasten one.

It's called the internet.

Remembering Finn's deadpan reply had Kendall chuckling. She could always search for a video. She just didn't want to get caught doing it. Finn was hard to impress, but she was determined to get there. She'd even written notes about good ranching practices on her hand in permanent marker to use to spark a conversation. She glanced at her palm now. Nothing was smudged.

Rebel nudged Kendall with her nose.

"You'll never tell, will you, Rebel?" Kendall obliged the mare with a scratch between her ears. "It'll be our secret."

A hissing noise had Kendall turning.

Little Boo stood in the bunk-room doorway, white hair raised and body arched.

Peanut executed the downward dog-yoga position, tail wagging, plus a doggy smile. He hopped forward, butt still in the air.

Lizzie giggled, jumping up and down behind Boo. "They're playing."

"Don't move, Lizzie." Kendall hurried over, keeping her tone even. "If you move too fast, Boo might scratch Peanut."

Peanut whined and trembled as if he wanted to pounce on Boo and give her a big furry hug.

Boo hissed again.

"They love each other, Miss Kendall." Lizzie reached out from behind Boo, as if she was going to pet her.

"Lizzie, no!"

But she was too late.

Lizzie touched Boo from behind. The kitten leaped straight up in the air, pivoted and scratched the little girl's outstretched hand. Peanut jumped forward, paws coming down on either side of the kitten, who landed on her feet, and scratched Peanut's big black nose. He yelped. Boo retreated, hiding under the bunk bed. The dog's yelps turned into excited barks as Peanut gave chase, knocking over a still screaming Lizzie.

Kendall dove into the melee, sweeping Lizzie into her arms and inserting herself between the bed and the dog. "Peanut, out!"

Peanut was still in the throes of the chase. For every step Kendall took, he dodged around, trying to crawl under the bed. Finally, Kendall managed to herd the dog out of the room and closed the door, shutting Boo in.

On the other side of the barn, Rebel had her back turned to them, perhaps unnerved by the ruckus. Kendall could relate, but she chose to face the situation head-on.

Finn was due back any minute. Kendall had to get control of the chaos.

"Waaaaaa." Lizzie was doing the post-trauma, dry cry, holding on to her scratched hand as if it was broken.

Leaving Peanut on guard duty at the bunk-room door, Kendall took Lizzie to the bathroom, where she washed and bandaged her scratch.

"Waaaaaa."

"It's all better now."

"No, it's not." Lizzie sniffed. *"Waaaaaa."*

"What happened? What's wrong?" Finn's broad shoulders filled the bathroom doorway. He held a little girl's straw cowboy hat, decorated with small pink and blue flowers and a thin ribbon. "Come here, love. Tell Daddy all about it."

"Boo scratched me." Lizzie began to shed real tears. "On p-p-p-purpose. *Waaaaaa.*"

Scooping her up, Finn's dark eyebrows lowered. His scars flushed the color of anger. His gaze landed on Kendall with a thud she felt in the pit of her stomach. "I told you—"

"It was an accident." Kendall held up her hands. "This is what my Grandpa Harlan would call a teaching moment."

"*N* is for no," Finn warned. "There's a time and place for everything."

"And now's the time for truth." Kendall came to stand in front of him, but it was the little girl she spoke to. "Now, Lizzie. Why don't you tell your father what happened?"

"Uh… Umm…" Lizzie wiped her tears with the back of her uninjured hand. "Peanut and me were playing with Boo, and then she scratched us. *Waaaaaa.*"

Finn looked toward the big dog with his nose stuck to the crack between the door and the floor. He sighed. And with that exhalation, everything about his face seemed to soften, even those scars on his cheek.

Finn dropped a kiss on top of Lizzie's blond curls and set her down. "What do I always say about baby animals, love?"

His daughter thrust out her lip. "That we have to treat them gentle."

"That's right." He kneeled down to her left, tipping back his cowboy hat. "Take a look at Peanut."

As if on cue, the dog scratched at the floor like crazy, possibly thinking he could dig his way to Boo.

"Does Peanut look like he wants to play gently?" Finn's voice was tender yet commanding, especially when he added, "Peanut, stop."

Lizzie lowered her chin, shaking her head. Peanut sank to the ground, panting and looking at his owner.

"Why is Rebel tied up with her bridle instead of a halter?" Finn got to his feet, shedding softness and reclaiming the jagged attitude those scars promised. "*P* is for process, princess."

"*Pro-cess?*" Lizzie murmured, carefully sounding the word out loud.

Finn grasped the halter and lead rope hanging outside Rebel's stall. "Process. Halter, then lead rope tied to a hook with a quick release knot—in case of emergency. Then a good brush-down of the parts that are going to be touching equipment." He used choppy motions to point out Rebel's chest, back and head. "Then it's a quick inspection of the hooves and saddle pad. Then it's saddle on. And finally—*finally*—it's the bridle. *Process.*"

Kendall crossed her arms and gave a brisk nod, keeping her troublesome pride and soft-sided ego locked tight inside. She needed this opportunity, which meant she needed Finn in a mood to impart advice. "Thanks for the refresher, boss. I won't forget the direction."

Finn made a sound deep in his throat. It sounded like a growl.

Kendall had never been growled at before. At least, not by a man. It was...*sexy*.

Shoot. She was drawn to this moody, intense man. How inconvenient. The sooner she learned what she needed to, the better.

"Daddy, are you mad at Miss Kendall?" Wiping her nose and looking thoroughly recovered, Lizzie beamed up at her father. "You know 'motions can be tricky. Do you need a time-out until you can be nice?"

"I DON'T NEED a time-out," Finn said tightly, trying his darndest not to look at Kendall. He knew he needed to tone it down and struggled to do so, taking a moment for a few deep breaths. "We're behind schedule moving the herd. Go get Pete, love."

When Lizzie darted off, Finn leaned closer to Kendall and whispered, "Ranch hands are supposed to create less work for me, not more."

"It won't happen again," Kendall promised, but those eyes…

They promised nothing of the sort. They promised laughter despite worries and workloads. They promised sass, not sharing. They promised long, slow kisses that made a man forget lists of chores and closing deadlines. If only they were the eyes of a woman ready to settle down on a mountain ranch.

Grrr.

Kendall smiled. *Smiled!* And it was an easy smile, too. One of those smiles that said there wasn't a tense or indignant bone in her body. How could that be? He'd just lost his temper, and even a child had noticed his displeasure.

Kendall stroked Rebel's brown neck. "I don't want to upset you, boss, but when it comes time…could you give me a little refresher on girth straps?"

His mouth dropped open. "This isn't a

training course. It's my life, my work, my livelihood."

"I know. I know. Just this once though?" That smile changed right before his eyes, became more forced, as if she was determined to charm him. "*G* is for girth strap and *H* is for how."

She was using his own tactics against him? *Grrr.*

And despite that feeling of being outplayed in a game of his making, his lips twitched, starting to inch upward.

Lizzie came out of Pete's stall, leading her little black pony with its halter properly on. "Did you have a nice time-out, Daddy?"

Finn swallowed another growl.

"He did," Kendall assured Lizzie. She reached up and patted Finn's whiskered cheek—*his scars!* "He can be a bear sometimes, can't he, Lizzie? But we find cranky old bears cuddly."

Cranky old bears? Cuddly?

Lizzie giggled.

Finn was tempted to step into the bathroom and look in the mirror, if only to see for himself what Kendall saw, because his self-image didn't jibe with cuddly old bears.

Before he acted on the impulse, Kendall disappeared into the tack room. Finn was tempted to follow her in, hold her in his arms and ask her to take another good, long look at him. His wasn't a face that inspired women to cuddle. And if his disfigurement didn't scare her off... Well, he'd give in to the impulse to kiss her.

I'd what?

Finn shook himself. This was trouble. Plain and simple. *She* was trouble. The Monroe princess was only looking to learn cowgirl skills. She wasn't looking for love with a broken man like him. And Finn wasn't interested in idle kisses.

Kendall emerged from the tack room with a brush and a hoof pick, which Lizzie promptly claimed. With a good-natured smile and a lyrical laugh, Kendall went back in the tack room. As princesses went, this one was kindhearted.

Still, when she came back out, he pointedly glanced down at her feet. "No riding in sneakers." And then he headed for his horse's stall.

"I'll get my booties on before we leave," Kendall told him. "And when I go into town tonight, I'll pick up a pair of cowboy boots. I saw some there, I think. Or at least, boot boxes."

"When you go into town..." He turned, frowning. "How are you getting back to town?" He sure as heck wasn't going out of his way to cater to her whims.

"I told you I'd find a ride. My brother's going to pick me up." Kendall was wearing that you-can't-rattle-me smile, which she flashed first to him and then to Lizzie, whose answering smile showed how much his daughter adored this woman.

I could adore her.

Oh, no. There was disaster ahead and it involved the right sort of attachment to the wrong sort of woman. The woman Finn wanted was straightforward, unassuming and a sure thing when it came to staying. Kendall was none of those things. "You're hanging by a thread here, princess." As was he.

Kendall laughed in that cultured way of hers. "Yes, but it's a thread that won't break."

RIDING TUCKER, HIS buckskin gelding, Finn led Lizzie and Kendall out to the main pasture to move fence. "We're an hour behind schedule." It was after nine.

"Sorry," Kendall replied in a singsong voice. Her chipper tone was going to be the death of him, along with those unflappable smiles, like the one she'd given him when he'd presented a girth-strap refresher.

Who knew he was a sucker for women

who could turn sour lemons like him into the sweetest lemonade?

"We're coming, Daddy." Lizzie rode behind Finn and in front of Kendall. Her blond curls ruffled in the breeze beneath her fancy cowboy hat. Pete was especially pokey today, having already fallen ten feet behind Finn and they'd only just left the ranch yard. "Why didn't we take the truck. We always take the truck."

"Oh, really." Kendall sounded overly interested in this piece of information.

"Really." Frowning, Finn sat rigidly in the saddle, resisting the urge to look back and see the expression on Kendall's face. "You said you needed a refresher, princess." Refresher? This was more like ranching for beginners. "You'll get a good, long ride in today." They all would.

This ride would challenge Kendall's determination and stamina. A true greenhorn would be saddle-tested at the end of a long ride, unused muscles aching in protest. And then there were her city boots. Besides having impractically high heels on, her boots had zippers on either side of her ankles. The stirrups were going to be unforgiving. He may not scare her away by lunch, but he was going to get rid of her soon. She wouldn't stay another night.

He took a deep breath and allowed himself a small smile.

"Is that why you're grumpy, boss?" Kendall asked from behind him. "Because it's going to be a long ride today?"

"Grumpy?" Finn turned in the saddle and frowned at her, pointing to his face. "This is not my grumpy expression. This is my everyday look, because every day I'm racing against daylight to get the necessary things done for the stock, for the ranch, for my daughter." And if he was really lucky, he'd have a sliver of time to work on the accounts.

"Grumpy," he muttered under his breath, feeling the pressure to juggle all his responsibilities and find himself a wife.

"Daddy needs another time-out," Lizzie said solemnly.

"I don't. Look. I'm smiling." He moved his lips until he was certain no one could argue that he wasn't smiling. He was the first to admit the stress of ranching life and being diagnosed with cancer were both getting to him. But the fact that his attitude was being picked up by Lizzie hit him sharply, the way an unexpected branch did when he rode too close to the tree line.

"Finn, you can't mean to say you run this place solo." Kendall looked ridiculous on horseback in her skinny jeans and city boots. *Ridiculously sexy.*

Facing forward once more, Finn drew the back of his hand across his forehead, trying to erase the attraction he felt for the most unsettling woman on the planet. Said woman trotted up next to him, practically bouncing out of Rebel's saddle.

Tucker's ears swung back and forth, clearly debating how to react to the mare's presence. He and Rebel often vied for the title of boss of the herd.

"Nobody runs a ranch by themselves," Kendall insisted. "It's impossible."

"It's hard, not impossible." Finn headed toward the road that dissected his grazing pastures.

"Feeding the stock alone takes a huge amount of time," Kendall said, still using that tone that indicated she doubted Finn's abilities.

"Now listen here," Finn began, just as Tucker reached over and nipped at Rebel, who quickly leaped sideways and out of reach, practically unseating her rider.

"Hey, keep your horse to yourself." Unperturbed, Kendall stood in one stirrup before righting herself in the saddle. One more un-expected move by Rebel and she'd fall out of that saddle like a sack of potatoes.

Finn tightened the slack in his reins and swung Kendall a quick glance. "If you can't sit a horse properly, at least hold on tight to the saddle horn."

"I sit well in a chair, not in a saddle." Squinting in the sun, she swatted at her cheek as if bothered by a bug.

"All it takes is practice," Finn muttered. She hadn't used the bug spray in the tack room. And without a hat, she'd be sunburned by noon. Not that there was anything he could do about it now. *Greenhorns!* "If you go out to Texas and ride with that old man you're so dead set on impressing, he's going to call you out for what you are—*a city gal.*"

"Can I add riding lessons to my list of re-freshers you'll give me?" she said sweetly.

He frowned—at the eagerness in her voice, at the way his mouth instinctively curved upward in response to her and at the increasing list of her so-called refreshers. "A ranching alphabet? Saddling processes? Riding lessons? And who knows what else you need to learn? At this rate, you won't be ready for Texas until Christmas."

"I have faith in you, boss." Kendall guided

Rebel closer to him to avoid a pothole in the road. "*Q* is for quick refreshers."

Tucker's ears snapped back, and he tossed his head.

Finn took a moment to turn the gelding in a tight circle, allowing Kendall and Rebel to move on ahead, allowing both horse and rider to earn some space. That's when he noticed how far back Lizzie was. He frowned. His daughter should be his first priority, not this princess. "Hurry up, love."

"Pete is walking," his daughter groused from thirty feet behind them. "And look at Peanut. He's gonna get lost."

Sure enough, their dog was racing through the brown grass ahead toward the smallest of their herds. Finn called him back.

"I need a big horse, Daddy. A fast horse." Lizzie kicked Pete with her heels, not that the pony increased his pace one iota.

"You can ride a big horse when you're five," Finn promised, same as always. He glanced ahead to Kendall, who was shifting in her saddle again. "Stop for a second and ride with your hips, no, seriously. Stop so Lizzie can catch up."

"Okay, but..." Kendall brought Rebel to a halt, smiling at Finn, although the expression didn't reach her eyes. "Ride with my hips? Is that supposed to be a joke?"

He was completely serious. "Out here, those boots are a joke. What I'm saying is that your hips are the shock absorber of the ride. Good shock absorbers aren't loose. They're held in place, the same way your feet and legs hold your hips in place."

"Got it." Obediently, and with a broader smile that reached her eyes, Kendall shifted her hips, her legs and her feet, earning a tail swish from Rebel. "Ouch. Better?"

He nodded.

Lizzie caught up to them. "Can I ride Rebel? Miss Kendall can ride Pete and work on her seat while he walks."

"No." Finn moved ahead, but not before he caught Lizzie yawning. "What's ranching rule number three, love?"

"Hang on. I just realized that you've numbered the rules." Kendall chuckled. "This explains a lot. Alphabets. Alliteration. Processes. And now rules. What's next? Pearls of wisdom? A treasure trove of knowledge? I'm going to walk out of here richer than I walked in." She flashed that winning smile at him.

"You use what you can to stay safe out here," Finn said, thinking he needed a rule for dealing with appealing, would-be cowgirls.

"Um…number three is… Don't fall asleep in the saddle?" Lizzie yawned again. "We should have taken the truck."

She was only saying that because she got to nap in the truck. He hadn't factored naps into his plan to get rid of the princess. And he had to get rid of her.

Or the riches she'd leave with would include his heart.

CHAPTER SEVEN

"WATCH WHAT I'M DOING," Finn told Kendall, turning to face her.

Kendall thought he had a nice back. A nice front, too, even with the damage to his cheek. In fact, he looked good from all angles. When he wasn't being grumpy. Although he had every right to be grouchy since he was single-handedly running a ranch and raising a daughter by himself.

She snapped a picture of Finn, using the cattle behind him as a backdrop.

Finn stood a few feet away from Kendall at a fence post with a small solar panel on top and a box mounted beneath it. His horse was tethered to a small tree, enjoying the shade.

"I turn off the electricity charging the fence here." Finn flipped a switch in the box, and then bent to step between fence wires to move into the pasture. "The wires aren't hot now, which means I can temporarily release the fencing wires where they're fastened to the post." He began squeezing yellow plastic fasteners on the opposite side of the anchor post, completely unfazed by the cattle that moved closer and closer to him.

"If you release the wires, there won't be anything separating you from the herd." Oh, yeah. That was panic in Kendall's voice. "Large animals make me nervous."

"And the real reason you didn't fit in on the family ranch in Texas becomes clear." The glance he spared her searched for confirmation.

"You don't know what it's like to be born into a family of overachievers." She sniffed. "You learn very quickly to stake out your areas of expertise and detach from the rest." With that smile Grandpa Harlan had taught her.

Finn bent his head to the fence once more. "I take it you fell, and no one encouraged you to get back in the saddle."

"Oh, they encouraged, all right." Kendall tried to make light of the past. "But I felt safer as a spectator." Physically and emotionally.

"This puts your smile in a whole new context."

"What's that supposed to mean?"

"We're late," Finn said. The man spent too much time watching the clock and not enough time talking about her smile. "Are you paying attention to what I'm doing?"

No. She wasn't. Smile discussion aside, there were at least fifty heifers—cattle…bovines…whatever—crowding the thin wires he was about to release and a couple hundred milling about behind them. If circumstances went south, from where she sat there wasn't anything Kendall could do to prevent Finn from being trampled.

Beside her, and at an extremely lower height, Lizzie slouched on Pete and yawned, clearly struggling to obey rule number three. Peanut sat at the pony's feet, watching with a bored expression on his face. Their nonchalance should have reassured Kendall that everything would be fine.

It didn't.

"Princess?" Finn straightened, the ends of both wires he'd unclipped in each hand. "Kendall? Did you see how I did that?"

"Sorry. I was too worried about the possibility that you'd be a victim of a stampede to pay attention to the mechanics, other than flipping the power switch off."

He made that noise in his throat, the one that sounded like a growl and gave her the good goose bumps. And then he gathered the wires together and hurried out of the way of his cattle. He didn't stop. He kept backing up and dragging wires away from heifer hooves.

Suddenly, the herd surged forward, passing through the ever-widening, makeshift gate, kicking up a light layer of dust as they passed, trotting out into the next pasture and beginning to graze. It didn't take long for Kendall's skin to feel gritty. She wiped at her face with the neck of her sweatshirt.

Miraculously, Finn wasn't trampled. Kendall began to relax.

When the last of the herd passed, Finn brought the wires back to the post. "All four hundred accounted for. Watch me refasten the wires."

"Why?" Kendall yawned. After that adrenaline rush, she was as much in need of a nap as Lizzie. "You think I might have to do this in Texas?"

"You want to learn, don't you?" Finn leaned into his task, creating tension in the bottom wire as he reattached it to the pole. "The best way to learn is by doing. We have three more herds to move. And chances are——" he attached the top wire "——Lizzie's going to need a nap soon. She's half-asleep already, which means we'll be riding double, so you'll have to do this."

Oh. Oh, no. "Lizzie can ride with me."

Finn bent and moved between the wires to exit the pasture. "You? Ride double? You can barely stay in the saddle by yourself. There's no chance I'm putting my daughter on a horse with you." He turned on the electricity. "I need a ranch hand right now, not a—"

"Princess. Yeah, yeah. I get it." Kendall was used to being a liability on a ranch. But nothing, not even her competitiveness with her brothers, had made her want to work harder at her skills on horseback and improve her knowledge of ranching than this man. Which reminded her of the plan she'd made earlier to impress him. "I still can't believe you run this place alone. Besides basic stock maintenance, there's branding and cattle transport," Kendall went on, holding her hand awkwardly on the saddle horn as she snuck a glance at her palm. "Plus, inoculations and tagging. Not to mention pregnancy verification."

He looked at her suspiciously, specifically at her hand. "Did you make notes about ranching on your palm?"

Kendall flattened her hand on the top of her thigh and glanced down at Lizzie. "Don't fall asleep, Lizzie."

Finn plucked a lethargic Lizzie from the saddle and settled her on his mount. He gave

Kendall a knowing look as he handed her Pete's reins. "Ranchers don't need notes."

"Hello? I'm not even a cowgirl." She gestured to herself. "It's why I looked things up on the internet." Thinking she might be able to get by.

"I was trying to impress you and failed. If you give me a test on ranching later, I promise not to write crib notes on my body. Cross my heart." She tried to make light of it.

Finn chuckled, adjusted his hat and stared up at her. "Ranchers learn the ropes. Plain and simple."

"Clearly, I'm not a rancher. I just want to play one on social media."

"Social media. There's a big waste of time." He scoffed, climbing into the saddle behind Lizzie. "I don't see the need for it."

Kendall laughed. And then laughed again. "Of course, you don't. You're probably ranching using the same methods your father and grandfather used and selling your cattle to the same suppliers you always have."

He drew his shoulders back and hit her with that hard look of his, the one that made him seem imposingly handsome. And yet, intriguingly attractive.

She refused to back down. "You probably

think the way to increase your profits is to increase the size of your herd."

"That is the best way to increase profits," Finn said, scowling as he urged that big horse of his forward.

"You could use social media to increase the productivity of your heifers." That was another one of her carefully culled research facts. "Ranchers are finding social media helps broaden their network of buyers and sellers, which results in stronger bloodlines and stock."

"Could you lower your voice?" Finn adjusted Lizzie's cowboy hat over her sweet, slumbering face, and urged his horse forward. "Let the kid snooze a little."

Kendall fell into line behind him on Rebel, holding the pony's reins. "What was it you said about my smile?" she asked in a low voice. "It needed context?"

Finn glanced at her over his shoulder. "You smile like you've faced hardship but you're refusing to let that keep you down."

He'd noticed? No one ever noticed. "You're… That's… I disagree. I have a nice smile!"

He shushed her, looking forward as Peanut trotted past before returning his gaze to Kendall and continuing in a soothing voice.

"You got that smile growing up with all those overachievers. It says you aren't going to quit, thank you very much anyway."

His words washed over her in a gentle wave of truth.

"You should be proud of that expression." His blue eyes glowed with that respect she'd been hoping for earlier. "It says you've got strength and character. It says you've gone miles down the road."

Kendall gasped. "Did you just say I'm old?" She was thirty-two and far from being over-the-hill.

He rolled his eyes and faced forward.

"You should have quit at 'character,'" she murmured.

They rode past several empty fields in silence. Even Peanut had slowed down, padding along ahead of them as if he was pacing himself.

Soon, they arrived at the next pasture. This one had a water trough near the power box, one that jutted into one pasture and was also accessible to part of the road. Again, the herd was waiting near the electric fence. Again, Kendall's heart beat faster at the thought of trampling. Only this time, it'd be her they flattened if she didn't do her job right.

"Animals sense fear, princess," Finn said, back to his usual gruffness.

"I'm not afraid." She gave him that smile he seemed to be a fan of.

"Sure," he said too quickly to be believed. "Anyway, I need you to dismount and give Rebel and Pete some water. And then tie them up over there." Finn nodded toward a slender tree bordering the pasture.

Kendall managed to dismount on shaky legs, silently cursing the blisters that were forming where her boot zippers rubbed her ankle bones. Still, she watered the pony and mare, then flipped the reins over tree branches without saying *"ow"* once. "What now?"

Finn brought Tucker to the water trough to drink. "Dig into my saddlebags. There's a dog dish for Peanut and water bottles for us."

Kendall handed Finn a water, took one for herself and then filled Peanut's water bowl. "And now I—"

"Do exactly what I did back there," Finn told her, his voice low but strong. His expression had a sort of grim confidence. "You can do it."

Kendall nodded. She cut off the power supply to the electrical fence, and then entered the pasture by climbing between the barbed wire—no small feat when each step caused her pain. "How friendly are your cattle?" They were awfully close, not to mention staring at her. "I mean, they're not meat-eating zombie cows, are they? They're staring at me like—"

"They're hungry. Yes. That's because they are. They just want to get to fresh grass." That was reassuring. "You'll be fine if you get out of their way quickly. Go on. Give them that smile."

"Like they'll be swayed." But it was enough that he was. Smiling stiffly, Kendall wrapped her fingers around a yellow plastic fastener and gave it a quick squeeze. The wire didn't pop free the way it had when Finn did it.

Her palms were sweaty. Her ankles throbbed. Her cheeks felt tight, like they were getting sunburned.

Shades of summers in Texas.

She glanced up at Finn, ready to ask for help.

"We rotate our cattle through the pastures daily," Finn said, not unkindly. He stared out over the valley toward the Sawtooth Mountains. "It gives us higher yield on natural grasses."

He was giving her ranching knowledge? Without use of the alphabet?

She couldn't quit. Not now.

"That's smart of you." Kendall made a mental note of the practice while applying a double grip on the fastener this time. She leaned into her task, falling to her knees when the wire popped free.

Sensing a change, the cattle crowded closer.

"Be quick about releasing the other wire," Finn cautioned. "The herd has a routine. We're late and they're impatient."

"Bear with me, boys and girls." Kendall repeated the process on the bottom wire—two-handed grip, leaning into it—and surprised herself when the wire fastener released easily. "I did it."

Something snorted behind her, and it wasn't Finn. She could almost imagine hot bovine breath on the back of her neck.

"Don't panic," Finn said in a soothing voice. "Just drag those wires out of their way. Hurry but don't rush or you'll spook them."

"I'm spooked enough for all of us," Kendall muttered, doing as instructed and getting out of the way.

The lead herd members trotted past, followed by the main herd at a slower pace, and then the stragglers.

Kendall managed to hook the wires back in place and get out of the pasture without snagging herself on the barbed wire or giving in to the pain of blisters. She turned the power back on, absurdly proud of herself.

"What's bothering you?" Finn's gaze performed an assessing inventory. "You're moving like you're hurt."

The last of her cool evaporated. "It's not that exactly. It's… My boot zippers gave me blisters." It wouldn't be the first time footwear had wounded her, but it certainly felt like the most inconvenient time. "I'll soldier on."

"There are bandages in my saddlebags." Finn regarded her sympathetically. "Those blisters have got to be killing you."

He was easy on the eyes, kind and compassionate, and he packed saddlebags for every contingency. Why was this man single?

Kendall quickly found the bandages—pink with white bunny rabbits—and applied them over her popped blisters, four in all. She pulled her jean leggings down lower to cover her bandaged ankles. "Thanks."

"You could have asked earlier if I had anything to help."

Not on her life. "Would you have laughed at me? Or just made another joke about royalty?"

He grimaced. "In my defense, I've never laughed at you."

That was true. She mounted Rebel and took Pete's reins in hand. "What's next?"

"Two more herds to move." Finn glanced down at the dog dish and her water bottle resting next to the water trough as he passed them. "I guess we'll pick those up on the way back."

"Oops." Kendall made a mental note not to forget to retrieve them later.

They rode in silence for a few minutes, after which, Kendall worked up the courage to talk shop. "You sound like you've instituted some smart ranching practices."

"I know you're surprised that this dinosaur knows a few new tricks." He'd tested her all last night and this morning, but this sounded like a tease, like a cowboy talking to his good friend.

"You're not a dinosaur. You're just ranching in an unexpected place." The life out here couldn't be easy. The winters were long and dumped several feet of snow.

"Most ranches are out of the way. All the good land and water resources are taken up by suburbia now."

"It's competitive." And he was doing it alone. On some level, their professions were similar. "I'm curious. Do you track each heifer's productivity?"

"Yeah. I cull heifers from the herd if they aren't regularly producing, just like everyone else." He deftly caught Lizzie's pretty little hat before a breeze carried it away. "I have a very extensive recording system—on a computer, no less."

"I'm learning a lot from you, boss, including not to underestimate a high country rancher." She grinned.

The corner of his mouth ticked, as if he was having a hard time not smiling back. "Those words would carry more weight if you meant them."

"I may sound like I'm teasing, but there's a grain of truth there."

"One grain in a whole big pile of—"

"Grains," she said, finishing for him. "Listen, I appreciate you. And not only for your bandages."

For things she couldn't begin to name and didn't want to.

"I THINK I'M getting the hang of this," Kendall told Finn as she got back in the saddle after moving a small herd of bulls without panicking or being gored or trodden upon. Success!

Peanut sat in the shade of a small shrub, seemingly as unimpressed with Kendall's work as Finn was.

"Good thing you're catching on because

we've got one more herd and it's the largest. We need to hustle."

"Why? Is it getting too hot? Are the horses tired?"

"No. It's nearly lunchtime. I only brought crackers for Lizzie to eat on the way back."

Kendall couldn't help herself. She laughed.

Finn gave her that cool stare that sent a delicious shiver down her spine. "Keeping a toddler well-rested and well-fed is just as important to a smooth ranch operation as appropriate footwear."

"Oh." Kendall couldn't argue with that.

He continued to stare.

She tsked. "That look won't work on me, boss. I already know your secret."

Finn raised his eyebrows.

"You're a softie." Just look at how he was cradling his sleeping daughter.

Finn scoffed, finally withdrawing that intense stare and guiding his horse forward. "You wish."

She did indeed.

Kendall urged Rebel alongside him, drawing Pete between the two horses like a buffer. Finn rode without speaking, scanning the landscape, the broad pastures, the pine-filled tree lines, the mountains in the distance.

"This place is a part of you, isn't it?" Kendall kept her voice low so as not to wake Lizzie. "My grandfather loved his ranch, even when he was too old to ride."

"My grandpa was the same," he said gruffly, gaze focused on the horizon. "I think the land works its way into your heart if you let it."

"Did your wife love the land, too?"

He nodded. "But she was from the mountains to begin with. Someone like you..."

"Someone like me?" Kendall scoffed. "There's a town full of someones like me up the road. City-dwelling Monroes transplanted to Second Chance. I never would have thought it could happen. But it won't happen to me."

Something cooled in his blue eyes and she had no idea why.

Her bewilderment made her babble. "My grandfather was born and raised in Second Chance. But he called several places home, including Texas, California and Pennsylvania. He embraced the different sides of himself. The small-town boy. The adventurer who discovered lost stagecoach gold. The hard-driving businessman. Whereas I feel..." She ground to a halt before she said too much.

"How do you feel?" Finn asked softly.

If the warmth hadn't returned to his gaze beneath that hat brim, she might have left then and there. Instead, she admitted, "I feel like I've elbowed my way onto a career path and now there's no way to branch off it." She patted Rebel's neck, comforted by the mare's softness. "I enjoy what I do, don't get me wrong. But is there more? I'm too old to change careers and—"

"Oh, come on. If I can't imply you're old, you certainly can't say it." Finn was sharp, this cowboy. And by the smirk on his face, he knew it.

"Okay, okay. Let me rephrase." Kendall sifted through her feelings. "I feel like my grandfather wasn't afraid to reinvent himself. Or afraid of failure. That's what makes people succeed, I think. They want something more than they fear going belly-up."

"And you fear…"

She held up a finger. "I want to do something important, to be *someone* important, other than just a Monroe. But if I fail, it wouldn't just be my brothers who wouldn't let me live it down."

"Now that's a stretch, even for you hoity-toity Monroes." Some of the gruffness had returned to his tone. "As a man with a kid sister, I feel the need to stand up for siblings everywhere. You don't tease family about things you can't laugh about together."

"You have a point." Although she was sensitive about things where her brothers were concerned. "But beyond the family angle, I don't want to flop and be labeled an heiress who couldn't stand on her own two feet."

He made a sound of agreement. "I suppose this is where I say 'Stick with me, kid. I'll give you the tools to land that client in Texas.' But that requires you to stick in the saddle, so to speak."

It was a challenge, plain and simple. "Princesses have backbones, you know." She adopted the smile he'd expressed respect for earlier.

Finn gave her one of those sidelong looks that searched beyond appearances, beyond creased sweatshirts and saddle-weary cowgirls. He saw her in ways others hadn't seen her before. "Now, see what you're doing? You're daring me to continue calling you princess, like it's going to be your rallying cry when you face something challenging."

That's exactly what it was going to be now.

She shook her head. "Boss, you sure know how to motivate a ranch hand."

He chuckled softly.

Kendall surveyed her surroundings, the land Finn loved so much. The pastures were vast and devoid of the pine trees in the thick, surrounding forest. Other than the plodding horse hooves and the occasional cry of a hawk, it was quiet. The grand Sawtooth Mountain range was just as imposing here as it was in Second Chance. The jagged mountains were as hard as she imagined the life here was. Or maybe that was just her perception as someone from the city. If their roles were reversed, who's to say that Finn wouldn't find life difficult in crowded, noisy Philadelphia.

A short time later, they reached the southern-most herd. Kendall dismounted and looped Rebel's reins around a fence post, following suit for Pete's reins. Peanut settled into the shade of a bush. It may have been September in the high country, but the day was getting warmer. She pushed up her sweatshirt sleeves.

"You're awfully quiet," she told Finn after she'd turned off the power, unnerved by his silence.

He glanced at Rebel and Pete. "Could be you've got me all talked out."

"Or that you're thinking about what else you could teach me?" she said hopefully. Kendall navigated her way into the pasture and proceeded to unhook the wires, barely looking at the hovering cattle. "Do you want me to do this tomorrow?"

"All by yourself?" He tsked. "I'll have to think about it."

Lizzie stretched in his lap. "Are we almost done, Daddy?"

"Almost, love." Finn righted her cowboy hat when she sank down again. "When we get back, I'll have you clean the tack room, princess."

It was Kendall's turn to tsk. "What happened to straightening the cupola?"

"It'll wait until tomorrow." Finn's gaze ranged over the herd the way it did when he was counting heads. He frowned. "One short." He scanned the herd again. "There's a heifer over there but no calf."

Kendall glanced up. Sure enough, there was one cow who wasn't hurrying through the gate. She lowed, looking back toward the forest and a fallen pine tree.

"Do me a favor. Circle around that heifer and drive her over here. And while you're out there, look for anything unusual."

Kendall picked her way through the pasture, ruefully accepting the fact that her boots were ruined by the mud and wet grass she'd walked in all morning. "There are tire tracks out here. Yours?"

"No. Rustlers." Two words. So much anger.

Peanut raced past her, nose to the ground.

Kendall followed the tire tracks to the back of the pasture near the downed tree. "They came through here." There was a makeshift gate and an overgrown dirt road leading into the trees.

"That's the federal fire road," Finn called back.

There were a couple of stray tufts of straw near the gate. Peanut sniffed them before running back to Finn. Kendall took out her phone and snapped a picture of the yellow straw. If someone had enticed the calf with an easy meal, maybe Finn could use the photograph as evidence.

She headed back to Finn and the horses. The sad heifer had gone through to the other pasture, but still seemed reluctant to move farther in it.

"Poor thing." Kendall got the first wire hooked and struggled with the second. She dug in her boot heels, putting pressure on her tender ankles. Finally, the fastener clipped in place. She let out a whoop of triumph, jumping up and raising her hands in the air.

Peanut startled, scrambling away from the fence toward Tucker, who jumped sideways toward Rebel, who gave a shrill whinny and lunged with teeth bared at Finn's horse. Her reins came loose. Rebel shook her head, sending the reins dangling. And then she whinnied, turned tail and ran back the way they'd come, bumping Pete, whose reins slipped free, too. The pony took a few mincing steps backward, and then galloped after Rebel.

Kendall glanced up at Finn, shading her eyes. "Shouldn't you run them down and bring them back?"

Finn shook his head. "They won't stop running until they reach the last gate." He turned Tucker toward the ranch. "Lesson learned, I hope. You've got to tie a horse properly."

"You knew I hadn't?" Kendall couldn't believe it. "Why didn't you say something?"

He shrugged. "Because now you'll have plenty of time to think about your mistake, such that it won't happen again. Enjoy your walk back, princess. I've got a stolen calf to report."

Finn kicked Tucker into a lope and left her.

CHAPTER EIGHT

"WHY DID WE leave Miss Kendall behind, Daddy?" Lizzie sat eating crackers on the bench outside the bunk room.

"She'll be along, love." Finn evaded the question, the same as he'd been doing the last few times Lizzie had asked. He didn't want to tell Lizzie that Kendall had to learn the hard way how to take care of her best partner on the ranch. That would only lead to more questions. And no way was he going to admit that he felt guilty about leaving Kendall at the end of the road.

He liked her too much. She was a smart woman, tough yet tender. But she'd said it herself. She wanted to be someone important. Important folk didn't run ranches in remote valleys in Idaho, much less want to settle down with a rancher in one. "You need to brush Pete."

"I don't wanna." Lizzie stood and put her hand on the bunk-room door. "I wanna play with Boo."

So did Peanut. He bounded to Lizzie's side, prancing a little.

"That's Miss Kendall's kitten, love." Finn paused, currycomb resting on Tucker's withers. He'd already unsaddled Rebel, brushed her down and put her away. "You don't have permission to play with that cat. Besides, you know the rules. No playing until the stock is taken care of."

Lizzie's shoulders fell. She stomped over to where Pete was tied. "Ranching rule number two. No playing until the stock is taken care of. I want a kitten, Daddy. I want a kitten of my own." Despite her complaining, Lizzie picked up a brush and set to work grooming her pony.

Finn's cell phone rang. He set down the currycomb and answered. "Hey, Sheriff. Thanks for returning my call."

"The message you left said a calf's gone missing? Have you ridden through the woods looking for it?"

"Not yet." He might have if Lizzie had been awake, or Kendall had tied the horse and pony properly.

"Maybe it slipped through the fence somehow." Given the way he was reacting to Finn's message, Sheriff Tate must have dealt with more reports of missing stock than theft.

"Cattle doesn't slip through my fence." Finn was determined to get his point across. "And the pasture it went missing from butts up to the fire road. There were tire tracks in my field coming and going from the federal gate. Not to mention, I haven't driven in that pasture since June. That calf isn't missing. It was stolen."

That got the sheriff thinking. His end of the line went quiet.

Taking the opportunity, Finn added, "And I saw Oscar Murray towing a stock trailer last night. He pulled into the general store to get gas. His rig was muddy, as if he'd driven across—"

"Let's not go jumping the gun with accusations against your father-in-law," Sheriff Tate said in a stern voice. "Sorry, Finn. But you know I can't even take a report until you know for sure that calf hasn't wandered into the forest."

The calf was gone. Of that, Finn was certain. Why couldn't the sheriff see who their best suspect was?

From her perch on the bench, Lizzie snuck Peanut one of her crackers. Last year, that bench was where he'd found his father-in-law, drunk and snoring outside the bunk room, unable to explain how electric fence wires all over the ranch were down. The herds had been all mixed together. It had taken days for Finn to sort them back into a semblance of order—his more productive heifers and their calves, his less productive heifers without calves, the bulls of all ages. Only then had he realized that he'd been robbed and that his father-in-law was most likely in cahoots with the thieves.

Déjà vu. Finn pressed his lips together.

"I'll reach out to fire management," Sheriff Tate Said. "And make sure they didn't come onto your property for an exercise or something. In the meantime, you check the woods. A paired calf will most likely work its way back to the fence line and its mama."

"Thanks, Sheriff. I appreciate it." Finn hung up.

Although he didn't have time to search the woods, he appreciated the sheriff's level head. And Kendall appreciated Finn. She didn't cringe when she looked at him or shy away from his stare. She thanked him for the tidbits of knowledge he imparted and teased him as if they were friends or...

Finn washed a hand over his face. Now wasn't the time to let his mind drift to thoughts about city women whom he had no future with. He picked up his currycomb.

"Daddy, is the stork going to bring me another little brother or sister?" Lizzie's question came out of the blue.

"The stork?" Finn rubbed the scar at the back of his neck.

Lizzie made big, sweeping nods. "I saw the stork bring babies on a cartoon."

"Well, if you saw it on a cartoon, then it must be true." Finn knew that wasn't a proper answer to give a four-year-old. But his daughter had succeeded in lightening his load. Levity was called for.

"That's right." Lizzie crumpled her empty cracker bag. "I bet Miss Kendall knows about the stork, too. She probably knows about lots of things."

"You will, too, when you get older, love." Finn gathered Lizzie into his arms. As he held her, something warm and pleasant spread through his chest, soothing the anger over being robbed. He may have a ranch to run and a daughter to raise. He may have a hard decision ahead about continuing cancer treatment. But just for a moment, he allowed himself to embrace the innocence and imagination of his precious little girl.

"SHANE! I'M SO happy to hear your voice." Kendall took her time returning to the ranch, snapping pictures and making phone calls, thinking about potential social-media posts for her fictional Second Chance Ranch and wishing she could just use a rideshare app to call for a lift to Finn's place.

The call from Shane, who was recuperating in the hospital after his car crash, was a welcome distraction. When she'd seen him yesterday, he'd been in a medicated slumber, with a tube to help him breathe.

She ached all over. But the worst of it was that her pride was stung. If she didn't keep calm and return to the ranch at a leisurely pace, she'd give Finn a piece of her mind—the piece that might get her kicked off the property altogether because...

He left me!

And if she didn't give him a piece of her mind, she might plant something on his kisser. With her kisser.

Kendall blew out a frustrated breath. She'd enjoyed talking to him and was intrigued by the reserved rancher. But kisses?

There shall be no kisses!

She forced herself to refocus on Shane. "How are you doing?"

"I'm good for a pincushion." Shane's voice was raspy, which she attributed to the tube being removed. "Breathing on my own...al-

beit with shallow breaths. On the mend otherwise. I hear you found a rancher to rescue
you."

"Not exactly a rescue, per se." Ha! Understatement. She'd been abandoned! "But I'm
learning a lot."

*Like being reminded not to trust cowboys
who made perfection seem easy.*

"Can we talk about that later? You're my
hero, Ken," Shane said somewhat breathlessly.
"Seriously. Thank you. You saved my life. A
coyote darted in front of me. That's why I
crashed."

"I know." He'd told Holden and Bernadette
when they'd found him, and Holden had told
Kendall.

"The coyote… It was a message," Shane
went on, gasping for air. "I need to stop—"

"All right. That's enough, honey." Franny's
voice came through in the background, firm
but loving. There was a pause and then his
wife came on the line. "Hey, Kendall. The
doctor said we need to keep Shane rested and
only allow him a few words at a time. You
aren't supposed to get breathless, Shane. I can
fill your cousin in. Hang on, Kendall."

There were sounds of hard-soled footsteps
and Kendall imagined Franny walking out of
Shane's hospital room in her cowboy boots.

"Shane came out of surgery with flying colors, but I'm not sure what to do," Franny continued in a low voice. "He keeps talking about swerving so he didn't hit a coyote because it was a message from your grandfather. Something about a story he told him on a camping trip."

"Grandpa Harlan told a lot of stories on camping trips." But Kendall didn't remember anything about coyotes. She stopped walking, numb for all the wrong reasons. "Is that the morphine talking?"

"I hope so. He told Holden the same thing an hour ago." Franny sounded worried.

She had every right to be. The injuries had been life-threatening.

But it was Kendall's job to soothe, not inflate, Franny's worries. "Shane's going to be okay, Franny. And as long as he's okay physically, we can sort out the meaning of one random coyote when he's better." And they lowered his morphine dosage.

Franny sighed. "Okay. You're right. But... oh, sure." Franny's tone turned brisk. "I don't mean to cut your call short, Kendall, but the surgeon is here, and I want to be with Shane when they talk next steps."

"No worries. Give Shane my love." Long after she hung up, Kendall stared at the Sawtooth Mountains and wondered what a coyote would signify or how it could be a sign from Grandpa Harlan.

It was better than letting her thoughts dwell on hard-edged ranchers and tough life lessons.

Besides, she'd been serenaded by coyotes last night. Should she be getting a sign, too?

CHAPTER NINE

"THIS IS LUNCH?" Kendall looked at the peanut-butter-and-jelly sandwich Lizzie had given her when she'd reached the barn. There were small fingerprint impressions on both sides of the soft bread and Finn was nowhere in sight. Lucky for him because she was still stewing about having to walk back to the ranch. "Did you make this, Lizzie?"

"Yep. Isn't it great?" Carrying a sandwich of her own, Lizzie skipped around Kendall as she trudged toward the bunk room, setting the dog dish and empty water bottle on a bench along the way. "I saw you come to the gate from the living-room window."

Peanut was lying on the floor bathed in a stream of sunshine. He sat up as they passed, gaze trained on Lizzie's sandwich.

Kendall had been hoping for a salad (chopped), a cup of soup (vegetable) and an ice-cold soda (diet). She wouldn't have refused homemade cookies or brownies for dessert. In her experience, households with small children often had homemade treats on hand. And based on that breakfast Finn had made, he had skill in the kitchen.

It was his skill with ranch hands he needed to work on.

"We can eat outside," Lizzie said happily. "I like eating outside."

"Outside it is. I just need to change my shoes first." Kendall entered the bunk room, removed her mud-caked boots and tossed them in the trash can. Her ankle blisters throbbed, and the soles of her feet would never be the same. She hadn't been this worn-out since she'd worked a three-day convention and co-ordinated booths located at opposite ends of the venue. "On second thought, I need to sit here a minute."

Or lie down and not get up for an hour or more. A nap sounded good right now. Too bad Lizzie had already taken hers. And too bad her bed wasn't empty.

Boo hogged her pillow—she was curled in a tight ball in the center. The kitten stared at Kendall through slitted eyes, as if to say "I'm not moving over."

Now who's the princess?

"I've been waiting to eat my sandwich with you." Lizzie came over to the bed and began petting Boo, who stretched and then wound herself into a tighter ball than before. "It took you forever to get back. Daddy and I put the horses away. We cleaned the kitchen. We put clothes in the washer. And after forever, I saw you come back. What took you so long?"

"When it comes to ranching, I have a feeling I will always be behind." Sighing, Kendall sprawled sideways on the bed, half-sitting, half-lying down. "Did you make brownies?"

"Nope. Daddy says baking is Grandma's 'sponsibility." Lizzie held her head over Boo and shook her curls as if they were ribbons Boo might chase after.

If Lizzie got another scratch, Finn would kick Kendall off the ranch for sure.

Kendall sat up with a groan and drew the little girl back a few feet. "We should eat lunch."

"Yep." Lizzie kneeled by Kendall's suitcase, gasping. "Are these your slippers?" She picked up Kendall's fuzzy pink slippers from where they sat beneath the bed. "They're pretty. Can I show Daddy? I want some."

"How about we take a picture and I'll show him later?" Kendall took the slippers and put them on her sleeping bag. "Those look rather plain by themselves." Her gaze caught on Lizzie's pretty straw hat. She plucked it from the girl's curls and placed it partially over the slippers. "Now that's adorable." She took a picture and then showed the girl.

Lizzie cooed over Kendall's screen. "Daddy will have to get me pink slippers now."

Kendall bet he would. She placed Lizzie's hat back on her wispy blond curls, drinking in her cuteness until a smile spilled out that had nothing to do with having chips on her shoulder. "If I were as cute as you when I was a kid, I'd have had my daddy wrapped around my finger, too."

Grinning, Lizzie waggled her fingers, then looked at them dubiously. "Okay. Come on." The little cowgirl hurried to the door, where Peanut sat waiting. The dog's gaze darted from the girl's sandwich to the kitten. "I always have lunch with the misfits. Daddy says I can't eat with them by myself."

Kendall didn't have the energy to get back on her feet. Had she learned enough about ranching and riding today to pass Old Man Connelly's test? She didn't think so.

"Come on." Lizzie returned to Kendall and grabbed her hand, giving it a determined tug. "Aren't you hungry?"

"Yep." Kendall stuffed her toes into her sneakers and followed Lizzie out. "Where's your dad?"

"He already ate. He's on the phone trying to

trade cows." Lizzie skipped ahead, blond curls bouncing, pink boots scuffing across hardwood. "Hurry up, Miss Kendall."

"Miss Kendall." That made her sound like a stuffy schoolteacher. "You can call me Ken."

Lizzie came to a halt and turned to stare at Kendall. "Ken is a boy's name."

"It can be. But in this case, it's a nickname, short for Kendall. It's what my family calls me sometimes." Kendall plodded forward. Her inner thighs protested all that riding. Her feet protested all that walking. Her blisters protested fashionable zippers.

"Ken." Lizzie gave a little shrug. "Okay."

They continued through the barn to the pasture out back, where the menagerie of misfits stood at the fence as if waiting for their arrival. If Finn had been here, he'd probably tell Kendall that they were late.

"I'm here!" Lizzie announced to the animals. She sat on a bench by the fence and unwrapped her sandwich. "And I brought Ken."

The emu strutted around a safe distance away, occasionally swiveling her long neck to look at them. The donkey raised his nose and sniffed the air. The goat and llama had none of their subtlety. The goat poked his nose between the narrow pasture rails, while the llama stretched his head over the fence.

Kendall was almost certain they were looking for food, not attention. Their gazes were too alert.

"They like you, Ken." Lizzie took a bite of sandwich and swung her cute pink boots, humming a happy tune Kendall didn't recognize.

Kendall sat down next to the little girl, fending off the llama's inquisitive nose. "Why are they all looking at us?" They hadn't been this laser-focused when she'd tossed out their feed this morning. "You don't give them your food, do you?"

"Farm animals don't get people food," Lizzie said, mouth full. But she grinned as she chewed.

Oh, farm animals get people food, all right. Little-girl leftovers.

She chuckled, imagining Finn's long-suffering expression.

"When we're done, the misfits get love." Lizzie had eaten the center of her sandwich, avoiding the crust. She held up the remains, which formed a *U*. "I'm done."

"Are you sure?" Kendall had only taken a few bites.

Lizzie pulled her crust into three pieces. She gave one strip of crust to Peanut, one to the goat and the last to the llama. And then she picked up a water bottle that had been sitting under the bench, extended the straw and drank deeply. She eyed Kendall's sandwich. "Are you still eating?"

"Yes." And she was so hungry that she didn't fancy giving farm animals anything, including her crust. "I'm going to eat all of mine."

"Ken…" Lizzie shook her head as if this was a bad thing.

Kendall kept on eating, fending off an attempt by the llama to nibble on her sandwich. "This is so good. I haven't had peanut butter and jelly in a long time." As tired and hungry as she was, she'd have scarfed down a baloney-and-pickle one and called it a feast.

"I have PB and J every day." Lizzie climbed the metal pasture railings, hooking her arms over the top. "The misfits love it."

Kendall tried not to dwell on the idea of a constant diet of PB & J. Instead, she focused on the adorable faces of the misfits. The llama nibbled on Lizzie's hair. It was a half-hearted attempt that made Lizzie giggle. The goat nuzzled her boots. Finding nothing of interest, he stared at Kendall with the most adorable expression of curiosity on his face.

"These misfits have 'video stars' written all over them." Sandwich in one hand, Kendall stood, whipped out her phone and toggled to the camera with her other. She moved closer to the fence. "Is Larry going to nibble on your hair again, Lizzie?" Kendall hoped so. She started the video, hoping to catch something magical. In her experience, adorable photos and videos could warm even the most jaded of audiences.

She imagined sharing the video with Finn, picturing his clear blue eyes the way they'd been this afternoon—unguarded.

Larry the llama looked at Kendall, blinking heavily lashed eyes with the utmost innocence. And then he swooped in, taking her sandwich, crust and all.

"Hey!" Kendall stumbled in a hole, careening into the fence. She dropped her phone into the pasture.

Gary the goat didn't hesitate. He picked up her phone with his teeth.

"Hey!" Kendall lunged for it, banging into the railing.

Both beasties ran to the opposite end of the pasture, followed by the emu, who Kendall suddenly remembered liked shiny things… like Kendall's rhinestone-studded phone cover?

"Come back here!" Kendall scaled the fence and hopped over. "Do not eat my phone!"

"WHAT IN BLAZES is going on here?" Finn flung open the gate to the misfit pasture and slammed it shut behind him.

Kendall ran toward him, long braid in unsightly loops, hands clasped in front of her chest.

Evie was hot on Kendall's heels. The emu's long neck was extended, putting her head next to Kendall's shoulder, where she seemed to be eyeing whatever Kendall was holding.

From the bench on the other side of the fence, Lizzie had an extreme case of the giggles.

Kendall stumbled into Finn, bodying up to him like a guard in a basketball game, hands roaming around his waist as she circled him and—

"Hey!" He leaped away. "You goosed me!"

"No." Kendall held up her now empty hands.

Evie strutted around them, making rat-a-tat-tat noises, head thrusting up and down. She surveyed Kendall as if looking for a point of attack.

"I don't have it." Kendall spoke to the emu.

This seemed to make Lizzie laugh harder.

"Why did you goose me?"

"I didn't." Kendall kept her attention on

the emu. "You're not so cocky now, are you, Evie?"

Gary the goat limped past Finn and head-butted Kendall's leg, although not hard enough to knock her over.

"Ow."

Instinctively, Finn reached for Kendall, drawing her into the protective circle of his arms. "What have you done?"

"Don't blame me," Kendall whispered into his chest.

Her head fit neatly beneath his chin. She smelled of flowery shampoo and peanut butter, of fireside chats and long walks in the moonlight.

Finn forced himself to loosen his hold on her.

Evie's circle tightened. Her inspection was unwavering, interrupted only by Larry, who poked his head over Finn's shoulder, gumming Kendall's hair.

Finn gently pushed him away.

"That llama is a nosy lookie-loo," Kendall grumbled. "That's a better name than Larry for a llama."

The llama continued his curious invasion of human space.

Doug was the only misfit who didn't want to get in Kendall's face. The donkey stood over by Lizzie and Peanut, swishing his tail as if nothing exciting ever happened in this field.

"Did you goose them, too?" Finn stared down at Kendall, realizing too late that he was looking into her upturned face with her mouth in kissing distance. "They're all riled up."

"Are you rescuing me or not?" Kendall demanded, as regal as genuine royalty.

"Save her, Daddy!" Lizzie called.

Save her? With what? A kiss? Then who will save me?

"I didn't goose you," Kendall said, frowning as she stared at his mouth. "See?" Her hands came around his waist again. "I used you for protection."

At her second touch, Finn dropped his arms and stumbled back, bumping into Larry, then rebounding and nearly tripping over the goat. "But—"

"Would you forget goosing? I was just reclaiming my property." Kendall waggled her phone before pancaking it between her hands. "I put it in your back pocket."

"Oh." He was oddly disappointed. "Didn't I tell you to keep shiny things away from the misfits?"

"You did." Kendall backed toward the gate. "I was sitting with Lizzie on the bench, eating lunch and minding my own business, when Gary stole my phone. I gave chase. He panicked and dropped it. And then Evie hammered it with her beak while Larry watched."

Evie, Larry and Gary were following her but allowing Kendall a wide berth.

Finn didn't know whether to laugh or reprimand his temporary ranch hand.

"Doug was the only respectable spectator." Keeping her eye on the more nosy misfits, Kendall opened the gate.

Finn joined Kendall in case the animals got any ideas about following her.

"Are you all right?" He pointed to Kendall's green sweatshirt, which had what looked like bird saliva spots on the arms and shoulders.

That was going to hurt later.

"I'll live but… Oh, no." Kendall brushed off her phone. "My screen's cracked." She tapped it with her finger. "At least, it still works."

Lizzie ran up to Finn and hugged his legs, placing her feet on his boots. "That was funnier than cartoons."

"But more dangerous." Finn frowned at Evie. What if it had been Lizzie that the emu had been chasing? Sometimes his daughter played with his cell phone.

"I'm to blame." Kendall came clean, proving her moral fiber once again. "I had my cell phone too close to the fence. Lizzie would never do something like that."

"I'm always careful around the misfits, Daddy," Lizzie said solemnly, staring up at him with those angel eyes.

Kendall had a similar look on her face, but her eyes werc a gentle, honest gray.

Finn sighed. There wasn't much more to say, except... "It's time to exercise the rest of the horses." He set down Lizzie, took her hand and led the way into the barn.

"Another ride?" Kendall trailed behind them, sounding drained, not that he blamed her. She'd had quite the day.

Earlier, he'd have been thrilled at having deflated her iron will. But that was before she'd confided her dreams to him and he'd learned more about what made her tick. She was no longer just another Monroe.

Still, there was work to be done and every experience he offered Kendall would only help her land that client in Texas. "No ride. Lunge line." Finn set Lizzie on the bench outside the bunk room. "And what can you do while we're lunging horses, love?"

"Play with the chickens or the misfits or with anything where you can see me." Lizzie swung her feet, grinning at Kendall. "Can I let Gary borrow your phone again?"

"No," Finn and Kendall said at the same time.

As they neared the bunk room, Boo extended a small white paw, claws out, beneath the bunk-room door, searching blindly for a playmate.

Almost immediately, Peanut lunged forward, offering his nose as a toy but scaring the kitten away before any damage was done.

"Can I play with Boo?" Lizzie asked, veering toward the action.

"No," Finn and Kendall said together again.

She fit in more places than his arms. They shared values, it seemed, about protecting precocious little girls and rambunctious kittens.

They fit? Finn frowned the thought away.

"I could take Boo with me to the chicken coop." Lizzie was determined to find new mischief to get into. "Peanut can't get Boo in the coop."

"Also, a no." Finn went to the tack room for his gloves, the long whip and a lunge line.

Kendall came in behind him. "Do I need to put my boots back on?" The resignation in her voice was telling.

"You could just wear your sneakers and watch."

"Thank you." She caught her reflection in a small mirror on the wall, the one Jenny had put up and Finn hadn't had the heart to take down. "Yikes, what a hair emergency." She unbound her braid and let her black hair tumble free in twisting waves.

His fingers itched to touch it, to learn its texture and measure its weight. With effort, he stuck to his role as her boss. "Have you ever lunged a horse before?"

"Yeah. Sure. When I was a kid." She had a way of making her experience sound as if she was just qualified enough that he could trust her with a task, like saddling a horse, which she'd also told him she'd done as a child.

"I'll go through it with you now. Tomorrow, when you have proper footwear—"

"Proper footwear," she said at the same time he did, smiling at him as if this amused her.

"—you can show me what you've learned." And then he'd see if she was capable of handling the task.

"I appreciate that." Her smile spread wider, the amusement reaching her eyes, which seemed to sparkle at him.

Finn turned away. He didn't think he could take any more appreciation from her. Not without showing his appreciation in return.

CHAPTER TEN

"NOW THAT'S THE face of a working cowgirl—
exhausted." Holden started in on the teasing
as soon as Kendall was in his truck. "Do you
want me to ask you how your day was? Quiz
you on ranch terms?"

"No." Kendall's body and spirit needed a
ranching sabbatical.

What she could stand more of was Finn's
lingering glances with that searching expression of his—the one that said he wondered
about her.

I wonder about him, too.

Like how he did everything alone. How he'd
picked himself up after his wife died. How
he kept himself together after setbacks, like
being robbed. She knew very little about what
made him tick. But she wanted to. And that
was unwise.

Which was why this dinner with Laurel
was imperative. Kendall had shed her work
clothes, showered and dried her hair. She was
wearing a pair of hip-hugging jeans, a scoop-

necked blouse and flat sandals. She'd lined her eyes and powdered her face. All in an attempt to remind herself that she wasn't cut out for the ranching life.

"What's with you?" Holden tsked, gunning his truck toward the highway. "Bad day at the office?"

"You could say that." Kendall gingerly patted her sunburned cheeks. "I need a pair of cowboy boots stat."

"And a cowboy hat or stronger sunscreen by the look of you." Holden chuckled.

She didn't argue with him. Her morning lotion contained sunscreen but clearly not enough.

"I need to order a new phone." Kendall held up hers, showing him the cracked screen and the broken cover. "Compliments of an old goat with a broken leg and an anxiety-ridden emu." As were the bruises beginning to develop on her arms and chest. Physically, she was a wreck. Emotionally, she was worn out. "Today was a reminder that I don't like ranch life." Just handsome ranchers.

"There must be something positive about this experience."

Again, handsome rancher.

"I got some decent ranch content. Photos and stuff," she admitted reluctantly.

The video she'd started had continued to record during the goat phone-jacking. It showed a bumbling escape, then a drop on a rock and a couple determined pecks from an emu. She'd probably post an edited version of the video online somewhere.

Kendall glanced back as they approached the highway. "Stop. I need to take a picture."

When he complied, she hopped out of the truck and snapped a photograph of the McAfee Ranch nestled in the valley with the austere Sawtooth Mountains in the distance. It was more than just a snapshot of Americana. It was the ranch that Finn loved.

She checked the photo for lighting and composition before climbing back in the vehicle. "The screen may be cracked, but my camera still works."

"So much for bad days at the office," Holden murmured, grinning. "You found a silver lining."

Handsome rancher...

Kendall shook her head. "Show some sympathy." She slugged her brother in the arm, although not hard. "You know, I could pick on you, urban cowboy. You wear cowboy garb and yet you don't own a ranch."

"Do we have to pick on each other?" He spared a hand from the wheel to rub his arm.

"Bernadette is the town doctor. We live *in* the medical clinic. I'm not likely to move to a ranch for a long time." He sounded wistful. "Finn has a nice spread."

"I know he has a nice spread. I've ridden from one side of it and walked back the other." Kendall caught herself, laughing a little at the day's mishaps. "But, brother, get it in gear. I wouldn't mind helping you on your ranch instead of aiding a grumpy cowboy and his menagerie of misfits." She sighed, running a finger over the largest of her screen cracks, thinking of Finn's face when he'd caught her after being chased by an emu. After she'd been left horseless, he'd probably thought her day couldn't get much worse.

What's worse was watching him exercise the horses.

When he'd said, "Eyes on me," he hadn't needed to tell her twice.

Something inside of Kendall gave a sigh of longing.

"Grumpy cowboy?" Holden's entire demeanor changed from teasing to protective brother. "Do I need to have words with this Finn?"

"No." Kendall dropped her phone into her purse. "He treats me the same as any not-quite-qualified employee." In fact, he treated her better than she deserved, considering how busy he was and how much about ranching she'd forgotten.

"Did he laugh at you?" Holden didn't sound appeased. "You hate when people laugh at you. You always have. It sours you to whatever you've got on your plate because you can't uphold the idea that you're perfect if someone laughs at you."

"Surprisingly, he hasn't laughed at me, despite my less-than-perfect performance. It's just... I'm not cut out to be a ranch hand. Which makes me question why I'd want the Connellys' business."

"Your bank balance comes to mind." Holden gave her one of his superior looks, honed after years of prospering on Wall Street.

"Spare me the lectures." She'd lectured herself enough for one day. "Seriously, I stink at the Western life. I even tried to study up last night and this morning, which only made things worse." She rubbed at the light traces of ink that hadn't come off her palm. "What can I bring to the Connellys?" Or Finn, for that matter.

"Would you stop."

"What?"

"You use designer labels and that fashion-magazine appearance to imply you're competent." Holden spared her a glance. "It's like you don't believe in yourself."

"That's not true." But her statement lacked conviction. She fell back on an old defense. "I have to do twice as much than—"

"That line doesn't work with me." Holden's tone turned commanding. "You're smart, with years of experience promoting people, companies, causes and brands. That's what the Connellys are willing to pay you for, not your ranching vocabulary. That only gets your foot in the door."

Kendall rubbed her palm where she'd written those crib notes. "Are you just saying that because you're my brother?"

"You're raising my blood pressure." Holden didn't need that. He'd had a health scare last summer. "Why would I tell you something I didn't believe?"

"Because you're fond of saying I'm a nuisance. A pain in the—"

"Yeah, you're that, too." He rubbed a hand over his chest.

He worried her. "We should talk about something else. How's Shane? I only got to talk to him briefly." And then she'd spent the afternoon mourning her phone and cleaning the tack room, which involved removing a large amount of thick, sticky cobwebs.

Holden was suitably distracted. "They got him out of bed today and made him walk the hall."

"That's always a good sign." Or so she'd been told. She ran her hands up and down her arms, needing to ward off the sudden chill. "He's still convinced that coyote was a messenger from Grandpa Harlan."

"He believes the coyote represents staying the course in Second Chance."

"Staying the course… What course?" They may have inherited the town, but they'd also inherited the leases people paid for their homes and businesses. Leases that were only one dollar per property. "Not the leases?" That made no financial sense.

Holden shrugged.

They were quiet on the rest of the drive into Second Chance.

Kendall thanked her brother for the ride and went to pick up Laurel in the Lodgepole Inn, which was currently experiencing a bit of a commotion.

Laurel was walking the floor with one red-faced, crying baby, while her husband, Mitch, walked with the other. Gabby sat hunched over her laptop keyboard behind the check-in desk with noise-canceling headphones on.

"Relief has arrived." Kendall took the infant

Laurel was holding and nestled her into the crook of her arm. "Hey, baby cakes."

The little tyke drew a deep breath, blinked up at Kendall and then heaved a weary sigh, lower lip trembling.

Kendall immediately went into action, talking baby talk and jiggling the infant.

"The twins have colic." Laurel's voice was nearly a shout. She reached for the baby in Mitch's arms. "Poor things."

The poor thing was Laurel. She'd brushed her hair and applied light makeup, but her red locks were limp and her mascara smudged as if she'd been crying, too.

"We've got this, honey," Mitch told Laurel, waving at his preteen daughter as he danced out of his wife's reach. "Gabby and I can handle the girls."

With a quick smile, Gabby dutifully closed her laptop, removed her headphones and approached Kendall with outstretched arms. "I'll take her. You guys head on over."

"Thanks, Gabby." Kendall transferred Hazel to Gabby. "Laurel?"

"I can't leave." Laurel stood in the middle of the lobby, lips wavering much like Hazel's had.

"Go on, honey." Mitch jiggled Hope like a trooper. "You need a break."

Frozen, Laurel stared at the front door as if she didn't dare step outside.

Kendall took a gentle hold of Laurel's arm and steered her toward a much-needed respite.

"I shouldn't go," Laurel said on the front porch when Kendall had closed the door behind them.

Kendall kept walking, towing her cousin from the porch and into the fading sunlight. "I came into town for dinner with you. We're having dinner. You'll sit in the peace and quiet of the diner. We'll have an adult beverage and—"

"No alcohol." Even if she refused a glass of wine, at least Laurel was moving with the tide.

"You can have a sip of my wine." Kendall deserved a pampering beverage to make her feel better after the day she'd had. "I bet there's dessert at the diner. Something decadent and chocolate." She certainly hoped so.

At the bottom of the porch steps, Laurel dug in her sneakers and stared at Kendall. Her cheeks were pale. "I can't leave my babies."

"Laurel." Kendall smoothed Laurel's red hair over her shoulders. "You need time for yourself. If you don't take it, you can't be a supermom. If Mitch and the babies need you, he'll send Gabby. Nod if you understand."

Laurel nodded, eyes watery. "This is my time to recharge."

"Precisely."

"You're going to make a good mom."

Laurel's comment took Kendall by surprise.

"Thanks?" The image of Finn's face came to mind. Kendall ignored it. "But that's a long way off."

The man of her dreams had always been a guy who wore classy silk ties and expensive leather loafers. He'd appreciate her footwear choices and her work in social media. He'd know the maître d' at her favorite sushi restaurant and the best vintage for pinot noir. They'd share similar friends and similar dreams.

Thinking on her dream-man criteria, it suddenly seemed rather shallow.

"Let's not talk about love and parenthood," she told Laurel. "I still need to establish my business, not to mention fall in love, get married and settle in with a guy. You know, that takes years."

Again, Finn's face came to mind. Again, Kendall banished the image.

"Ha!" Laurel found this amusing. "Love and kids don't abide by life plans or timelines."

"Mine will." Kendall led the new mom to

the general store. "I just need to make one stop before dinner."

"Oh, the store." Laurel perked up. "We're almost out of milk for Gabby. And diapers. The girls fly through diapers." She walked faster.

Faster than Kendall!

Kendall hauled her cousin back, slowing her down. "No. This isn't a stock-up visit. Remember, this is two adult women taking time out for themselves."

"In the general store of Second Chance?" Laurel sounded doubtful. And why wouldn't she? You could buy anything from motor oil to groceries to sewing supplies in the store.

"I know it's not exactly a department store on Fifth Avenue in New York." Kendall chuckled. "But I need boots, a hat, bandages and sunscreen, and if we don't go now, the store will be closed after dinner."

Laurel rolled her eyes. "How is your list of purchases any different than picking up milk and diapers?"

"Shoes," Kendall said as if that explained everything.

And her fashion-loving cousin must have agreed because she stopped protesting. At least, until they'd picked up the other items

Kendall needed and reached the small shoe section of the general store.

Laurel held a bright red boot with white piping, staring at it in disapproval. "You should order something online."

"I can order whatever you like," Mackenzie shouted from the front of the store, where she'd been unboxing and pricing coffee mugs.

"That woman has excellent hearing," Kendall muttered, holding a hot pink boot with hot pink fringe and an explosion of rhinestones away from her body as if it was an emu that might strike. Wearing them would put Holden's opinion of Kendall to the test. Still... "Why on earth did she order these?"

"All those boots were on clearance," Mackenzie shouted back. "You'd be amazed what people will buy for full price when they're desperate. I sold a lot of cowboy boots of every color in June, when we had the Western Festival."

Although Kendall admired the woman's business skills, she couldn't help but think either pair of boots would erode her confidence, not to mention her credibility, with Finn.

"There's a reason all these boots were on clearance. They're hideous." Laurel put the red boot back in the box. "Don't get either pair, Kendall. This is a fashion crime waiting to happen."

"Agreed. But I need Finn to open up to me, and to do that, I need to be a productive ranch hand with the proper footwear." Kendall was torn. She tipped back the straw cowboy hat she planned to purchase. It fell off. She hoped that wasn't a bad omen. "Should I 'eeny, meeny, miny, moe'?"

Laurel handed Kendall the box with the red boots. "Get some good socks and the larger box of bandages. I have a feeling these boots aren't going to be comfortable."

"A few days from now, I'm going to win the Connelly account and reward myself with a massage and a pedicure." Kendall could almost believe it. "And then I'm going to sleep in late and walk on concrete sidewalks in my high heels."

And forget about handsome ranchers with strong arms.

She hoped.

"You'll be pampered and rested while I'll still be sleep-deprived and walking the lobby of the Lodgepole Inn in my sneakers." Laurel headed to the front of the store.

"Stop that." Kendall rubbed her cousin's shoulder. "You wouldn't have it any other way.

Three adorable children and a husband who dotes on you. You hit the jackpot."

"You're right." Laurel straightened. "I need to reframe my life now. Family requires a little sacrifice and a little forgiveness, including of myself." That was something their Grandpa Harlan used to say.

"Atta girl." Kendall paid for her purchases, and then they walked next door to the diner. Laurel insisted on a booth by the window, despite Kendall's protests that they sit where she couldn't see the Lodgepole Inn.

A young cowboy with a green-check shirt, a mangled straw cowboy hat and worn-in cowboy boots paid his bill, leaving them as the only customers in the diner.

"I'm good here." Laurel flashed their cousin Cam a smile when he came over to take their order. "I'll have the special."

Cam frowned. He was wearing his chef's jacket and black trousers, looking like the Michelin star chef he once was, not the diner cook he'd become. "I haven't told you what the special is."

Laurel waved off his comment and then seemed to notice that she had spit-up on her blouse. "Look at me. You can't take me anywhere." Her eyes filled with tears.

"Baby vomit is nothing," Kendall quickly

reassured her. "Earlier, I had cow manure stuck on my Gucci boots, ground-in mud on the knees of my favorite leggings and emu spit on my sweatshirt. At this rate, my new red boots won't be shiny and red for long."

That got Laurel to smile. "We both need to reframe our situations."

"Exactly," Kendall said. "No rough patch lasts forever." Another one of their grandfather's sayings. But try as she might, she couldn't remember any about coyotes.

Cam cleared his throat, tugged down his chef's jacket and faced Kendall. "The special today is—"

"I'll take it, Cam," Kendall said, in solidarity with Laurel.

"But—"

"Two specials," Kendall said firmly. "Surprise us, Cam. We trust you."

Cam ran a hand through his dark hair and stared at the table, looking less the confident chef and more a man who'd had his bubble burst.

Kendall took pity on him. "Would it make you feel better, Cam, if you told us what the special is first?"

"It would have." He regained his composure, smoothing his hair and giving them a mischievous grin. "But now I'm going to make you wait to discover what's on the menu. Two chef's surprises. And I guess I won't tell you how I decided on a menu to please you, Laurel."

Laurel glanced up at their cousin, teary-eyed. "You designed a special dinner just for me?"

"I did." He laid a hand on her shoulder. "You deserve some fine food and a lot of pampering. And Kendall... Well, Kendall gets to reap some of the benefits."

"What? I don't deserve a little pampering? Just look at me." Kendall gestured to herself. "My nose is sunburned, my butt is sore and my ankles are rubbed raw."

"You can take it." Cam shrugged.

"I can take it," Kendall muttered with a thick layer of sarcasm. "Why does everyone think I'm tough? I'm a city girl, as soft as they come."

Laurel released a shout of laughter, which was heartening to Kendall after witnessing all her mommy angst.

"In your dreams. You're so stubborn. And stubborn means strong, at least in my book." Cam grinned and headed for the kitchen, where two young boys were no doubt waiting for him. RJ and Nick revered their soon-to-be stepdad.

And wasn't that the problem with Second Chance? Everywhere Kendall looked, there were couples and families. Not to mention Monroes settling into new careers and reaching for new dreams, while she was still pursuing her first career path. Kendall put her elbows on the table and her chin in her hands. "Do you think I hide behind my wardrobe?"

"Yes, but I can relate." Laurel rearranged her silverware. Of course, she'd understand. She used to live and work in Hollywood. "That doesn't mean you're shallow."

Kendall fell back in the booth. "I didn't ask if I was shallow."

Laurel laughed. "I'm not saying you are. If you were shallow, you wouldn't have bought those red boots just now. Or saved that kitten."

Or gone to work for a grumpy rancher with scars on his cheek.

"Rewind for a second. Who accused you of being shallow? Holden?" Laurel's laugh mingled with the sizzle of Cam frying something in the kitchen.

Kendall hadn't heard her laugh this much since her wedding to Mitch in June. "Holden didn't say I was shallow. He said I hid behind my wardrobe."

Laurel sniffed her disdain. "Well, he wouldn't

have said that if he saw your manured boots, muddy leggings and emu-spittle sweatshirt."

Their eyes met and they shared a long laugh. Holden's fiancée, Bernadette, entered the diner and came over to their table. "I'm here to pick up take-out. Seems like I'm doing that a lot lately. I would have sent Holden, but I saw you ladies here and it gives me a chance to socialize." She patted her prominent baby bump and then pushed her black glasses up her nose. "How are you feeling, Laurel? I'm asking as a friend, not your doctor."

"Good. Tired, but good." Laurel almost looked it. "I'm taking an hour for myself."

"An hour or two when you need it is a life-saver." The doctor beamed.

"Kendall came in from…" Laurel trailed off. "Which ranch are you working on?"

Both women turned toward Kendall.

"The McAfee Ranch. It's just a temporary thing." Kendall pointed to the boot box and cowboy hat on the seat beside her. "I'm sure Holden told you."

"He mentioned something, but he didn't say you were with Finn." Bernadette's face lit up.

"I'm not *with* Finn," Kendall quickly corrected, although the image of Finn exercising horses on a lunge line came to mind. He'd been putting his skill and strength on full display.

Yowzer. She'd snuck a picture of him when his back was turned. What woman would blame her? But she still had to squash any potential rumor. Second Chance was a very small town, after all. "We're not together."

Bernadette was quick to apologize for the assumption. "I'm just so glad to hear you're working there. I wish Finn would hire someone full-time so he could..." She seemed to catch herself. "All I can say is that Finn needs to take time for himself, just like Laurel's doing. He's got a full workload running the ranch and taking care of Lizzie. If you could stay for a month and free up his mornings—"

"A month?" Kendall blurted, trying to wipe the image of Finn glancing at her mouth from her mind. "I can't stay a month."

"A month does seem like a long time." Laurel studied the doctor's expression. She added pointedly, "A specific amount of a long time."

"Forget I said anything." Bernadette turned, and then spun back around. "Or, maybe don't." She moved to the register.

"What was Bernadette trying to say?" Kendall ventured. Finn didn't look like a man in need of medical care.

"That you should have a four-week fling with this Finn fellow." Laurel grinned mischievously.

"Stop." But Kendall grinned along with her cousin. And blushed.

Laurel leaned forward. "You like him."

Noting Cam's approach, Kendall shushed her, then whispered, "It's more like appreciation than liking. We just met."

Cam presented them their salads, which were a work of art—small, edible cups containing mixed greens. "Ladies, Caesar salad in Parmesan bowls."

Laurel gasped. "You made the bowls out of fried Parmesan cheese?"

Cam nodded. "Your favorite. I know."

Kendall didn't care if each serving was only cupcake-sized. She liked them, too. "This beats peanut butter and jelly or burnt eggs any day."

"Such high praise." Cam chuckled and returned to the kitchen.

Kendall and Laurel had an enjoyable dinner—carrot coconut soup, salmon on a bed of peas and mushrooms, chocolate cheesecake bites—and an even more enjoyable conversation, although Laurel didn't miss an opportunity to tease Kendall about Finn. Kendall snapped photos of their food, of course, and showed Laurel pictures on her cracked phone screen of the new designer shoes she'd purchased in Philadelphia, as well as the video made when the goat stole her phone. Laurel showed Kendall baby pictures along with photos of their renovation. She and Mitch were updating and soundproofing their apartment at the inn, as well as extending into an upstairs guest room to be used as Gabby's bedroom.

"I love the before-and-after pictures so far." Kendall thanked Cam for bringing a second plate of chocolate cheesecake bites. "People love renovation stuff online. Although in this case, I don't think it would benefit the inn's business."

"You know everything about online content." Laurel picked up another decadent dessert bite. "You should create a social-media account for Finn's ranch as a test run for the Texas job."

Kendall stared at her plate, not ready to admit she'd already done so, although under a pseudonym. "Finn would hate it."

"Would he?"

"He's the kind of man who needs proof." She didn't think he'd be swayed by counts of likes or link clicks.

"Faith is hard to find when exposed to something new. Just look at me. I didn't think selling quilts and crocheted goods would help support us." Laurel glanced out the window toward the mercantile she'd opened. And then she sat up, as tense as she'd been when their evening began. "I suppose it was too much to think this dinner would last." She took a final bite of dessert, some of the stress returning to her face.

Kendall turned, leaning closer to the window.

Mitch and Gabby were walking toward them. They each carried a baby, and from the happy looks on their faces, this wasn't an emergency interruption.

Kendall got up to hold the door for them.

"The girls are exhausted and content." Mitch angled the baby he held so that Kendall could see her peaceful face. "Hope even fell asleep."

"We came over to pick up dinner," Gabby said quietly, handing Hazel to Kendall. "We didn't want to press our luck and put them in their cribs since Hazel is still awake."

Hazel blinked bright blue eyes up at Kendall, working the pink pacifier in her mouth.

"Finish your dinner, honey," Mitch told Laurel. "We've got this."

"My hero." Laurel beamed, vanquishing all evidence of stress.

And although Kendall was happy for her cousin, a part of her wished for a hero of her own.

CHAPTER ELEVEN

FINN AND LIZZIE had just sat down to dinner when the front door opened.

Peanut sat up but didn't bark, a sign that someone familiar was entering. Kendall?

Finn felt a grin expand across his face. He'd been pleasantly surprised by the way Kendall kept bouncing back from adversity, often without complaint. And he couldn't help but smile when he thought about her experience with the misfits. He wouldn't blame her if she came back to give notice. But he didn't want her to leave yet either.

"Hello! I've brought a chicken casserole. But I imagine you've already eaten." Finn's mother, not Kendall, entered the dining room carrying an insulated tote and sporting short gray hair that looked like the wind had taken a turn at styling it. She always moved like she was in a hurry, which she always was, and that pace probably explained her lean frame. "Traffic leaving Boise was terrible today. I'm sorry I'm late. Are there leftovers? I'm famished. Oh, beef stew and corn bread. Yum."

"Late?" Finn glanced at Lizzie in confusion and then at his mother, who sailed past them and into the kitchen, giving Peanut a pat along the way. "Did I forget you were coming?" He'd been on the phone most of the afternoon after exercising the horses, setting aside other chores as he spread the word that a branded McAfee calf had gone missing. He'd had no idea he should have been expecting his mother for dinner.

"You didn't forget a visit, Finn." His mother puttered about the kitchen—putting away her casserole, setting some papers on the kitchen table, rinsing dishes that had been soaking in the sink and giving the stew a good stir before dishing some for herself. "I've been thinking about you since our call a few days ago. I figured I'd breeze up here and surprise you with some food. And I know the kitchen and bathroom can probably use a good cleaning. Don't you worry about a thing. I want you to save your strength whenever you can."

Save his strength. For the energy-sapping medical treatment he kept putting off?

"Mom, you didn't have to come." He didn't want her constant reminders.

His gaze drifted to the six empty seats at the

dining-room table. If he delayed the therapy, he could fill some seats and the empty bedrooms upstairs, packing the house with laughter and talk of the ranch's future. He could put off the follow-up treatment for years...

Couldn't he?

Finn sucked in a heavy gulp of air. He might not be that daring.

"You're my son." Mom cut a thick slice of cornbread. "I'm allowed to help you out when you're sick."

"I'm not sick." Finn took a bite of stew, trying to stop an argument.

"Do you have a fever, Daddy?" Lizzie got out of her chair and came to Finn at the head of the table. She pressed a palm to his forehead. She'd already taken a bath and smelled like her grape bubble bath.

"No fever, love." He ruffled her curls and shooed her back to her seat. "Mom, I told you I don't want to make a big deal out of this."

"You can't just carry on as if nothing's changed." His mother sat next to him, directly across from Lizzie. She flashed his daughter a significant look before leaning toward Finn. "Finn, you have ca—"

"I'm well aware of what I *had*. Dr. Carlisle said—"

"When Mr. Pickersgill, you know our

neighbor on the corner, battled prostate cancer, he was at half-strength for weeks." Mom peppered her stew liberally, as if Finn hadn't adequately seasoned it. "He had a wife and two adult sons nearby when he had the surgery and the follow-up radiation treatment. You're out here alone and—"

"We have a ranch hand now." Lizzie mopped up stew juices with her cornbread. "Ken."

"Ken..." Who was Ken? It took Finn a moment to connect *Ken* to Kendall. He latched on to the ruse. "Yeah, Ken started today. We'll be fine, Mom." Who'd have thought the cowgirl princess would come in handy?

"How convenient." Mom's malarkey meter must have gone off. She didn't seem convinced Ken existed. "You've been looking for someone to replace Daniel for months and suddenly... Ken."

"I got lucky. We met Ken in town yesterday." Had she only been with them a day? It felt a lot longer. He checked his watch. "Are you going back home tonight?" If she didn't, the "Ken" situation was going to get awkward.

"Turn around and go home now? Are you kidding? It's almost seven. I'm spending the night." She speared a bite of carrot. "Is Ken around? I want to introduce myself."

And give his new ranch hand her contact information, no doubt, in case Finn happened to collapse or something, which he didn't plan on doing because he was going to postpone the daily dose of hard cancer-killing chemicals as long as possible. "Ken went into town for dinner tonight."

Mom seemed more relaxed than when she'd come in. "I'll spend the night, and in the morning, I'll meet Ken."

"And Boo." Lizzie grabbed a piece of potato with her fingers and shoved it in her mouth. "Ken has a kitten named Boo." She chewed, beginning to smile. "Ken has a kitten, Daddy." She emphasized the *K*s.

Finn drew a deep breath, setting aside his discomfort over his mother's concern and his worry over the lost calf, beaming at his daughter the way any proud father would. "And the *kah* sound is made with the letter…"

"K-k-k… K!" Lizzie beamed and chewed her potato while receiving praise from both Finn and his mother. "Grandma, do you know what a andvarkle is? It starts with the letter *A*…"

Later, after the dishes had been done and Lizzie had been put to bed, Finn joined his mother in the living room.

She set aside her knitting and muted the

television. "Before you lecture me on boundaries and such, I just want to say the house feels empty without Jenny."

"Mom…" Finn rubbed a hand over his face.

"Your father is doing better after his stroke." His mother scooted forward in her seat. "Maybe we should move back."

"Mom…"

"Hear me out. We miss the high country. And this house…" She glanced toward the hearth, where there were pictures of five generations of McAfees, including Jenny.

"Mom." Finn took her hand. "The house is fine. I'm fine. This is exactly where I'm meant to be. Dad needs to be closer to medical care than he could be up here. Besides, we don't have a downstairs bedroom." And his father was still using a walker. "You know this."

"I know this," she echoed. "It's just—"

"Mom." He stood and drew her to her feet and then into his arms, giving her a tender hug. "Let it go. I'll find a wife. Someone who wants kids as much as I do. And then, later on, I'll get the treatment." The one that could possibly leave him sterile. The one that he didn't dare delay for too long for fear that the Big C would make a second appearance.

"All right." His mother's gaze seemed drawn to a picture of Jenny on the hearth.

"I've canvassed my bunco group. They came up with a good list of several single ladies. They're very excited to hear about your interest, but I'm not so sure. Are you ready to date?" She gestured toward Jenny's picture.

He didn't look. "Whether I'm ready or not, it's time."

FINN TOLD HIMSELF he wouldn't go out to greet Kendall when she returned from town.

That would send the wrong message.

He didn't watch her get out of the truck that dropped her off. Or watch the truck drive away. Or watch her stare at the farmhouse before walking to the barn.

Not on purpose anyway.

After she was home safe, he did close up his laptop, having arranged one small stock trade—a young, untested bull for an older one with a record of high yields. He shut off the living-room light, walked upstairs and checked on Lizzie.

She was asleep under her cowgirl bedspread, arm around Peanut. The dog gave a gentle tail thump as if to say "good night." He was such a good dog. He'd washed out of training as a guide dog for the blind. He'd been another of Jenny's misfits and had bonded with Lizzie from day one.

Sometimes, that connection made Finn feel left out, which might have explained his fascination with his new ranch hand. He had to set that attraction to the side. She was temporary, destined for important things. The next woman Finn had a relationship with was going to be experienced with ranch life, a woman who loved the mountains, the simple life, large families and misfit animals. Pursuing feelings with anyone else was just a waste of everyone's time.

And yet, despite the need to find another love, no one called to him the way his Monroe princess did.

Finn should lock up and go to bed. Tomorrow was another busy day, one that would begin with his mother around. Who knew what would happen when Mom met "Ken."

Best give Kendall a heads-up tonight.

Now that he had an excuse—correction: a reason to talk to Kendall—with purposeful strides, he walked out the back door, down the steps and toward the barn. The floodlights came on, illuminating a clear path for him.

Coyotes yipped in the distance, distracting him as they called to each other. There was a pack that sometimes swung through the valley, especially when the weather began to cool. He'd reiterate that the kitten be kept indoors at all times for safety reasons.

Finn swung around behind the barn to make sure the chicken-coop gate was firmly latched. It was. He proceeded to the rear barn door. Only then did he hesitate—it was late, nearly nine o'clock—and Kendall might be getting ready for bed. But then again, the barn was lit up like it was Christmas. As the ranch owner, he had every right to investigate if there was a reason the lights were all on, to check that the stock was okay, or that his employee...

Finn shook his head. He'd just seen her return. His employee had looked fine. Mighty fine.

Get a grip, McAfee.

He was here to warn Kendall that his mother would want to meet in the morning.

He slipped into the barn and froze. "What are you doing?"

His question startled three beings.

Kendall straightened and whirled to face him, damaged phone in hand. Rebel shifted around to look at him, brown ears cocked forward. Boo, who was on Rebel's bare back, lost her footing and tumbled to the ground. She landed on her feet and came to a stop a short distance away from Finn, blinking at him almost the same way Kendall was.

His ranch hand's cheeks had turned an attractive shade of pink. "Do you have to barge in like—"

"I own the place? So, yes." Finn marched toward her, scooping up the kitten and bringing Boo to his chest, which was a mistake. She scaled him like a tree, perching on the back of his neck and releasing a mewling complaint.

"Traitor," Kendall muttered, pressing something on her phone before tucking it in her pants pocket. "Hang on. I'll get her. She can cling with those sharp little claws. Wouldn't want to be responsible for my boss getting a bad acupuncture treatment." Kendall circled around behind Finn. "Don't move." She lifted Boo slowly from his shoulders. "Oh. Did she…?" Before Finn could turn or move away, Kendall traced a finger across the back of his neck. Her touch was warm and featherlight where it rested on his skin. "I thought Boo might have scratched you, but… You had something cut out here? What was it? A mole?"

"Yes. It was…"

Cancer.

Finn refused to give the toxic word voice. But instinctively, his hand came around to the fresh scar. Their fingers touched. He jumped forward as if scalded.

That heat...

Her touch ignited something inside his chest that tried to compel him back to her. It was instinct, this longing.

"I didn't mean to startle you," Kendall said slowly.

"I should've been paying more attention to what was happening." He shoved his hands in his pockets in case instinct gave him a stronger kick and he reached for her. She was beautiful standing there in her city clothes with her mouth in a small *O*. Her slightly distressed expression practically invited him to tease. "How are your ranching studies coming along? Anything new you want to quiz me on? Or can I start quizzing you?" Somehow, he'd managed to return to her side—*when had that happened?*—and was reaching for her left hand, turning it over to look at her palm. "No new notes, I see." Her hand was devoid of writing. Not even a K ♥ F.

What is happening to me?

Finn stepped back, washing a hand over his face. This woman wasn't a cowgirl or a woman of the mountains. She wasn't going to fall head-over-heels for him, Lizzie and the McAfee Ranch. She was here just to beef up what little ranching skills she had and move on to Texas, and then back to wherever she was originally from on the East Coast. Any attraction he felt for her, or she for him, was a dead end.

Kendall's cheeks were flushed and for the first time since they'd met, she wouldn't meet his gaze.

He was grateful for that. On so many levels.

Only now, he couldn't remember why he'd come.

To kiss her, you fool.

He squashed that thought like a bug beneath his boot and searched his brain for a purpose. "Hey, uh, my mother showed up tonight for dinner."

"That's nice," Kendall said too quickly, still staring down.

Not since before his accident overseas had he wanted someone to look him in the eyes so desperately. He wanted to know what she was feeling. About him.

"It is nice," he said in a voice that sounded far off. "She came all the way from Boise." *Stop babbling.* "She even brought chicken casserole." *Shut up.* "It's her specialty. The casserole. You know the kind with green beans and those breaded French onions?" *For the love of Mike...* "She loves to cook, you know. And I love...to eat."

He wanted nothing more than for the earth to open and swallow him whole.

Rebel blew a raspberry. Even the livestock knew he was floundering.

"I can't wait to meet her." Kendall set Boo on the ground and walked back to the brown mare. "Or have some of this famous casserole." She untied Rebel's lead rope and returned her to her stall.

Which reminded Finn that something had been going on when he'd entered. Something that had nothing to do with ranch chores or lessons. He waited for Kendall to emerge from the stall, then asked, "What were you doing when I came in?"

"Taking a picture. Boo keeps sneaking into Rebel's stall." Kendall hung the mare's halter on its hook. Only then did she turn and meet his gaze. Her cheeks were still flushed, but that smile was back in place, the one that said she could weather any storm with good humor, even Hurricane Finn. "I thought it'd be a cute picture."

"There are so many ways that could have gone wrong." The terror at the strength of his attraction to Kendall was receding, replaced by the responsibility of a rancher. "Rebel could have panicked. Horses are flight animals. They try to run when startled."

Her smile never wavered. "But it didn't go wrong. At least, not until you came in. And even then—"

"Please don't do it again." She could have been hurt. The kitten could have been worse off. And then he'd have to tell Lizzie and… "Just don't do it again."

"I won't," she said too quickly, agreeable as always.

Kendall was the most courteous when he wanted nothing more than to argue and put distance between them. For his sake, not hers.

Grrr.

They were back to staring at each other. She, as if nothing at all awkward had happened between them—not the innocently heated touch or the resulting urge for another. He, as if her very presence angered him, as if he didn't have the overwhelming desire to take her in his arms and kiss her.

He hesitated for a moment but then jumped in. "This was not how I thought my life would go." Having only one kid. Losing Jenny. The grind of working alone. The cancer. The unorthodox ranch hand he couldn't seem to fight his attraction to.

Having said too much, having thought too much, Finn spun on his heel and left her.

Her. His ranch hand. Ken.

The first woman he'd wanted to kiss since Jenny had died.

"THOSE LOOKS HE gave me were hot," Kendall told Boo after Finn closed the door behind him. "And awkward." Because she wasn't looking for love in Second Chance, not by a long shot.

Boo was licking her paws, uninterested in Kendall's problem.

And the growing attraction between her and her boss was a problem.

He's not my boss.

"Like that makes any difference." Kendall wanted to learn from him and offer good old-fashioned hard labor in reciprocation, not kisses.

And from the horrified look on Finn's face after she'd touched him, and then again after he'd taken her hand, he found this connection between them as unappealing as she did.

I don't mind it.

"I need to silence my inner voice, Boo." Kendall shut off the main lights in the barn and prepared to go to bed.

Or at least to sit on her bunk and create some social-media posts for Second Chance Ranch. She put her pillow in her lap and rested her elbows on it, scrolling through her picture gallery, a task made more challenging with a cracked screen. The phone she'd ordered online wasn't going to arrive for several days. She had to muddle through with this one until then.

"Boo, the photographs of the misfits are cute but hardly something a traditional ranch would post." What would a traditional rancher post? Kendall tried to channel Finn.

Would he post a picture of me?

Kendall scoffed. That was unlikely unless it was a picture of Kendall learning ranch lessons the hard way, in which case, the selfie she'd taken walking alone on the road back to the ranch would do.

Not on your life!

It was too embarrassing. Her faux ranch page needed to imply a traditional and successful ranch.

She scrolled back through her photographs, making some decisions.

The grass is always greener on the other side, she posted with a picture of the herd waiting for Finn to let the fence wires down.

Have stock. Looking for trade, she posted with a picture of a calf's inquisitive face.

Ranch hands wanted. Must love long hours and scenic views, she posted with a picture of the ranch with the Sawtooth Mountains in the background.

Bunk houses make for strange bedfellows, she posted with a picture of Boo sitting on Rebel's back.

Kendall was almost tempted to post the picture she'd taken of Lizzie's hat and her slippers. "Holden's words aside, that picture would be proof that I'm not meant to work for the Connellys. And by the way, Boo, cattle aren't as photogenic as you."

Perhaps drawn by her voice, Boo hopped up on the bunk and came over to sit in Kendall's lap, purring and kneading the pillow as if looking for a place to bed down for the night.

"Don't tease me, Boo. You'll be up and climbing the walls in another minute or two." Kendall scrolled to the picture she'd snapped unobtrusively of Finn with Boo perched around his neck. His bemused expression was endearing. "He's such a good person. A good dad. And a good rancher. Because of his scars, he has no idea how handsome he is. What a catch he is. How much a girl might want to kiss him..."

Good listener that she was, Boo kept purring and kneading.

"What does it matter?" Kendall searched through the rest of her photographs, but nothing inspired her that felt ranch-worthy. "His life and mine are worlds apart. I don't even know if these posts are any good. Carol might hate them. Burger by the Layer might hate them. I might not get the job." If she didn't get work soon, she'd need to let go of her apartment and move…somewhere else.

No. Not to Second Chance. I'm Philly through and through.

She thought back to the laughter she'd shared with Laurel at dinner, the way those babies felt in the crook of her arm, the way Finn teased her. And a myriad of other memories made in the last day or so. Her attention drifted from the phone in her hand to the remembered warmth of Finn's hand when he'd touched hers.

Her phone pinged, scaring Boo, who leaped to the floor and stalked away. It was a text message from Carol.

Taking Daddy to the clinic tomorrow for his procedure. We're so excited to see what you can bring to our business. Talk soon!

All things considered, Carol was the kind of rancher Kendall wouldn't mind working with. She had big dreams—admittedly vague, but big—and was determined to make them come true. Unlike Finn, she was going places.

All it took was one job, one success, one endorsement, and she'd be on her way.

She drew a calming breath. A lot had to happen between now and success.

Kendall turned her phone on silent and plugged it into the charger. She knew better than to dream about jobs that might not come through. The stars had to align.

Kind of the way they did when people fell in love.

CHAPTER TWELVE

KENDALL WOKE TO the phone alarm in the wee hours of the morning, Boo's small paw on her cheek, and the memory of warm, scarred skin beneath her finger. In the drowsy state between waking and sleep, she imagined tracing the scars on Finn's cheek, leaning forward for a tender kiss, then Finn's melting gaze flaring into shock.

Her eyes flew open.

"He knows we're not meant to be." Kendall sat up, oblivious to the morning chill, consumed with one question. Why did he think she was wrong for him? She rolled her eyes.

That's so me. Placing blame at my door.

It could just as likely be his hang-up. Maybe he still loved his wife.

"Boo, this is why I need to learn how to be a ranch boss and move on. The man is more irresistible than chocolate to me. And I'm like day-old bread to him." She slid her feet into her pink fuzzy slippers, shoved her arms into her champagne-colored bathrobe and shuffled across the barn to the bathroom.

Along the way, horses snorted or poked their heads over stall doors.

"Don't gawk," she told them. "And don't beg for breakfast. I'll be back after I get coffee."

Toothpaste and a hairbrush had Kendall feeling more like herself, although she'd applied a facial mask to combat the dark circles under her eyes. While it dried, she headed back to the bunk room to change.

"Oh…" A petite, older woman with short gray hair stood in the main barn doorway. She held a big mug of coffee and stared at Kendall in a way that was reminiscent of Finn. "I was looking for… *Ken*?"

"Um." Kendall touched the stiff mask drying on her face. "That's… *Ow*."

Boo had been hiding behind a feed barrel and pounced on one of Kendall's pink fuzzy slippers as if it was her prey.

"Boo, stop." Kendall shook her foot, trying to thwart the kitten's attack. "Sorry. That's me. Ken. Kendall. You must be Finn's mom. I'm new." If not for the kitten on her foot, she might have walked over and offered to shake Mrs. McAfee's hand. Instead, Kendall shook her foot harder and wished she wasn't vain enough to apply a facial mask.

At least, she can't see me blush.

Boo leaped free, raced to Rebel's stall, turned and did a full-body wiggle, preparing for another attack.

"Oh." The woman looked Kendall up and down, and then said more significantly, *"Oh."* Her smile grew. "I brought you coffee."

"Thank you." Kendall moved quickly to accept it. The coffee was black and smelled strong enough to grow hair on her chest. "I'll get dressed and—"

Mrs. McAfee's smile showed no signs of abating. It was alarming, that smile. It was the expression a parent made upon meeting their child's significant other and approving of their choice.

There was no choice. There hadn't even been kisses.

The older woman swayed up on her toes, practically giddy. "I'll go back to the house and make you breakfast."

This wasn't good. Didn't she know there were rules about breakfast?

"Please don't go to any trouble on my account." Although Kendall didn't argue as arduously as she should have given her poor cooking skills.

"No trouble," Finn's mother said in a sing-song voice as she left the barn, practically skipping the way her granddaughter did.

Boo raced across the floor and planted all four paws on top of Kendall's right slipper, gnawing at the thick fringe of pink fuzz.

"Somehow, I don't think Finn is going to be happy to see me this morning." Not when his mother had visions of wedding nuptials in her head. Kendall walked to the bunk room with the kitten on top of her foot.

A few minutes later, Kendall was dressed, facial mask replaced with makeup and sunscreen. She planted her bright red-and-white cowboy boots on Finn's front porch and raised her hand to knock, determined to clarify her presence at the ranch.

Finn's mom threw open the door before Kendall's knuckles connected with wood. She smiled as if Kendall was an elf delivering presents on Christmas morning. "Come in. Come in. I'm Julie. I forgot to introduce myself earlier. It's so unusual to have a female ranch hand. Dale and I never had one when we ran the ranch. Nice boots."

"What? Those old things?" Kendall grimaced at her reply. What was she thinking? She padded after the woman in her new thick socks. "Actually, I just picked those boots up in town. Mackenzie has a unique inventory."

"That's a nice way of putting it." Finn's mother had already moved into the kitchen and moved on from boots. "Are you single? Of course, you are. You wouldn't be working and living on a ranch so far up here if you weren't." Julie laughed as she hurried toward the stove. "Sit down and tell me… How did you two meet?"

"Uh…"

"She picked me up at the general store in the bubble-bath aisle." Finn entered the kitchen, giving Kendall a wide berth as he beelined for the coffeepot.

"Actually, *Finn* picked *me* up in the kitty-litter section." If his version was a big pile of malarkey, hers could be, too. Kendall sat down where a place had been set, presumably by Julie, who had eggs in the pan and bread in the toaster, bless her. "Whatever you're making smells delicious, Julie."

Finn sipped his coffee as he leaned over the stove. "You know the rules, Mom—you *made* the rules. Once you turn ten, you make your own breakfast." His hooded gaze slid around the room, stopping on Kendall. "I wouldn't want to guess at a woman's age, but I think my ranch hand is at least ten."

"At least," Kendall murmured, tucking her feet beneath her chair.

"*Ken* is a guest." Julie stirred the eggs with angry strokes.

"*Ken* is an employee." Finn popped the slice of bread that had been cooking in the toaster and put it on a plate.

"Unpaid," Kendall murmured, really hoping Julie would win this argument.

"You're so stubborn." His mother took the plate from him and added eggs to it. She handed the breakfast to Kendall. It looked and smelled better than anything Kendall could make. "Were you plagued by bad dreams last night? Finn has bad dreams, you know." She said this last bit to Kendall.

"Everyone has bad dreams." It wasn't a denial. Finn gave Kendall one of those smoldering looks that said he might be interested in kissing her if she was a better ranch hand and followed his rules.

"Every man for himself." Kendall sighed and handed the plate to Finn. She knew what side her toast was buttered on. "Much as I appreciate the gesture, Julie, rules are rules." Kendall moved to the piloting position in front of the stove. A little dab of butter in the pan. One egg on top. She dropped a slice of bread in the toaster, determined not to burn anything this morning. "I've got this."

Finn's mother glowed. She went to sit down next to Finn at the table. "Finn's lucky to have found you."

"Don't look so happy," Finn grumbled. He'd sat in Kendall's chair and was making short work of what was supposed to have been her breakfast. "This is a disaster, coming and going."

"Finn…" Julie began.

"Disaster," Kendall muttered as the McAfees bantered about her. Much as she tried to cook her egg over easy, she broke the yoke and overly browned it. Not to mention her toast was the dark brown of the almost burnt. She didn't try a second time, but she did add cream to her coffee before sitting, still trying to shut out the back-and-forth of Julie and Finn.

Her presence at the table didn't go unnoticed by Finn. "I see practice doesn't make perfect." He nodded toward Kendall's breakfast.

Julie studied Kendall's plate. "Finn, hers looks better than yours did when you were ten and first learning how to cook."

"She's not ten," Finn pointed out, smirking at his mother.

"I realize it's not exactly five-star," Kendall said, thinking of her excellent dinner last night in town. "But—"

"Ken isn't really suited to the ranch life." Finn sat back, drinking his coffee and staring at the stove.

"And that's why *Ken* is here," Kendall said firmly, more than happy to talk about herself in the third person. "To learn about the ranch life she doesn't live."

"Oh?" Julie passed Kendall the butter and jam.

"She's temporary," Finn said in a detached tone. His gaze swung around to Kendall once more. "When is it you're leaving?"

"When my internship is complete." Kendall slathered her bread with butter and jam. "I have to pass a test given by one grumpy rancher—not Finn, but a Texan. I think the whole process is rigged."

Finn hid his smile behind his coffee mug. "Says the woman who made crib notes on her hand."

Julie poked his arm. "Don't make fun of her. She might leave you."

"I will anyway." Kendall took a bite of toast, taking a moment to chew on the thought and the bread. She'd miss Finn's sly humor and unguarded, heated looks. "I've got an opportunity in Texas."

"I like a woman with drive." Julie refused to be deflated. "Don't you, Finn?"

Finn mumbled something that sounded like "she drives me around the bend."

Kendall frowned at him. "Really?"

"Are you done eating, Ken?" Finn's smile was so fake he could sell it with knock-off designer bags in Times Square. "Can you feed the stock this morning by yourself? I need to make some calls."

"Still trying to make a stock trade work?" Kendall tsked. "If you had a social-media presence, it'd be easier." She was tempted to show him some of her work.

He rolled his blue eyes.

"I'm serious." Kendall huffed. He could be so annoying. "If people know you, even from social media, they're more likely to do business with you."

"You don't need to tell me twice." Finn carried his dishes to the sink. "Oh, that's right. You've already told me twice. This is the third time."

Without thinking, Kendall made a sound in her throat, a sound not unlike Finn's unhappy growl.

"Listen to her, Finn," his mother said. "She has drive."

"I have enough drive for both of us." He walked out, but called over his shoulder, "Thanks for breakfast, Mom."

"I'll get back to you about those dates," she called in return.

Once he left the room, Kendall felt like she could breathe easier. "Dates?"

Julie hurried over, rinsing the dirty dishes left in the sink. "Friends of my friends. No one you need to worry about. You saw him first."

"I'm not worried." Kendall grinned. "Are you trying to fix Finn up?" Because she should take herself out of the running. And she'd gladly do it, too...

After she experienced a few kisses.

Kendall rubbed a hand over her forehead, trying to erase her train of thought where Finn was concerned.

"Why would I arrange blind dates for my catch of a son?" Julie ignored her, humming while she put the cream in the refrigerator.

"I guess I misunderstood." Not likely, but still. It was time to move along. Kendall cleared her dishes. "Thanks for trying to make me breakfast, Julie."

Finn's mother put her arm over Kendall's

shoulder and gave her an enthusiastic squeeze. "He likes you."

Kendall couldn't contain the little burst of happiness at that statement. However, it didn't mean she shouldn't discount it. "That's kind of you to say, but—"

"He likes you," Julie insisted, taking over dish-rinsing duty and gently pushing Kendall back toward the table. "But he'll never do anything about it because he has cancer."

Kendall's legs gave out and she sank back down in her chair. "That explains so much." The scar on the back of his neck. His reluctance to tell her more about that mole he'd had cut out. Even Dr. Carlisle's enthusiastic reaction to Kendall helping Finn at the ranch.

"Finish your coffee, dear."

"I can't." She needed to step up her game where her ranch contributions were concerned and make Finn's life easier. She got to her feet. "I have a lot of work to do this morning."

FINN WENT THROUGH the rest of his contacts, desperate to find someone to do a stock trade and trying not to think of soft gray eyes and long silken hair.

Kendall and her wit were extremely distracting. Not that it mattered. He was quickly running through his list of possible ranchers in the state of Idaho, and his goal of reducing the herd by at least fifty before winter set in was looking impossible. The theme of responses was consistent:

We already optimized our herd for the winter.

I'm looking for an infusion of larger stock.

We're culling our herd because beef prices dropped.

Finn grumbled between phone calls about never having enough time, the low demand for calves not fully grown and the declining price of beef. Later, he grumbled about greenhorns and ranching tests. And later still, he grumbled about slim profit margins and rising electricity costs.

He very carefully did not grumble about the Big C and treatment plans, the search for a wife, or his well-meaning, meddling mother.

When he was done calling and grumbling, he realized his mother had fed Lizzie and Peanut, and was getting ready to leave. The morning sun was up and trying to chase away the morning chill.

Finn walked his mother out to her car with Lizzie skipping alongside. "Thanks for the casserole. Tell Dad and the rest hi for me." His younger sister, Joy, a nurse, and her family had taken Mom and Dad in after the stroke. Joy watched over Dad while Mom was gone.

"I like her." Mom grinned at Finn the way she'd done when he'd told her she was going to be a grandmother for the first time.

Finn sighed. "Can't you let this go?"

His mother's smile didn't dim. "A woman like that... She'd understand the choices you're facing. She wouldn't fault you if you asked for kids right away."

"Mom," he said sharply, gesturing toward Lizzie, who had one hand on the trunk of a nearby pine and was circling the tree, singing softly to herself. That didn't mean she wasn't listening.

"All I'm saying is that she's the one," Mom said. "There were sparks this morning. And when there are sparks..."

Mom thought Kendall would make allowances for all his brokenness.

"I appreciate you wanting to speed up the dating process to pave the way for—" he glanced toward Lizzie "—other things that need to be done. But you need to move on from this."

Mom had selective hearing. "Nonsense. Ken is going to surprise you." And then she laughed as she stepped into his arms. "Don't make excuses or love will pass you by." She drew back, staring up at him. "I'm glad I came and I'm glad I met Ken." She called Lizzie over and kissed her cheek. "You take care of your father."

Lizzie's brow wrinkled. "Is Daddy sick?"

"No, love. Grandma just wants you and I to look out for each other." He held on to Lizzie's hand as his mother got in her car and drove away. And then he had no more excuses to avoid his ranch hand. "Time to move fence."

"Every day the same thing." Lizzie sighed dramatically. "Are we taking the truck today? It's so much faster than riding Pete."

"Yes, but someday, you'll be riding the fastest horse out here and you'll remember Pete fondly."

And someday Kendall will be gone, and I'll remember her fondly, too.

By the time they reached the barn, Kendall had their mounts groomed and saddled and Boo shut in the bunk room, a fact confirmed when Peanut planted himself in front of the door and pressed his nose to the crack between the door and the floor.

Shoot. I should have told Kendall we were taking the truck today.

"Pete!" Lizzie ran to a feed barrel full of oats and grabbed a handful, holding it out to her pony. "You're my favorite even if you are slow."

"Hey, oats are for *after* your ride." Finn tipped his cowboy hat back and weighed the effort it would take to unsaddle the horses and deal with Kendall's hurt feelings, versus the time spent riding to move fence instead of taking the truck.

Too much trouble, he decided, not wanting to acknowledge how much weight Kendall's feelings factored into his choice.

"The stock is fed and watered." Kendall emerged from the tack room. She was wearing cowboy boots and… It was hard to look at anything beyond those unnaturally red cowboy boots. "The stalls are all mucked out. I would have collected eggs, but it looks like your mother did it. What else can I do for you?"

"Look at her boots, Daddy." Lizzie went over to Kendall and kneeled at her feet. "I bet they make you ride better, Ken."

"I hope so." Kendall pivoted as if modeling. "At the very least, they're attention-getting."

Finn tore away his gaze, noticing for the first time that Kendall had a straw cowboy hat on. It was ill-fitting, sitting high on her forehead. One gust of wind and it'd fly off, possibly startling the cattle or spooking the horses.

Lizzie ran into the bunk room, miraculously keeping Peanut out.

Finn's gaze returned to Kendall. Those loud boots... That ill-fitting hat... She may look like a cowgirl, but not like the cowgirl a rancher would have by his side.

I can't be attracted to this woman.

She was everything he didn't need at the ranch—a distraction and a safety hazard.

But to kiss her...

Lizzie darted out of the bunk room and ran over to Finn, carrying a fuzzy pink slipper. "I want cute pink slippers like this, like Ken's. Can I, Daddy?"

His gut clenched, bracing for the fear and foreboding. Not because his daughter wanted something overly feminine. Not because fuzzy slippers were somewhat impractical. But because somewhere along the line, his sister Joy had grown to appreciate such things, had looked for happiness and fulfillment beyond the McAfee Ranch.

Why am I working so hard if not to preserve the ranch for Lizzie and my future children?

Finn's mouth went dry. He couldn't force anyone to love the ranch the way he did.

What if no McAfee besides me wants this life? He'd be postponing treatment for no reason.

He met Kendall's gaze, searching for something. Reassurance or confirmation—of what, he didn't know. The moment he stared into those gray eyes, everything from last night came rushing back—the spark when she touched him, the need to draw her into his arms, the urge to kiss her. The compulsion to build a relationship on this attraction and have Kendall in his life, no matter the cost.

At the cost of his way of life?

Finn wanted to say no. Kendall was to him what those fuzzy slippers were to Lizzie—something exotic, tempting and new.

It was the spark between them that scared him. He almost pulled out his phone and called his mother back. That's how badly he wanted an adult chaperone. With effort, he dragged his gaze from hers.

"Impressive work, don't you think?" Kendall said, although, lost as he was, Finn had no idea what she was talking about until she added, "I did all the morning chores and saddled our mounts. If you want, I can get on the roof and see what needs to be done with the cupola this afternoon. After Lizzie and I lunch with the misfits and I exercise the other horses, that is."

She was disproving his theory that she didn't fit into this life. His life.

And she did so with an energy he envied, having lost sleep last night to bad dreams and fears of mortality. He tried to remember how much coffee she'd had at breakfast and couldn't, possibly because his brain kept being distracted by those red boots, by her cute pink slipper, by everything that was the opposite of what he wanted in a ranch partner.

"Daddy?" Lizzie thrust the slipper toward him, waiting for him to respond.

"We'll put slippers on your Christmas list, love. Put that back where you found it."

While she did as asked, he checked the pony's girth straps, elbowing Pete to get him to blow out air before tightening the strap a bit more.

"Did I pass muster?" Kendall was still grinning, and that proud look invited him to smile right back.

It took effort, but Finn didn't smile. "It'll do." He moved over to Tucker, checking that every buckle and strap was properly in place.

It was.

"*P* is for process, boss." Kendall joined him at the buckskin's side, opening a saddlebag flap as Lizzie exited the bunk room and gave Peanut a good ear rub. "I even restocked this with bandages and snacks."

"You raided the kitchen when I wasn't looking?" It was hard to think of her as wrong for him when she was doing such a good job.

She nodded, glowing with pride. "Your mom caught me."

He bet she had. He bet his mother would be talking about Kendall and missed opportunities for romance. He could put an end to that by dating someone else. But when faced with Kendall's beauty and rapidly developing ranch skill, that held little appeal.

"Why are you looking at me like that?" Kendall whispered. "Do I have something on my face?" She rubbed her nose.

"Yeah." The word came out as gruff as a dog growl. "Your lips."

Almost immediately, her cheeks flooded bright red and her soft pink lips parted.

Finn cleared his throat and tried to clear his mind of attraction. "What I meant is that your smile slows me down because..." This conversation wasn't productive. Needing something more to occupy his mind and line of sight, he marched over to Rebel, checking her bridle and saddle placement. He picked up one of Rebel's hooves. It was clean and dry. A glance into her stall confirmed that it had been cleaned.

Kendall crowded his space again, this time with a gentle touch to his shoulder. "I know my being here is a pain. But I did all the work we did together yesterday morning so you could devote more time to conserving your strength."

For a man with kissing on his mind, she was too close.

And yet, he didn't hear a word she said. He forced himself to turn and face her.

Of its own volition, his hand reached out and smoothed a stray strand of black, silky hair behind her ear.

She sighed.

He jerked his hand back. "Sorry, I... You had a piece of hay in your hair."

"I don't see no hay." Lizzie peered at the ground, having snuck up on her kiss-obsessed father.

"Any hay," Finn corrected absently.

The color in Kendall's cheeks was still high. "If you need more time to make those calls, I can take Lizzie with me to move the herd. You could use a break, I think."

"No." He didn't want Kendall to spend the morning away from him.

I am in such trouble.

Finn looked deep into her big gray eyes, wondering at the attraction. Not only was she a greenhorn and out of her element, but she also approached everything differently than he did. Social media to help him market cattle? He shouldn't respect her for suggesting it, but he did. Boots that would never look the same after one walk into a muddy field? She knew nothing about appropriate ranch footwear, but that was part of her charm. He should admire her the way he admired fancy sports cars, the ones that had no place at the ranch—from afar. He couldn't.

She had pluck. And obvious skills in many realms that were foreign to him. She had a big heart, and an ability to challenge him with her sunny façade when he tried to throw obstacles in her path. And possibly the most important and telling aspect of her personality and character? She treated him as if he had no visible scars—inside or out. Could he say the same of his mother's dating candidates?

Kendall tilted her head to one side as she regarded him. "You look like a man at the end of his rope. No luck selling off cows?"

"No." He'd had no luck putting distance between them either. Somehow, his hands had come to rest on the gentle curves of Kendall's hips. He stuck his hands in his back pockets instead.

"Let me help you," she said softly.

"And here we go with the social-media argument again." He rolled his eyes. It was easier to back away now, to shift his gaze to Lizzie leading her pony out to the ranch yard, although the magnet that was Kendall drew his attention back around.

She wrapped her fingers around Rebel's leather reins the same way she'd seemingly wrapped her fingers around his rapidly beating heart. "Hey, if a ranch in Texas is willing to give social media a try to help land a burger chain's business, you should keep an open mind."

He didn't want to keep an open mind. Social media would just complicate his life further, adding to his to-do list and he was already a technophobe, using his phone and computer for only the most basic of things.

"Tell you what." Kendall led Rebel outside and then swung into the saddle. "I'll race you to the gate. If I win, I have your approval to start a social-media campaign for you, one designed to promote stock sales."

"My horse is faster than Rebel." Finn grabbed Tucker's reins.

Kendall took off, laughing and bouncing in the saddle. "Come on, Lizzie. It's a race."

Lizzie whooped, and managed to urge Pete into a trot.

"That's cheating," Finn said when he caught up to them at the gate.

"The rules of the race weren't spelled out." Kendall was cockeyed in her saddle and holding her hat on her head with one hand. "I win!"

"Go ahead then. I doubt your social-media posts will make any difference." He backed Tucker toward Rebel, keeping him under tight rein until he was close enough to grab Kendall's hat and move away before the two horses started a fight.

"Hey!" She protested the hat theft, but didn't urge her horse forward.

He guided Tucker to the far side of the road with Pete a buffer between them and opened Kendall's headband. "You have to adjust your hat to your head or you'll lose it." He removed a strip of padding in the front, tucked it into his jeans pocket and then flipped the headband back in place. "See if this fits better." He handed the hat to Lizzie, who handed it to Kendall.

She put it on her head, pushing it down until it sat midway on her forehead. "Oh, this is much better. Thanks."

He leaned over to unlatch the gate, aware of Kendall's gaze upon him.

"Are you sure you don't want to stay behind and rest?" Kendall asked.

"Rest?" There was a theme to Kendall's comments, a theme he'd been overlooking since he'd been blinded by attraction. He opened the gate, riding through and turning Tucker around so he could give Kendall the coldest of cold stares. "I'm not sick."

Kendall blushed. "Oh, but..."

"Pete and I almost beat Kendall." Oblivious to the tension between the two adults, Lizzie called Peanut and rode through the gate, and kept on going at Pete's typical, slow pace.

Kendall followed on Rebel, sneaking cautious glances at Finn.

"Don't believe what my mother tells you," Finn said in a voice meant to stop any and all arguments. "Dr. Carlisle got it all."

"So you don't need four weeks of rest?" Kendall's gaze roamed over him.

"No," he growled, closing the gate.

"I can't wait until I'm old enough for a fast horse," Lizzie hollered. She'd turned in her saddle to beam at the adults. "How much longer until I'm five, Daddy?"

"Yes," Kendall said quietly, snapping a picture of Lizzie with her infectious grin. "How much longer?"

"She'll be five in six months and starting kindergarten in a year." Which was a reminder that Finn needed to start the search for an appropriate mount for her. The pursuit would probably take months, made more challenging by winter, when the passes were intermittently closed. He'd need to carve out more time to develop her riding skills. And knowing Lizzie, the more proficient she became at riding, the more she'd want to venture out on her own, which created an entirely new set of problems for him on a day-to-day basis.

Overall, that was a more pleasant dilemma than trying to decide which local woman he might date and how long to postpone medical treatment.

Kendall was staring at him.

"What?"

"That expression you wear sometimes… It reminded me of someone, and I couldn't think of who until now."

"My mother?" She was fond of saying he took after her side of the family in the looks department.

"No. There was something about your expression that reminded me of my cousin Laurel. She gets that faraway look in her eyes when she's thinking about how hard parenting is and wondering if she's making the right choices."

Finn grunted.

"Everyone knows Laurel's doing a good job," Kendall continued. "Just like anyone can see that you're doing a good job. But that doesn't mean you don't feel overworked or overburdened with responsibility, wondering if you're making the right choices or worrying about the future."

She'd hit the nail on the head. But rather than agree, he grunted once more.

Lizzie, Pete and Peanut were farther up the road, with a head start, one that wouldn't last long based on the quick strides Rebel and Tucker were making.

"Hey, you need to remember that your hips are a shock absorber." Finn gestured toward Kendall's midsection. "And no slouching."

Kendall sat up taller.

"If you want to pass my ranching test, much less pass one for that place in Texas, you need to live and breathe the cowboy life."

"Got it." Kendall nodded. "Shock absorbers. Breathe." She slid him a speculative glance. "How, exactly, are you going to test me?"

He laughed at the loaded question and the multitude of ways a man could answer. "You'll just have to wait and see."

They reached Lizzie.

Finn checked his watch. For the second day in a row, they were late setting out. "Stop for a second, love." He dismounted and removed a lead rope from one of his saddlebags. "We're going to speed up Pete today."

"Goody." Lizzie gave Pet's neck a pat.

"What are you doing?" Kendall leaned over to look, her long, dark braid spilling over her shoulder.

"Pete has an endurance bridle that converts to a halter." A feature he'd used more often when Lizzie was very young. "I release his bit and clip the lead rope beneath his chin. That way I can lead him without pressure on his mouth."

"Clever." Kendall's praise made him feel less broken.

"To save time we're going to trot today." Given their rider skill levels, that was as fast as he trusted his girls to go.

His girls.

Yeah, it was going to hurt when Kendall left town.

CHAPTER THIRTEEN

"I'M SO GLAD this is the last herd to move." Kendall clung to Rebel's saddle as she dismounted to move fence. Her knees were stiff, and her toes felt cramped in her new boots. "My shock absorbers have quit."

Her declaration was met with silence. She glanced over at Finn, who sat tall in the saddle despite holding a sleeping toddler in front of him, as well as Pete's lead rope. He was scanning the pasture where the cattle were milling about, waiting to pass through.

Was he thinking about cancer?

Kendall sighed, tying Rebel to the post with the mare's reins in a quick-release knot. She worked out the kinks as she walked to the fence post with the solar-panel unit.

"Are you saying your seat is sore?" Finn said in a deep, smooth voice with a hint of a tease.

"That's a very polite way of asking if all that trotting hurt my sit-bones." Kendall shut off the fence power and climbed in between the barbed wires, snagging her straw cowboy hat and catching her hair on a barb. "Ow."

"You munched your new hat," Finn noted.

Kendall removed it, not exactly ruing the broken hat brim on the back. Nubby strands of straw littered the grass beneath the fencing. "That's exactly what I saw at the pasture yesterday."

"What?" Finn tried to lean forward in the saddle, obstructed by a slumbering Lizzie.

"Those short pieces of straw." She tried to straighten out her rear brim, only succeeding in more straw falling. "Do you think the rustlers broke their hats when they came through the fence?"

Finn frowned. "Are you sure that's what you saw?"

"I took a picture." She found the photograph on her phone and angled the screen his way. "It looks the same. Maybe the sheriff can use that."

"Maybe…"

Kendall didn't like the defeat in his tone. "Talk to me about branding." Kendall popped off the top wire and moved to the bottom fastener. "Specifically, I want to know how many people you need. I'm pretty sure you can't do it by yourself." Out of the corner of her eye, she watched Finn adjust Lizzie in his arms.

"I hire a crew of…" He sounded peeved. "I lost count."

He'd been counting cattle? Kendall glanced at Finn while she dragged the wires out of the herd's way. His eyebrows were drawn down and his mouth made a thin line as the herd ambled past. She didn't say anything more.

Finn's gaze shifted to the cattle in the back. He frowned. "I think I counted wrong. I'll start over in a second." His horse shifted so he was facing her from his left side. The scar on his cheek was flushed. "Branding, was it?"

"Yes," she said.

"Okay. The next time I move the herd…"

"We," she said firmly, because despite what he said about the cancer being gone, there was the comment Dr. Carlisle had made about staying home for four weeks. She wasn't leaving until she had to.

"…the veterinarian might be here to check my heifers, I'll…"

"We'll," she corrected again.

"…separate the calves for branding and inoculation, and schedule a crew to help with that. Five or six ought to do it." He rolled his shoulders back, as if preparing for hard work ahead. "At the same time, heifers that aren't pregnant but were last year will go into a pasture with my best producing bull. Those that aren't pregnant and weren't last year will need to be traded."

Kendall found this fascinating. "Who would take a heifer that isn't producing?"

"Someone who can afford artificial insemination or maybe someone looking to infuse their stock with new bloodlines."

"New bloodlines…" That reminded her of the Connellys. "What do you think of Gelbvieh?"

"It's an expensive breed. They've become the flavor of the month. Why do you ask?"

"That's the cattle they breed at that Texas ranch I'm trying to impress."

"Which explains why they can afford to pay for professional social media." His statement was delivered with equal parts envy and annoyance. "They can probably also afford artificial insemination, which can eat one tenth to one third of a rancher's profits, depending on what a cow sells for."

Kendall let several cows pass by before she said more. "I have to admit I've never paid much attention to ranch profits."

His gaze landed somewhere behind her and his expression hardened. "Do you want to know how a poor rancher like me manages his herd? On a wish and a prayer, that's how. This is why my count was off." Finn nodded toward the nearly empty pasture and a calf who trotted along the far fence line, crying in a high-pitched, melancholy voice. "There's a heifer gone this time. I'm so mad I could do more than just spit."

"Oh, that poor thing. And you, too." From the way he was talking, this was going to hit his bottom line. Kendall wished she could console him. "Do you want me to circle around and shoo the calf along with the herd?"

"Yes, please." He couldn't do much but hold his sleeping daughter.

Kendall made her way to the calf, making all sorts of noise and clapping. "Come on, sweetheart. Move along."

The calf kept staring toward the herd, and then circling around toward the back corner of the pasture.

Now Kendall was curious. She walked all the way to the rear corner of the field.

As before, there were tire tracks, but they didn't enter this pasture. They were only in the field closest to the fire road, the one the cattle had been in the day before. However, this time, there was evidence that wires had been cut and mended, as if they'd used the fire gate and then needed to cut this fencing to steal more cattle.

"How could they cut this?" Kendall drew

closer. "Isn't this part of the electric fence?" She reached out with the flat of her bare hand and tapped the wire once. *"Ow! Shoot—ow!"*

Kendall stumbled back.

Unfortunately, she stepped in something fresh. Her feet slid out from under her, and she landed flat on her back.

"Moo-ooo." The calf nearby seemed sympathetic to her plight.

"I'm okay, buddy." Still, she took a moment to stare up at the clear blue sky because she could feel the electric tingle up her arm and a buzzing in her ears. Kendall took a deep, shuddering breath.

Footsteps pounded, coming closer. "Kendall, are you hurt?" Finn's face came into view. He bent over her, resting his hands on his knees. "Did you get shocked?"

Kendall nodded, fighting back an unexpected surge of tears. She blinked rapidly.

"Daddy, I'm scared," Lizzie shouted from the other side of the fence. "Is Ken alive?"

"Yes, love," Finn called back.

"Don't laugh. The jolt startled me." Kendall's right arm was cramping, and she had no urge to move just yet. "I'm okay."

"Are you sure? You're not getting up. And why would I laugh?" Finn continued to survey her for injury, which was kind of nice, all things considered.

Maybe if she lay there longer, he'd pull a Prince Charming and kiss her.

Finn stared into her eyes with an understanding gaze. "The fence operates on a pulse system, primarily so if something gets a shock, they can move away quickly before they get another."

"That's what I did." When it became apparent no kisses were forthcoming, Kendall heaved herself to a sitting position. "I used my ninja moves. *Wah-pow.*"

"Yay, Ken is still breathing!" Lizzie did a little dance from the safety of the road.

Finn helped her to her feet. "No ninja ever had footwear like yours."

Her red boots were smeared in muck, which, in the scheme of things, wasn't a great loss. But it still choked up Kendall a little. She prided herself on being put-together, regardless of the situation. She bent to pick up her cowboy hat, which was also mud-stained. She decided to focus on the fence rather than dwelling on the condition of her clothing. "They cut your wires. I thought there wouldn't be any charge since they were cut."

"They probably wanted to get in and out quick, so they had gloves or something to stop the energy conduction." Finn held on to Kendall's arm and led her toward the fence. "They spliced the wires. And they did a pretty good job of it."

"That was nice of them. Is there such a thing as nice cattle rustlers?" The damp from the ground had begun to seep into Kendall's pants and the back of her shirt. A touch of her hand to her hair revealed it to be mud-soaked.

"There are only evil cattle rustlers who try to cover their deeds so ranchers won't notice right away." He was back to sounding angry.

She wanted to soothe him—first with a touch to his cheek, and then with a gentle kiss to his lips. But she was in no condition to touch anyone. She wiped her hands on her jeans. "Should we call the sheriff? Maybe he can make a plaster cast of those tire tracks."

A bird cackled in the trees. Thunder rolled across the valley.

She glanced around nervously. "Are they still around? Watching?"

"They're long gone. And I don't think the sheriff is going to do anything about the tire tracks. You've been watching too much television." Finn's expression was stony, his stance tense and still.

Kendall slipped her cracked phone from her pocket and snapped a picture of the spliced wires and the orphaned calf, then turned to take a picture the other way. His way. "This is where they came in the other day, too?"

"Yes. Did you take a picture of me?"

"Why would I do that?" Other than to have something to post—the silhouette of a strong cowboy. Or at the very least, something to remember him by when she was gone. She tucked her phone away.

Thunder rolled again.

"Change in plan," he said, nodding up at the sky. "We're going to bring the entire herd closer to the ranch proper today." He marched back toward Lizzie. "Which means I'll have to start using my hay stores sooner than I planned."

Kendall knew enough about ranching now to realize this would be another hit to his slim profit margin. "We're moving the entire herd because of the cattle thief?"

"That, and because of the fire danger. If lightning strikes the woods, it could race down here, and they'd be trapped." He stopped marching and turned, seemingly waiting for her. "So much for pasture management."

Sometime, probably months from now, Kendall was going to marvel at how much she'd learned in such a short time. But not now. Not when Finn was hurting, scowling like this was the worst-case scenario, because it probably was. "Is this the first time you've been robbed?"

"No. But it's the first time I've been robbed two days in a row." He fell into step next to her, taking her hand, fierce expression easing. "Someone is desperate."

From the tone of his words, she thought he knew who.

BY THE TIME they finished moving his cattle closer to the ranch and arrived back at the barn, Finn was antsy to do something about the cattle thief. He wasn't just going to call Sheriff Tate. He was going to confront the man who was stealing from him—his father-in-law. A man who had a mangled straw hat and a muddy rig and trailer.

"Can you put away the horses, Kendall?" Finn helped Lizzie to dismount, then looped Pete's reins through the hook near his stall. Kendall had proven herself capable today. He turned when she didn't immediately answer.

"Put up the horses? No problem." Kendall moved slowly, as if every muscle in her body was on strike. Her back half was covered in mud, including her hair beneath her equally filthy hat. Her red boots were mostly brown, the white piping no longer visible. "I can manage the horses." Even her voice sounded bruised. "And clean my saddle."

He wanted to enfold her in his arms. He wanted to help her to the bench to rest. He wanted to pamper her, to hold her hand the way he had in the pasture, lending her strength and taking some of hers. But like everything on the ranch, the clock was ticking, and compromises had to be made.

"You're in no shape to work." Finn tamped down his urgency. If he was right about the cattle thief's identity, the man wasn't going anywhere. "Grab a hot shower and change. I'll take care of it." He reached for Pete's halter.

"The heck you say." Moving faster than he'd given her credit for, Kendall tugged the pony's halter and lead rope from his hand. "I can do this. Maybe not as fast as you'd do it, but I'll get it done."

"I'll help." Lizzie squeezed between them and grabbed Pete's lead rope.

Not to be left out, Peanut wiggled into the middle of the human circle and stared up at them all.

"I'm a big girl and we can't eat until the stock is cared for, right, Daddy?" Lizzie's stomach growled.

Finn took in the two females—trail dust lined their faces, but their chins were thrust in the air. He was proud of his girls. Yes, his girls. "All right, Kendall." He gave in. "I'm going to go into town, but Lizzie's coming with me."

"Daddy, I'm a big girl. And Ken needs me." His daughter jutted out her lip.

"You'll come into town with me, Lizzie." Finn pitched his voice as a no-arguments command. He hadn't taken on Kendall as a babysitter. And he doubted she had experience watching precocious kids who made it a habit to find trouble.

"Daddy," Lizzie scoffed, four going on forty. "Ken doesn't know everything about horses. I do."

Finn caught Kendall's eye, trying to gauge her openness to taking on ranch duties and babysitting. Because, on second thought, he didn't want Lizzie to witness the confrontation he planned on having with her grandfather, the man he was certain was pilfering his cattle. "Could you…?"

"We'll be fine." Kendall smiled in that unflappable way of hers. "We've got Boo and Peanut. No worries."

He wanted to hold Kendall to that promise of no worries, but he knew his daughter too well. Even now, Lizzie was grinning like she had something up her sleeve. "Lizzie, you be good. I'm leaving Miss Kendall in charge, not you."

"But, Daddy…" Lizzie scuffed her boots, kicking up dust. "I'm a McAfee."

He headed for the door. "Miss Kendall is in charge."

"Oh, hey," Kendall called out. "Can you do me a favor?"

Finn turned in the doorway, waiting.

"Can you pick up another pair of boots at the general store? I'll pay you back." Kendall rattled off a size.

He shook his head. "Just hose those down. They'll dry." Maybe not by tomorrow, but a working rancher's boots were never clean and seldom completely dry, at least not up here in the high country.

"No. It's…" Kendall grimaced. "These boots pinch my toes. I should have bought a roomier size."

He came back to her and kissed her nose, surprising them both. "I'd think you of all people would know how to buy shoes."

Her eyes were wide and her lips slightly parted.

"Did you just kiss Ken, Daddy?" Lizzie blinked up, looking from one to the other.

"Yes, I did." Finn spun on his heel and left

the barn, grinning because for once Kendall was speechless.

"Don't judge," Kendall yelled after him when he'd almost reached the house. "Boot sizing can be tricky, you know."

BY THE TIME the horses were put away and oats doled out, Kendall's toes were crushed into the points of her new red boots. That wasn't the worst of it. Her clothes were like a sheet of dried mud rubbing against her skin. And her hair was similarly caked, seemingly glued to the shoulders of her shirt. And her hat… She'd taken time to hose it off, but now it had lost its shape. The brim was drooping.

All in all, it would have been completely demoralizing if not for the memory of Finn's hand encompassing hers as they crossed the pasture and his lips brushing her nose when he'd bid her goodbye.

Kendall couldn't stop smiling.

But that didn't mean she could ignore reality. "Lizzie, I need to take a shower." And it wasn't like Kendall could bring the girl into the bathroom with her. It was a wet room with no shower privacy. "Can I trust you and Peanut to stay out of trouble while I do?"

"Yes." Lizzie stood next to Kendall, dirt streaking across her face and arms. Her gaze was trained on the bunk-room door handle. "Can I play with Boo?"

Beside them, Peanut gave a little whine of agreement, thumping his tail.

This had disaster written all over it. Kendall couldn't leave Lizzie unsupervised. Anything could happen to Lizzie or Boo, which in turn might upset every horse in the barn. Not only that, but she could also just imagine Boo scampering off to escape the dog and little girl, leaving Lizzie to wander out to the pasture with the misfits, possibly leaving the barn door open. Boo, of course, would innocently find it, thus becoming a coyote snack.

What a nasty what-if scenario.

Kendall contained a little shudder. She needed something to occupy the girl. A larger bathroom or... Inspiration struck. "Why don't you take a bath while I shower?"

Lizzie rolled her eyes. "It's not even lunchtime."

"I know, but we're both dirty. Let's get cleaned up. In the house. In *your* house." Surely, Finn wouldn't mind that she used his bathroom while Lizzie was cleaning up in the other one. That brought up another issue. "You do have two bathrooms, don't you?"

"Yes, but I take baths before dinner." Lizzie held out her hands, half-shrugging.

"You could show me your room. Did your grandma sleep there last night?"

"No." Lizzie bent to pet Peanut, sounding as if this was the most ridiculous thing. "She slept in her room. Take a shower, Ken. I'll be in charge." She stared at the bunk-room door once more.

Yeah, I'm not buying that, kid.

"I'll make a deal with you." Kendall was spitballing ideas. "I take a shower. You take a bath. And then I'll make you a special lunch."

Lizzie eyed her suspiciously. "Something the misfits will like?"

"Grilled cheese." Kendall tried to make it sound like a gourmet treat, when it was more likely she'd burn the bread. "Do we have a deal?"

The miniature ranch boss thrust out her hand.

CHAPTER FOURTEEN

"WAIT FOR ME to talk to Oscar, Finn."

Finn hadn't heeded the sheriff's words from their earlier phone call. He rolled onto his father-in-law's property with too much speed and too much resentment, coming to a stop in a cloud of dust and getting out of his truck in a cloud of anger.

Oscar Murray lived in a house that many would have condemned. There was a tarp over the roof. One end flapped loose in the wind. The sidewalls leaned outward as if tempted to give up supporting the roof. Back when Jenny had lived here and her mother had been alive, it had been painted a cheerful blue, but only traces of that paint were visible around the rotting window and door trim.

Next to the house, the old man's ancient truck had a stock trailer hitched to it. Both had mud-splattered fenders. Evidence, as far as Finn was concerned.

Finn marched up to the front door and

pounded on it with his fist. "Oscar! Open up, man."

After several more angry knocks, his father-in-law opened the door wide, blinking bleary eyes as if he was in a drunken stupor. His stringy gray hair hung limply around his face. Behind him, the living room had the dingy, dust-filled look of despair that matched the exterior.

"Late night?" Finn demanded. "Just getting out of bed for the day?"

"Yeah." Oscar ran a thin hand over his face.

"Where are they?"

Oscar rubbed the sleep out of his eyes. "Who?"

"Who?" Finn drew a breath, trying to contain his rage. Not succeeding. "The cattle you stole. Don't pretend. I know you did it."

The old man's eyes widened.

The sheriff arrived, parking his SUV behind Finn and blocking him in.

"Don't lie to me," Finn said, not even attempting to be civil. "Or the sheriff."

The old man said nothing.

Sheriff Tate joined Finn on the porch. He was young, wearing a pressed uniform and the benefit of the doubt. "Afternoon, Oscar."

Pleasantries were exchanged. Finn was

practically biting his tongue, past being pleasant, needing answers.

"You wouldn't happen to know anything about some missing cattle?" Sheriff Tate was too nice. He was new at the job and came across as gullible. In Finn's experience, treating Oscar with respect just allowed him to walk all over you. "Finn's missing a calf and a heifer."

"I'm not welcome on the McAfee Ranch," Oscar said slowly, not looking at either man.

"Especially now that you've stolen from your granddaughter *again*." Finn was beside himself with anger.

Oscar's bony chin jutted out. "I didn't steal anything. Not now and not back then."

"Then why do you have a stock trailer?" Finn jabbed his finger toward the evidence. "You don't own any stock." Not so much as a goat or a pony, much less a horse or a heifer. "Why is your rig all muddy?"

"I got a job at the cattle auction in Boise." Oscar stared at the sheriff, chewing his lower lip. "I transport stock around the mountains for them. It's their trailer."

"Right." Finn wasn't buying it.

"Check the registration," Oscar said, again directly to the sheriff. "I got a legit job because I want to see my granddaughter. Plain and simple. She's all I've got left now that Martha and Jenny…are gone."

Finn rolled his eyes. Oscar was so good at playing the hurt card. "And what about your straw hat? The cattle rustler mangled his straw hat on my fence, and I noticed your favorite straw hat had a broken brim."

"A bull knocked me against the side of the trailer." Oscar rubbed the back of his head. "A broken hat means nothing."

But Sheriff Tate nodded, like he believed Oscar. "I'll have to check out your employment, along with the trailer's registration, Oscar."

Grrr.

Finn must have growled out loud, because the sheriff urged him to wait inside his truck while he verified Oscar's statement.

His father-in-law went back inside. Finn was left to stare at the house, his thoughts inevitably turning to memories. In high school, he'd enjoyed coming to the Murray house. Jenny's parents were friendly and seemed to approve of him dating their daughter. At the time, Martha had worked for the forest service and Oscar had worked as a ranch hand for the Clarks at the Bucking Bull. They'd invite him over for Sunday supper and then Jenny would walk him out to his truck to say goodbye.

Later, after they were married, Jenny had been so perfect, greeting him at the doorway when he was done for the day, filling the house with the warm smells of hot meals and baked goods, with sweet embraces and comfortable conversations. Jenny hadn't said or done much that had surprised him. She'd been content with life on the ranch and content with him.

Kendall was nothing like his wife. She was spontaneous on multiple levels and had the power to get under his skin. She wanted more out of life, to make something of herself, to be considered important by her peers. Life with her wouldn't be easy or predictable.

The soft feel of her hand in his… The way her eyes widened when he'd kissed her nose… Finn allowed himself a soft smile. She wasn't the only one to bring surprise to a relationship. If they had a chance at a relationship.

He blew out a breath, staring through the windshield at the dark clouds overhead.

Sheriff Tate tapped on Finn's window. "His story checks out. The trailer belongs to the auction yard. Not only that, but they confirmed Oscar works there. He's thought of as a good employee. Dependable. Trustworthy. Never a whiff of alcohol."

"Doesn't mean he isn't using the trailer to

steal." Finn clenched the steering wheel. "He might even be selling *my* stock to the auction yard." Which was a stretch considering they'd been branded, even the calf that was a yearling, and a legitimate auction yard had to clear all stock sales with documentation and brand identification. But Finn wasn't ready to put anything past the old man.

Sheriff Tate hooked his thumbs in his utility belt, looking like he was winding things up, at least in his mind. "Finn, I know you're upset, but you can't go accusing everyone of cattle theft when there are facts that say otherwise. Oscar has an alibi. He didn't drop off the last of his deliveries until late last night in Aspen."

Finn swore. How could it not be Oscar?

"Go home, Finn." The sheriff didn't sound like he was asking. "I put the word out about the stolen calf yesterday. I'll put out the word about the heifer this afternoon. It's suspicious enough that we should file a report. Let me do my job." He laid a hand on Finn's door. "Head back to the ranch. Take a beat. I'll call you tonight."

Finn waited for Sheriff Tate to check back in with Oscar and then leave. Finally, Finn was able to do the same. He was still trying to wrap his head around the fact that the thief wasn't Oscar when he stopped at the general store to pick up milk, nearly bumping into a cowboy coming out the door, one who looked like he'd been working the range too long for too little pay. His clothes were dirty, and his straw-hat brim was broken in the back.

Come to think of it, Kendall's straw-hat brim was also broken. There was probably many a cowboy too poor to replace a mangled hat.

If that didn't go to prove that Oscar might be innocent, Finn didn't know what did.

"How are things?" Mackenzie peered over the wall separating the front window from the rest of the store. She was creating a display of winter coats and blankets. "Is that Monroe working out for you?"

"I'd say yes if she had no issues with her footwear." Which reminded him that she needed a new pair. Finn selected a gallon of milk and considered claiming he'd forgotten Kendall's request.

"I just sold her a new pair of boots." Mack stepped out of the window display and latched the wall in place. "Just. As in last night."

"They were too small." He didn't share the unfortunate incident in the pasture. "I'm supposed to pick up a size nine." He rummaged around the boot display, opening a box that was her size. "Holy cow, Mack. Why would you stock these?"

The boots he'd found were pink, a tone hotter than Lizzie's boots, and they had leather fringe with sparkles. If he bought them, Kendall might assume he was making fun of her.

Don't laugh, Kendall had told him after she'd fallen in the pasture this morning.

"Why would I stock those?" Mackenzie worked her way to his side, presumably to explain. "Finn, when you live in the middle of nowhere at a junction between two small mountain highways, I can stock just about anything people need and they'll buy it because they need it now, not two or three days from now, when the big online companies can deliver it." She grinned, finger-combing the sparkly fringe. "Besides, the wholesale cost of something like this is next to nothing, which means my profit margin is a livable wage."

"Does that mean you'll give me a local-customer discount?"

"Shoot. What good does being honest to a customer do me if they ask for a markdown?" But Mack grinned. "Sure."

Finn continued to hold the box of boots away from his body, but there was a kind of kismet about them. They were the style of faux cowgirl boots a greenhorn might buy. Or someone who wanted to make fun of a greenhorn who was trying her best to do the work.

Finn sighed, wanting a pair of boots with more cowboy street cred for Kendall. "Don't you have any other nines? Something less shockingly neon?"

"No. What's your problem?" Mack took the box from him and straightened the boots inside, covering one boot with tissue paper. "It's not like you have to wear them."

"No. But I have to look at them."

"Kendall is pretty. Focus on her face." Mack laughed and headed toward the checkout counter. "Problem solved."

That didn't solve his problem. Not at all.

"KEN! HELP!"

Peanut barked.

Kendall had been toweling her hair dry, enjoying a shower in a real bathroom while Lizzie took a bath. "I'm coming!"

Kendall ran down the hall and into the bathroom, slipped on the wet floor and landed with a thud. "Ow."

Immediately, she was soaked and sore.

Another bruise to add to my running total.

"I can't turn the water off," Lizzie cried in a panic, standing in the overflowing tub. She spun the handles above the claw-foot tub back and forth.

There was close to an inch of water on the floor and more coming. Soap bubbles were as high as the rim of the tub, spilling over like a bubbly waterfall. The air smelled of sweet grape soda. There were bubbles on top of Lizzie's head and on Peanut's nose. The dog sat in a puddle and didn't seem to care. He glanced from Kendall to Lizzie as if to say "I've got priorities here."

Kendall scrambled over to shut off the taps and thrust her arm in the water to release the drain despite part of her brain saying this would make a great social-media post. She got to her feet, tugging her phone out of her wet back pocket and setting it on the counter. "I ran the water for you, Lizzie. You weren't supposed to turn it back on." In fact, the little girl had promised not to.

"The water got cold," Lizzie said tremulously.

Kendall tossed the towels hanging from the rack on the floor, hoping they'd soak up the water before it drained into the walls and to the kitchen below. "Bath time's over."

"But, Ken…" Lizzie sank in the tub, sending a wave of water over the rim. "I'm not done."

Kendall gave the little girl a stern look. "Didn't you just call for help?"

"Yes." Lizzie sounded guilty, but made big puppy-dog eyes, as if she was innocent. "But now it's okay."

It was far from okay. Kendall looked in the cabinet beneath the sink for spare towels. "Honey, is water supposed to get out of the tub onto the floor?"

"No." Lizzie's lower lip popped out. "Am I in trouble?"

"I hope not." More likely, Kendall was. Any hope of additional kisses from Finn went out the window. "Stay in the bathtub while I clean up." Kendall hurried into the hallway and to the linen closet, where she'd found towels for her shower. She grabbed all the towels and came right back, laying two towels on the sink before spreading out the rest on the puddles. The water soaked through quickly. Kendall suspected she was going to have to wring out towels to mop up the water completely.

Unconcerned about the flood she'd caused, Lizzie giggled, thrashing about in the tub as it drained, creating big waves. Luckily, the water level was low enough now that nothing sloshed over the top.

Kendall indeed wrung out towels and tossed them back on the floor until it seemed as if the tide was stemmed. She held up a dry towel to Lizzie. "Time to get out, cowgirl."

"I don't wanna." She sat in the bottom of the tub surrounded by a mountain of bubbles and the empty bubble-bath bottle.

"You have two more minutes while I dry Peanut." Kendall used the towel to dry the dog's hindquarters and paws.

"Can't I turn on some water?" Lizzie reached for the handles.

"No!" That came out more forcefully than she'd intended. Kendall modulated her tone and repeated, "No. We still have to feed the misfits." She offered the girl another towel. "Aren't you hungry? We're late for lunch."

"I'm starved." This time, Lizzie allowed Kendall to wrap her up and lift her out of the tub.

A door downstairs opened and shut. "Hey, where is everybody?"

Finn.

Lizzie squealed and ran to her room, trailed by Peanut. She slammed the door.

"Up here!" Kendall put the last of the wet, heavy towels in the bathtub and turned to face the music, smile firmly in place. "I can explain."

When Finn reached the bathroom, he didn't say anything for a good minute. He took in the pile of towels in the back of the tub, the steamy mirror and Kendall's damp appearance. All in silence.

If he'd been one of her brothers, he'd be laughing right now. At her. At the popping mountain of bubbles in the tub. At the amount of towels it had taken to soak up the water. At her wet jeans. At her inability to keep one little girl out of trouble.

Finn didn't laugh. Finn didn't grin. He just looked rather wooden as he said, "You let Lizzie take a bath unsupervised?"

"Um…yeah. I learned my lesson though and…" Kendall pushed sincerity into her expression. It was an uphill push. "I guess you could say I'm good in a crisis."

That must have been a stretch because Finn's expression pulled closer to a frown.

And she loved him for it—that contained emotion. It made her feel safe. It made her feel like she could try anything—and fail at anything—without him having a laugh at her expense.

She stared deeply into those hooded blue eyes.

I love him.

And then she caught herself.

Strictly in a friendly way.

Could you love somebody in a friendly way?

"Hey, Daddy! I'm all clean." Fully dressed, hair still wet, Lizzie charged out of her room and ran to Finn, wrapping her arms around his legs. "I had the best time with Ken."

Tail still damp, Peanut walked up to his owner, sat and stared up at him with equal adoration, as if knowing adorable affection was what the situation called for rather than Kendall's weak attempts at excuses and lessons learned.

Finn's mouth worked before he said, "Did something happen that you needed a bath in the middle of the day?" He sounded dazed, not that Kendall blamed him.

"Yes." Lizzie nodded vigorously. "Ken needed a shower, and she didn't want to leave me in charge of the barn while she showered. So we came back to the house, and I showed her your shower and then I made lots of bubbles." She glanced at the bathtub. "Next time we go to town, we need to buy bubbles."

"No more bubbles," Kendall said, earning an almost smile from Finn. "That's my recommendation." She clapped her hands. "Hey, I'm hungry. Aren't you hungry, Lizzie?" At the girl's nod, she edged past Finn. "How about I make us some lunch?"

"You're going to cook?" Finn asked, still in a stupor.

"Of course." Kendall tossed him a look as if offended. "Not grilled cheese though. Peanut butter and jelly. My specialty."

"My favorite." Lizzie ran past her to the stairs.

CHAPTER FIFTEEN

"It's only three and already it's been quite a day," Kendall told Finn after she'd made them all PB & J sandwiches and hadn't burned anything or flooded the house.

Lizzie had been given her sandwich first, taken three bites and pronounced herself full. She'd left the adults in the kitchen to watch cartoons in the living room.

And Finn had let her because in the course of just a few hours, Kendall had nearly caused a disaster and words had to be spoken. The problem was… Finn had no idea what to say to her.

Lizzie was safe. She might now come to understand that she didn't need to use the entire bottle of bubbles in one bath. She might have even learned a lesson about turning on the taps by herself—something she always tried to do under his watch. All in all, the bathroom was dry and the towels in the wash, and no serious harm had been done.

Kendall sat at the kitchen table across from

him, a stack of bills and Lizzie's artwork at the opposite end of the table. Kendall hadn't complained about wet jeans or anything being sore. She hadn't even dashed off to the barn for dry clothes. And she wasn't wearing that can't-rattle-me smile like she had the first night she'd arrived. But she was smiling. She was smiling at Finn as if he'd saved her from something unpleasant. He just couldn't figure out what.

"Thank you," Kendall said simply, although nothing with Kendall was ever simple.

Finn had been dutifully eating his sandwich—which had a choking amount of peanut butter. He managed to swallow, washing down his latest bite with a lot of water and taking advantage of Kendall's opening. "What are you thanking me for?"

"For picking up a pair of boots for me."

"You haven't seen the boots yet." He'd left the box with the hot pink explosion in the foyer.

Kendall set down her sandwich and rolled back her shoulders, nodding all the while. "I was in the general store the other day. I know the only other boots in that size were...not exactly my style and not what you'd consider footwear for a *real* cowgirl."

She knows? What a relief.

"To be fair, my daughter wears pink boots and she's a real cowgirl." Or she would be one day if Finn could keep the ranch going and make ends meet, which meant finding the cattle thief. It was a shame it hadn't been Oscar.

"And I'm grateful you didn't lose your temper when you realized the bathtub overflowed on my watch," Kendall said quickly, as if triggered by his frown. "Someday, you'll laugh about this."

"Uh…" He wasn't ready to laugh. In fact, he wanted to say something about it. But how could he when Kendall had admitted the tub debacle was her fault?

Yes, how could I when she showered in my bathroom?

Finn swallowed thickly. And he hadn't even been eating peanut butter.

Her clothes are probably still up there.

Finn stared at his plate. There were crumbs scattered around his sandwich the same way his best intentions about Kendall were scattered around the ranch. His gaze lifted to her face and that rattle-me-not smile she'd brought back. He wished he knew what had happened in her life for her to create such an enduring expression. At the same time, he wished she'd tell him she was leaving so he could wish her and this longing a fond farewell.

The longing won't go away when she leaves.

Finn picked up his sandwich, torn between what he wanted and what he needed. "You got the horses put away okay?"

"Yep." Kendall seemed happy. She picked up a stack of Lizzie's artwork and began to leaf through it, turning the pages over. She focused on one page in particular. "What's this?" Kendall held up his hospital-discharge papers, the ones with the recommended follow-up treatment, the back of which Lizzie had been using as a sheet to color on that morning while his mother was here.

"It's nothing." Finn reached out to pluck the papers from her hand.

Kendall leaned out of reach, continuing to read them. "This was dated a month ago."

"Yeah."

"You were supposed to do a follow-up procedure." Kendall kept her voice down, but the shock was there on her face. "A four-week series of—"

"It's optional," he said quickly, finally succeeding in snatching the pages from her.

Kendall frowned. "That's not what it says. It was under follow-up instructions, no optional about it."

He turned the discharge pages over on the

table, artwork side up. "You read all that in the few seconds it was in your hand?"

Kendall nodded. "I'm a speed reader."

"You're nosy."

"That, too." She didn't apologize. She just stared at him like he was a lab rat whose behavior confused her. "You're not going to do it."

"Like I have time? I have stock to sell. Heifers to buy. A ranch to run. A daughter to keep safe every day. And poachers." Hard stop. He wasn't willing to tell her more. Finn tried to stare her down.

As usual, Kendall wasn't one to be cowed.

In that case, he wasn't going to sugarcoat his excuse. "Do you know how draining it is to put chemicals that kill cancer in your body?"

"Not personally." Kendall wrapped her arms around herself. "But I had a friend, a very talented and kindhearted friend. Elizabeth chose not to do all the recommended treatments for her cancer."

I had a friend...

Finn swallowed. He didn't want to hear about this friend.

"Elizabeth said she had no time for more treatments. She said they clouded her head and impaired her creativity. And she... And I—I went to her funeral two years ago." And that was where Kendall dropped the mic, raising her eyebrows at him. But it was the tears in her eyes that had a stronger impact on him, sending a shaft of pain directly to his heart.

"It's not the same thing," he said thickly, standing and shaking Lizzie's artwork as if by some miracle it proved his point. "When a doctor says they've got it all, you're supposed to believe them." But his words sounded empty.

"And when they say that to make sure they catch all the bad cells you need a follow-up treatment, you should believe them then, too. Cancer is relentless, Finn. It doesn't care what intellectual alibis you tell yourself."

He knew what she said was true. He knew, but... The house was quiet except for the sound of cartoons in the living room. The house was quiet...

He stood at the trash can with his back to her, holding his daughter's artwork in his hands. She'd drawn two buildings—the house and barn he supposed—and three stick figures—the biggest had brown hair, the middle-sized one had long black hair and the smallest had blond curls and what looked like pink boots. She'd also drawn something gray in the sky. A bird? It seemed to be carrying an ice-cream cone—at least, that's what he associated with a triangle and half circle. Only...

She'd drawn a family and a stork delivering a baby!

Finn put his hand over his face.

"How do you know you have the luxury of choice, Finn?" Kendall didn't rail at him like his mother did. Or box him in gently the way Dr. Carlisle tried to. No. Kendall came to stand next to him, giving him an inquisitive look as if she truly wanted to understand his point of view.

"I don't," Finn said softly. "But there are things I have to do before I take the treatment."

Kendall rolled her eyes. "Like catching a cattle thief?"

In the living room, Lizzie laughed. Finn stared at her artwork once more.

"Finn..." Kendall took his free hand in both of hers. "You're a handsome, single man with an established business and a strong work ethic. Guys like you are few and far between, just so you know. You could make a go of it with any woman if not for this one thing."

"Any woman?" *Her?*

Kendall blushed, getting the message. She dropped his hand and made a fuss over dumping the remains of her sandwich in the trash.

The knowledge that she found Finn attractive made his chest swell with manly pride.

"However, you'd have to find the right woman to take you on." Kendall put her empty plate in the sink and lowered her voice to a whisper. "Someone who'd be willing to understand your perspective regarding your health and love you anyway."

"Who might this woman be, I wonder...?"

Leaning against the counter, Kendall fell right into his trap. "Someone who finds you irresistible. Someone who appreciates your humor, your passion for this ranch and your love for your daughter. A woman who can take the hard life out here in stride."

He didn't dare speak because everything Kendall had said might just describe her. His gaze traced the graceful lines of her face.

A man could spend a lifetime looking at that face.

His eyes brushed over her lips. They were a soft pink and seemed oh, so kissable.

But Kendall wasn't done. "Someone who's willing to take a gamble that the cancer isn't coming back." Kendall's gaze didn't shy away from his. "Or someone who knows that whatever you've got to offer is enough for however much time they have together."

"We could all die any day, Kendall." Finn

was whispering now, too. "It may sound harsh or even cold, but that's just the way it is. I have responsibilities here. To the ranch." To his dream of family. To his family legacy.

"Are you trying to convince me—" Kendall took a step back "—or yourself?"

Although his instinct was to reach for her, Finn didn't move. He held his medical paperwork with his daughter's artwork on the back over the trash, hesitating. Lizzie would be upset if he tossed it.

Lizzie will be upset when she's older that I didn't do the treatment.

Torn, Finn put her artwork on the fridge with unicorn and fluffy cloud magnets that reminded him of his young daughter. "Maybe I'll do it next year. Lizzie will be going to kindergarten in the mornings. And I might have things here on track by then." A wife, a baby on the way.

For a moment, he dared to wish Kendall was that person.

His phone rang. Finn was grateful for the diversion. It was the sheriff.

"Just wanted to let you know that none of my contacts have seen or heard about cattle with your brand being sold." Sheriff Tate sounded apologetic. "That might mean they're holding on to your stock, waiting for a good time to sell."

"Or setting up a ranch of their own." With his cattle as seed money. Finn gripped the kitchen chair back. "Any calves they have next spring can be marked with their own brand." He needed to catch these guys because Sheriff Tate wasn't about crime prevention. He wasn't even about solving a crime after the fact.

"They'll need bulls next." Kendall had her back to him while she rinsed her dish, but she clearly considered herself part of the conversation. Despite that, when he hung up, she asked, "What did the sheriff say?"

"You got the gist. It was nothing of use." Finn placed both hands on the table and hung his head. "I need to catch this guy."

"How are you going to do that exactly?"

"I'll stay out all night waiting for them. I can do it this Saturday when my mom comes out next. But I have a feeling that the thief will show up again tonight. He's already hit me two days in a row."

"He? So you suspect someone?"

"He… They…" Finn explained about his suspicions regarding his father-in-law and how Sheriff Tate had crushed them. "Oscar moved into the bunk room after Jenny died. It seemed like the right thing to do. Mutually beneficial grieving. I didn't realize he was drinking so heavily. And then later, I thought I could make him stop."

"What happened?"

"I took Lizzie down to Boise to visit my parents one weekend, leaving Oscar in charge. We found his truck out on the highway, along with an empty stock trailer. He was passed out in the barn and didn't remember how the truck and trailer had got out there, or why there were multiple fences down in the pastures."

"That's no proof he stole from you."

"But it was proof that he had a serious problem and I couldn't have him watching Lizzie while I was working the ranch." His voice had grown in volume. Finn swallowed back the pain of the past. "I should stake out the herd tonight."

"Do it, Finn. You have me," Kendall said. "I'll sleep in Lizzie's room. No more baths, I promise. Except... I'm suddenly worried that it could be one man or several. You shouldn't do this alone."

Before he had a chance to argue, something rattled outside. It sounded like a car door slamming. And then an engine roared to life.

A high-pitched birdcall reached Finn, louder than a rooster and nearly as earsplitting as an upset baby's cry.

"What's that?" Kendall shut the dishwasher. "A delivery truck? Some kind of custom car horn?"

"Not likely." Finn heaved a sigh and headed toward the front of the house, suspecting they had a new misfit on their hands.

"Daddy, come see!" Lizzie hopped off the couch, where she'd been looking out the window. "It's so pretty."

He hoped whatever it was didn't eat much.

A peacock was strutting along the side of Finn's truck, feathers fanning out behind him like he was royalty. And then he attacked Finn's hubcaps with his beak, releasing another screech.

"What's he doing?" Having put on her pink-fringed boots, Kendall drew Lizzie back on the porch.

Finn sighed again. "He thinks his reflection in my hubcaps is another male."

"He's not too bright," Kendall noted.

"Peacocks are known for their plumage, not their brain power." Right now, Finn was questioning his own brain power. Because he knew he was going to keep the beautiful bird. He just didn't know if he could keep him safe from coyotes.

The peacock launched another attack at Finn's truck.

"Hey, not my fender!" Finn stomped toward the bird, noticing a bag of bird feed with a note taped on top. "'Please take good care of Charles.'"

"Daddy, he's a *pea*-cock. *P*. Like Pete or..." Lizzie floundered.

"Patrick. Pedro. Prince." Kendall was full of ideas, including how Finn should run his ranch and manage his health.

"Sorry, love. Sometimes you have to honor someone else's wishes." Finn caught Kendall's gaze. "Even if you don't agree with them."

KENDALL WAS DOWN to her last pair of ranch-appropriate clean clothes, so she wasn't changing just because her seat was wet and there was a peacock in the ranch yard she wanted to photograph. The latest misfit and her limited wardrobe weren't even the biggest of her concerns.

There were cattle rustlers. And there was the issue of Finn not seeking follow-up treatment to his cancer surgery. It was her friend Elizabeth all over again. She wanted to talk about this further, but it wasn't any of her business.

It would be if we loved each other.

She was falling for him. She wouldn't be so

emotional about that treatment he was ignoring if she wasn't.

The peacock squawked.

Kendall moved across the ranch yard, cell phone out, boot fringe swinging. She set up a picture with the peacock, the ranch house and that slightly askew cupola. The sky was a clear, rich blue and the tall pines behind the house were a deep green. Both colors picked up on the shimmering colors of the peacock's plume.

Finn and Lizzie moved with Kendall, still having a debate about whether Charles would stay Charles, or if a peacock deserved the same loving alliteration they'd bestowed upon their other misfits. Finn was adamant the peacock remain Charles, cautioning Lizzie not to get too attached in case the bird wasn't capable of defending itself against coyotes.

"Peanut and I will protect him." Lizzie marched off to take up vigil on the front porch.

"You know what I didn't expect?" Kendall waited for Finn to guess, but he simply shrugged. "I didn't expect there never to be a dull moment here."

"That's all part of my master plan." Finn tilted his head back as he stared at the ranch house. "When you look at it from this angle, it looks like the situation is more urgent."

Kendall glanced at him, confused. "Your follow-up treatment?"

"My cupola," he said gruffly.

"Are we fixing it this afternoon?" Every time they talked about it, she couldn't imagine how they'd get up there or what they'd do to straighten it. But it always felt as if she should ask.

"Fix the first thing you noticed was wrong with my ranch?" He tsked, regaining some of his dry wit. "Not today. I need to take Lizzie to see her grandfather." He didn't sound happy about that.

"Your former prime cattle-rustling suspect?"

Finn nodded. "I'm going to ask him to join me on the stakeout tonight."

"That's one heck of an olive branch."

"In a way, he owes me, because of the drinking." Finn sighed. "And in a way, I owe him because I shut him out of Lizzie's life, when she was the last thing he had left."

"My Grandpa Harlan used to say that a man who pays his debts is a good man."

"I met him once." Finn glanced at Kendall, a slight smile on his face. "He was at the Bent Nickel Diner when I came home on military leave. He bought me a cheeseburger and thanked me for my service." He touched his scarred cheek self-consciously.

Kendall was convinced Grandpa Harlan would have bought Finn the world, if he'd seen his scars, but she wanted to keep things light. "He was a good man, my grandfather."

"Most grandfathers are," Finn said, although he frowned, perhaps thinking of Oscar.

"Do you want me to call some of my family to help on the stakeout?"

"No. Too many people will increase the likelihood of being noticed and scaring the bad guys away." But how he squared his shoulders and raised his head implied there was pride at stake, too. "I need to get going."

"Be careful." The words were out of her mouth and a kiss planted on his cheek before she realized what she was doing.

He didn't move.

"I mean…" What did she mean? "Be aware that it's not just your pride at stake, but Oscar's, too. Choose your words carefully, especially since you'll have Lizzie along." She beamed up at him.

"Are you saying I can be…abrasive?" He raised his dark eyebrows and allowed just a smidge of a grin.

"How about brutally honest?" That felt

closer to the truth. He was a man who lived by the clock. She knew firsthand that he had no time for dancing around an issue, and therefore, he could be brusque.

"I'm leaving now. Lots to do before sundown." But he continued to look at her warmly.

She gave his shoulder a little push. "Get going. It's not like I don't have chores to do myself." Kendall hurried toward the barn as Finn headed toward the house. She'd take the opportunity while he and Lizzie were gone to check on Boo and do a load of laundry.

As soon as she was in the bunk room, she kicked off her pink boots and sorted her dirty things. Boo was fascinated with the sparkly fringe, batting it until she couldn't stand it anymore and then pounced on an entire boot.

Her cell phone rang. It was Carol Connelly.

"My daddy had his ingrown toenail successfully removed," Carol announced by way of greeting.

"What a relief." Kendall tried to sound suitably concerned. After all, there was a big retainer at stake and her apartment rent was due in a few days.

"No lie, honey. That and bunions make a workin' man's life a misery." Carol sounded as feisty as ever. "When are you coming to Texas?"

Was she ready to take the test? Kendall didn't think so. Although, that might only be because she wasn't ready to walk away from Finn, Lizzie and the ranch.

She moved to the window. "I'll visit soon, Carol. There was a family emergency. My cousin—you know Shane—was in an accident. I flew out to Idaho, where he's recuperating."

Carol expressed all the right condolences but wasn't to be dissuaded. "I suppose it's better if we wait a tad longer. That way, Daddy has more of a chance to get better. He was on his feet too much today and was such a bear that two new ranch hands and my French chef quit. Do you know how hard it is to get a good French chef in East Texas?"

"About as tricky as it is to get a good ranch hand in the remote mountains of Idaho?" Through the bunk-room window, Kendall watched Finn load Lizzie into his truck.

"I can't vouch for your reference, but I feel we're speakin' the same language." Carol laughed. "Can't wait to meet you face-to-face. I'll call you next week and we'll make all the travel arrangements."

Kendall agreed and then hung up, watching Finn drive away.

She wrapped her arms around her waist and acknowledged one thought: she didn't want to leave.

CHAPTER SIXTEEN

FOR THE SECOND time that day, Finn pulled up to his father-in-law's house. It didn't fare any better. But this time, Finn looked upon the house with concern. It wasn't safe to live here.

Oscar didn't show himself when they parked. But Finn was convinced he was home. The old man's truck was still there, stock trailer still hitched to it.

Finn got Lizzie out of her car seat and set her on the ground. Peanut bounded after her.

"Grandpa O!" Lizzie headed for the front door. "Grandpa O, it's me. Lizzie."

The door opened slowly, and Oscar stepped into the sunlight. He was wearing the same dingy clothes he'd had on earlier. When he caught sight of Lizzie, his entire face lit up, making him look years younger.

Finn grimaced. To honor Jenny's memory, he should have taken care of her father.

"Grandpa O!" Lizzie threw herself into her maternal grandfather's arms. "You never come visit."

"Sunshine, I've been busy with a new job." Oscar set Lizzie on her feet, coming down to rest on his knees to be at her level. "Didn't mean I didn't miss you."

"We have so many new misfits," Lizzie said, always the more talkative McAfee. "Today we got a peacock. His name is Charles and Daddy won't let me change it because he might get eaten." She gave her standard I-can't-get-my-way lip pout.

"Oh?" Oscar knew better than to get involved in the argument between Lizzie and Finn.

"*I* say he should be Pedro. None of our other misfits with good names get eaten. So he should be Pedro." She paused, checking the reaction to her logic with Oscar, and then Finn. "But Daddy thinks he'll be eaten by morning."

"I didn't say that." His daughter had the gift of embellishment. Or maybe she just knew when and how to push his buttons the way Kendall did. For a moment, Finn imagined what it would be like to have Kendall in his life permanently. His days would be full of light banter, intelligent questions and possibly all kinds of little disasters. Her being chased by Evie came to mind, bringing a smile to his lips.

"Butterfly!" Distracted, Lizzie waded into the overgrown flower garden, followed by Peanut.

"What brings you by, Sunshine?" Oscar may have directed the question to Lizzie, but he had his eye on Finn.

"Visiting." Lizzie was too busy plucking at wildflowers to turn around.

"I need your help, Oscar." Finn took a few steps closer. "I've had cattle stolen two nights in a row. Makes me believe I might get robbed again tonight. I need someone with me in case I'm right and in case there's more than one thief."

Oscar took his time considering the request. Finally, he hitched up his pants and spoke. "I see where this is going. If the real thief shows up while I'm with you, you'll believe me."

"I believe you anyway," Finn said, if only half-heartedly.

"But if the thief is a no-show, that proves nothing about my innocence," Oscar observed.

"I believe you," Finn said again.

But Oscar wasn't hearing. Or maybe there had just been so much bad blood between them that he didn't believe Finn. "Some things can't be proven, Finn. I told you that a year ago when you accused me of the same thing."

"I believe what you said back then." It was too little, too late, where Oscar was concerned.

Oscar put his hands on his thin hips. "If I help you, I want to be able to visit."

"You can join us for dinner this Saturday." His mother would be around to ease any tension.

"What's the catch? You were just here this morning and—"

"The sheriff cleared you." Did the old man have to make this so difficult? "Join us for dinner Saturday." He wasn't going to beg.

They settled on a time for Oscar's arrival that night.

"Time to go, love." Finn held out a hand for Lizzie, who had a bouquet of wildflowers that were faded past their prime. Finn hoped that wasn't a sign of something ill-fated.

Lizzie dragged her booted feet. "But Grandpa and I didn't get to play checkers." Checkers had been their game when Oscar had lived on the ranch.

"We'll play this weekend," Oscar promised, smiling. "Saturday night. I'm coming to dinner."

Lizzie looked to Finn for confirmation.

He nodded. "Dinner and checkers."

It wasn't the Saturday he'd been thinking

they'd have. But then again, Kendall wasn't the ranch hand he'd imagined either.

"ROMEO, ARE YOU going to be good to me today, buddy?" Kendall entered the dapple gray gelding's stall with a slight case of nerves. "I'm a rookie on the lunge line." And she'd chosen Romeo to try first because he'd done such a great job with Finn yesterday.

The gelding lowered his nose to her boots.

"Yeah, buddy. Everybody does a double take when they see hot pink fringe and sparkles." She slipped on Romeo's halter and led him out of his stall.

It was a perfect afternoon. The warm sun. The light breeze. The willing horse at her side. It didn't matter that her boots were a sight and her cowboy hat was damp and droopy.

"I can do this," Kendall told Rebel as they passed her stall.

The brown mare put her head over the stall door and nickered.

Kendall chose that as a good sign.

They passed the bunk room. Boo stuck her paw beneath the door and moved it around with a light pouncing motion, looking for someone to play.

"That's a kitty high five," Kendall told

Romeo, leading him to a small field located between the misfits and the chicken coop.

The misfits wandered closer as they passed. Evie the emu came right up to the fence, looking at Kendall's boots and making a low noise, a quick rat-tat-tat-tat. Kendall moved another foot or so over on the path, just in case Evie held a grudge.

She'd left the pasture gate open and put the lunge line and whip inside. It made it easier to get Romeo there, close the gate and switch his lead rope for the lunge line. She walked out to the middle of the pasture, where Finn had stood the day before.

"We should document this moment." Kendall held up her phone for a selfie, positioning herself near Romeo's regal head. She snapped the picture, checking the shot before putting away her phone. She chuckled. "We were photobombed by Larry the llama."

The llama's sweet face had made it into the frame.

The gelding pawed the ground with his front hoof, ready to go.

"You're right. It's the moment of truth, Romeo." She coiled the extra lunge line in one hand and held the long, sticklike whip in the other. "You're a veteran at this. Let's go, buddy."

She gave him some slack and tapped his hindquarters with the whip.

Romeo politely did as she asked, walking in a quick circle around her.

"I'm doing it." Kendall tapped his hindquarters again to make him go faster.

Romeo moved into a trot.

"I'm doing it," she said again, knowing full well it was the well-trained horse that should get all the credit. She gave him more line, enlarging the circle. "Don't get cocky," she murmured to herself, a little dizzy because she was spinning in the center of the circle Romeo was creating.

After a few minutes, she turned Romeo around, switching the rope and whip in her hands. The gelding resumed his trot without much prompting.

"I'm doing it." Pride filled each breath, edging aside those old fears created in Texas. Maybe winning the C-Bar-C business wasn't such a stretch. She could feed stock, groom and saddle horses, manage electrical fences and exercise horses. She could talk herd management and about the impact of cattle rustlers, at least on one level. By next week, she'd land in Texas, pick up a better pair of legit cowboy boots and hat and show the Connellys that she was the perfect choice for their business.

Charles fluttered to the top rail of the pasture and let out a gnarly shriek that startled Romeo. He sprang out of the circle, pulling the nylon rope through Kendall's hand so quickly she fell to her knees. She dropped the rope and Romeo galloped to the corner of the field near the misfits.

"Ow." Kendall cradled her palm where the rope had left a rapidly reddening burn. "The reason I hate ranching is coming back to me." The dirt. The pain. The feeling of being defeated by even the smallest of tasks.

Charles hopped down and shrieked again.

"Charles, you have the worst timing." Kendall picked herself up. Her thin, fashionable jeans had a rip in the knee. She'd lost some skin. And her rope burn was, well...burning.

She hobbled across the length of the pasture to Romeo. "It's okay, buddy. It's just one of Lizzie's misfits." She was feeling like one herself.

Romeo was all the way back in the corner. The lunge line was lying along the fence line.

Kendall bent to pick up the end. But before she wrapped her finger around it, something jabbed her ankle from the side, knocking her over.

Evie strutted along the fence line, a bit of fringe and sparkly sequins dangling from her beak.

"Don't eat that." Kendall climbed the fence and hopped into the misfit pasture, ignoring her aches and pains. "It's bad for you."

Evie dropped the strip of fringe and made that rat-a-tat-tat noise in her throat.

"Good girl." She spoke too soon.

Evie lowered her head to boot level and hurried toward Kendall.

"Bad girl." Kendall took a step back, and then another. "Bad girl. No!"

Before she could fully retreat, Gary boxed her in from the other side. The goat was also staring at her boots.

"Hey, not fair." Kendall waved her arms and raised her voice. "Back away from the greenhorn, people!"

Where was a hero when she needed one?

"I'M GLAD WE BOUGHT TWO bottles of bubble bath, Daddy." Lizzie skipped up the porch stairs carrying her purchases, Peanut close on her heels. "Can I take a bath?"

"You already had one bath today." He followed her inside and stopped.

Kendall was walking down the stairs barefoot and wearing a blue dress—an impractical city dress that Jenny never would have worn—that draped softly over her curves. Her hair was wet, and she had a bandage on her hand. "To be clear..." Kendall held up her hand as she reached the landing. "I showered in the barn. I was just doing laundry upstairs and put my things in the dryer."

"You had a second shower." Lizzie gaped. And then her gaze swiveled to Finn. "That means I can have a second bath, Daddy."

"If your towels are dry," he told her.

"I took them out to dry my stuff." Kendall slid into her sandals. "They'll probably need another hour after that."

"After dinner then, love." He watched Kendall walk past him and out the door. "Why did you need another shower?"

Kendall's shoulders drooped about the time she reached the bottom porch step and turned. "Um... I tried to exercise the horses, starting with Romeo. But Charles enjoys jumping up on the fence rail and shrieking. Loudly. So Romeo was the only horse to get exercise because I made an executive decision to call it a day." She held up her bandaged hand.

Finn hurried down the stairs to her side. "Are you all right?"

"I'm fine. I..."

He gently took her hand in his, wanting to check her wound, wanting to ease her pain.

"I need to get back to the misfits." Kendall slowly pulled her hand free. "Evie and Gary managed to eat a beaded fringe or two from my boot and I want to make sure they don't suddenly need veterinary attention."

Finn stared at her feet in those delicate sandals. Her toenails were painted a deep purple. He was momentarily distracted by the color. He blinked. "Did they eat your boots?" There weren't any others her size at the general store.

"No. Just a mouthful of trim."

He was having a hard time understanding how they'd consumed boot fringe.

"Ken, come smell my bubble bath." Lizzie carried an uncapped bottle toward the porch stairs, stumbled and squeezed the bottle too tight, spilling bubbly bath on the porch's wooden floorboards. "Oh..." Her lips trembled and her big blue eyes began to water.

"It's all right, love." Finn came back up the steps, drawing Lizzie away from the spill.

Kendall was right on his heels, taking possession of the plastic bottle. "Is that coconut I smell? Your last bubble bath was grape."

"Yes. We got grape and coconut." Lizzie was recovering her equilibrium. "I'm getting a second bath with coconut."

"I bet your sheets smell like coconut in the morning." Kendall gave one of Lizzie's curls a gentle tug. "Cool."

She'll be fine with Lizzie all night.

Something inside of Finn eased. Worry, he supposed. He was worried all the time lately, but especially about Lizzie.

Finn spared Kendall a soft glance before he went inside to get something to clean up the spill. Kendall was going to stay with Lizzie tonight while he waited for cattle rustlers, and he wasn't going to worry if she could keep Lizzie out of trouble. Lizzie was going to be Lizzie. She was bright and curious and had an enthusiasm for life that would always get her into some kind of mischief.

Kind of like Kendall.

KENDALL SAT ON her bed in the bunk room in a dress and replayed the look on Finn's face when he'd seen her come down the stairs earlier.

"He looked like he cared, Boo."

I'm talking to a kitten.

And she had been since she'd rescued the kitten from the curb.

"You like it here, don't you?" Kendall snapped a picture of Boo on the floor batting at the sparkly pink fringe of the boots Finn had purchased. "I do, too." But there was her business to launch and noteworthy things to do. Finn struck her as a man who needed time to get used to new things and new feelings. Like a cancer diagnosis. Like a new woman in his life.

He wouldn't ask her to stay.

"We'll come back for Thanksgiving." Shane was planning a big holiday event. It was a good excuse to see Finn again. They'd take it slow.

And as their love grew, maybe he'd decide to follow Dr. Carlisle's advice about the follow-up treatment.

"I'm being optimistic, Boo." Which wasn't like Kendall. "And getting attached." Which wasn't like Kendall either. She was selective about whom she let get close.

With a little bootie wiggle, Boo pounced, tipping over the boot. She didn't give up. She just kept on biting and attacking.

The peacock shrieked somewhere outside. Boo ran for cover beneath the bunk beds.

"It's okay, Boo. Charles puts us all on edge." Kendall had spent over an hour sitting with the misfits, during which time neither Evie nor Gary had shown signs of choking due to eating boot leather. But during that time, Charles had made his way through every bit of brush and every lower-limbed tree, and called out his displeasure.

The main barn door opened and closed with its distinctive creak.

Kendall set aside her phone and walked out into the breezeway, still wearing her flat sandals.

Carrying a stack of folded clothes, Finn froze at the sight of her. His cheeks flushed with color, which was about the most adorable thing ever. "Oh. I'm sorry. Lizzie's napping and I thought you were still with the misfits."

"Evie and Gary seem fine. Are those my clothes?" The ones she'd left in his dryer. Now it was her turn to blush, since it included her underthings. "I forgot all about them. I'm sorry. You have enough on your mind without doing my laundry."

Outside, the peacock shrieked. The sound fit how Kendall was feeling inside—embarrassed and unsettled. Horses shifted in their stalls. None of them stuck their heads out to greet Finn. Charles was wearing them all down.

Finn executed a laundry handoff without touching Kendall. "I did a little peacock research. Looks like they can be noisy when they first arrive to a new home and during mating season."

She hurriedly dropped the laundry on her bunk and returned to him. "Is it mating season?"

"No. That's early in the summer." Finn gave her a tentative smile. "For peacocks. For humans…"

Impulsively, Kendall pressed a palm to his forehead beneath his hat brim. "Are you feeling all right? Seems like you've been off your game all day, ever since we discovered the heifer was stolen."

He reciprocated, placing his palm on her forehead. "This from the woman who was shocked by an electric fence earlier?"

They stared at each other for a moment before both lowered their hands.

"Of all the things that have gone wrong for me the last couple of days—the blisters, runaway horses, electrical charges, rope burns—"

"Rope burns?" He took her wounded hand and gently unwrapped the bandage. "Is that what happened? I was worried Evie got you with her beak."

His touch both soothed and excited her. "I told you I'm not a ranch person."

"That wasn't what you said." He examined her wound. "You said you didn't like your family ranch. That doesn't bother me. Every ranch is different."

"That's not the point. Besides the fact that just about everything I touch around here turns into a disaster—"

"Only on the first attempt." He rewrapped her hand, winding the bandage around carefully. "And disaster might be extreme."

"—you never laughed at me."

Finn held on to her fingers, studying Kendall. He had such an interesting face, such a beloved face. At least, to her. Each bend and twist of the scars on his cheek could have turned him sour and bitter. But he was a gentle and compassionate man, a rancher who wanted to do what was right for his family and the animals in his care, even animals that had been left in his care. Or misfits, like Kendall, who never quite felt they belonged.

I could love him.

Love. She wanted to broach the subject with Finn. Not just love, but a future together. Somehow. She held herself very still, circling around the idea of staying with the seriousness of a mathematician working on a new solution for pi squared. She could work anywhere. She could return from visiting the Connellys and stay in the bunk house. If Finn felt the same… If Finn was falling in love with her…

That was a lot of *ifs*. He'd never credit her feelings ran so deep. They'd only just met.

But we've spent the last few days together.

Her gaze roamed over him some more, remembering something she'd said to Laurel the other day about finding Boo.

I looked into her eyes and I just knew.

Knew that they were soul mates, that their personalities and values aligned, that they could trust each other. Could it be the same with Finn? They'd had a connection from the moment they'd met in the general store.

It might be something that could last if they were on the same page about his health. Increasingly, she was realizing that was important to her.

He was staring at her face with an intent expression on his, eyebrows slightly lowered as if he was puzzling out a problem. "My scars don't bother you." It wasn't a question.

"Your scars don't detract from your presence in any way." She didn't hesitate in explaining. "You're handsome, maybe more so because there's this mystique about you." The words tumbled out without her thinking about them. It was on the tip of her tongue to apologize.

But he smiled.

Oh, my.

She wanted to say more, to put herself out there.

"When you smile at me like that, I want to kiss you," she whispered, quick-like, pulling the reins on feelings.

He didn't stop smiling at her. In fact, his smile grew.

It made her keep talking. "It's just that you have such kissable lips and that whole cowboy vibe…" She finally caught herself, closed her mouth and took a step back.

He took a slow step forward. "Earlier today, you told me that I had you."

"I meant in your corner," she said slowly, editing her words. "Like the saying, you know? You have me in your corner."

"I'm familiar with the saying. But… You want to discuss the meaning of words when I have such kissable lips?" His eyes sparkled with humor and invitation.

Was he waiting for her to make the first move? Kendall wasn't normally a first mover. "What's come over you?"

"You." He took another step closer. "You've made me look at things differently."

"I'm sorry, I—I can be a little overzealous." Everyone in her family said so.

"I like overzealous." Finn placed his hands on her hips, curling his fingers until they fit just so. "I like feisty. I like honesty. The thing is, Miss Kendall Monroe. Despite your fancy shoes... Your lack of ranching skills... And your strong opinions... I still want to kiss you. In fact, if you were to leave tomorrow and I didn't have that kiss, I think I might regret it."

Oh.

Her blood raced and her brain fogged, and only one thought emerged.

I'd regret it, too.

He lowered his mouth to hers and kissed her gently, sweetly, the way a man kisses a woman after a first date.

It had been a long few days. Kendall didn't want a first-date kiss. She wanted heat and fire and passion—everything that their first few encounters were made of.

Her arms came up around his neck and she snuggled closer, kissed him deeper, tried to express the budding feelings she had. And that what they could have was worth working through the obstacles because on some profound level she couldn't identify, they were like-minded, like-hearted, alike in almost every way a couple should be.

"Daddy! Ken! Where are you guys?" Lizzie's adorable little voice drifted to Kendall. "Daddy? Did Kendall leave?"

We're right here, Kendall thought happily.

She sighed into Finn, knowing this first kiss was going to end, realizing they had hard discussions and decisions ahead. But whereas before, she'd been worried she was leaping forward too quickly, now she was certain they were headed down the right path.

Finn took a step back, ending the kiss, ending the embrace.

And if the look of regret in his eyes was any indication, ending any future they might have had together.

For the life of her, Kendall couldn't figure out what had gone wrong.

CHAPTER SEVENTEEN

THE BRAVEST MOMENTS in Finn's life had also been the hardest.

Crawling out of a Humvee after a blast in a foreign land, dazed, ears ringing, knowing that he was in better shape than the rest of his unit and needed to act to save others.

Clawing away the airbag after he and his father had been hit by a drunk driver, ears ringing with a now familiar and foreboding warning while Finn went into rescue mode.

Comforting Jenny in her last days while doing nothing more than sitting next to her and telling her everything would be all right, that he'd be the rock for the family and do right by their little girl. He'd told her he was strong and had endured hard things.

He didn't admit that after great feats of bravery always came periods of defeat and fear.

With only scars on his face to mark the IED, he'd been loath to go back on patrol and relieved that his tour was close enough to being over that he could return home and retire from the military with his pride in tatters. He'd also walked away from the car crash he and his father had been in, carrying more guilt as he took on full responsibility for the ranch while Dad retired. And after Jenny died, he'd failed to care for her father properly. Instead of driving Oscar to rehab, Finn had driven him from his life.

Cowardly acts, all.

And now, he'd gone and fallen for a woman who wasn't right for all the people and things he needed to be strong for. After that kiss, he'd left Kendall standing in the barn in her city clothes and run to Lizzie. Setting Kendall away from him had taken courage, but it was just another patch in the quilt of bad dreams he'd face alone at night. Loving her would only get in the way of finding a woman who would stick by him and the McAfee Ranch. She had important things to do. She'd said so herself.

But instead of telling Kendall why he'd retreated, Finn let cowardice kick in. He'd avoided any conversation they might have by asking Kendall to sit with Lizzie while she took a bath and he cooked dinner. He'd evaded her further by loading his truck with supplies for the evening. And then finally, he'd called his father-in-law and asked him to arrive earlier than planned so that he could leave.

He was a coward, plain and simple. It was a good thing he was on cattle guard duty tonight. He wouldn't have been able to sleep.

When Oscar showed up looking showered and rested, he took one glance at Finn and said, "You look like you've been struck by more cattle rustlers."

"Get in the truck." Finn had already kissed Lizzie good-night and left Kendall with written instructions. He could feel her watching him from the house, feel her questions like a palpable weight on his shoulders. He owed her an explanation and he didn't want to give it.

Oscar seemed transformed. He had pep in his step and excitement in his tone, crossing the ranch yard as the sun set. "Got everything you need?"

Finn grunted. He was prepared. He'd packed two thermoses of coffee, several large bottles of water, one extra large flashlight and a cooler of food, which did not include peanut-butter-and-jelly sandwiches.

Oscar got in. He'd only brought a jacket. "Giddyap."

And his sarcasm.

Finn wished his father-in-law would have left that behind.

"Did you bring a gun?" Oscar poked his nose in the back, where there was no gun. "I guess not. I guess this means we're going old-school." He held up a fist.

"We'll call the sheriff if they show." He'd abide by the law.

"Sure thing." The old man chuckled and hopped into the truck.

Finn was in no mood for laughing.

Thirty minutes later and they were parked on the road next to the last pasture, the one the rustlers had been using to get on Finn's property. The sun had set, and clouds were coming over the mountains to the west, bringing much-needed rain and, more importantly, cover on a night with a full moon.

"I bet they used the fire road last year, too," Oscar said in a voice tinged with anger. "Don't know why they waited until this year to return."

"I made a fuss last year," Finn explained. "And now that winter is around the corner, they're probably thinking about herd management."

"You're giving this outfit too much credit." Oscar sounded so certain. "Cattle thieves aren't that smart. They're lucky."

"If they supplement their breeding stock with mine, they're smart enough." Finn's fingers curled into his palm. He hoped whoever was rustling his stock showed up tonight. He hoped he had a chance to deck someone.

Grrr.

"I know I was drunk when you came back," Oscar began in a tone that promised confession.

Stop talking. Finn didn't want to rehash the past.

"We're going to be here a long time, son—"

Don't call me that. He didn't deserve the title after casting the man out.

"—and you *will* hear me out."

Finn slouched in his seat and crossed his arms over his chest, wishing the crooks would show up sooner rather than later.

"I'm an alcoholic." Oscar clutched something around his neck. "I attend meetings now and that's what you're supposed to say. 'Hi, I'm Oscar and I'm an alcoholic.'" He blew out a breath. "That's my burden to bear. I should have turned to Jenny for help after Martha died, but I turned to my pride and a bottle instead. And then mere months later when Jenny died, I should have turned to you for help. But you had Lizzie to care for and my pride was used to leaning on the bottle." Oscar sat up straighter in his seat, still clutching whatever was around his neck.

"I let you down," Finn admitted. "Jenny was worried about you those last few months, and I should have acted sooner...differently." But he'd retreated into survival mode, taking care of things that clearly needed to be done.

"The regrets are mine to carry, son." Oscar drew a deep breath. "If we'd have been able to have more children, Martha and me, maybe I'd have had someone else to lean on."

Finn sunk lower in his seat. This was partly why he wanted another child. Life was hard and full of unexpected curves. If Finn didn't have more kids, Lizzie would have to deal with the burden of the ranch alone or opt to sell. "I should have stepped up, not back, where you were concerned."

"You did the right thing." Oscar turned to face him. Even in the shadowy darkness, Finn could see the man's deep frown. "A person has to take care of their own. And if that means hunkering down and staying the course without falling apart, that's what needs to be done. Don't apologize for it."

Finn wanted to. He wanted to go back and do better after every act someone had labeled courageous. But life handed you no do-overs. There was only the moment and the aftermath and maybe...

Kendall's beautiful face came to mind. She

was giving him her enduring smile, the one that said she could handle hardship with grit and grace.

And then her voice filled his head. "I'm sorry," she'd say, followed by a laugh that told him she couldn't quite believe she'd done something that required an apology, but she was more than happy to give it.

It seemed like Kendall understood that best.

"I'd like to think that deep down you know I'm right." Oscar shifted forward again, perhaps believing he'd gotten his point across. His point being that Finn was a better man since he hadn't found solace in alcohol.

Knowing he hadn't really found solace—he only pushed the pain into a ball that he rolled with on the daily—Finn closed his eyes. "Are you going to be like this all night?"

"Possibly."

"If I apologized, would you change your mind?"

"Possibly."

Finn smiled the way he imagined Kendall might, with just the right amount of sincerity. "I'm sorry about the last year. And about the year before. And for not being there when you needed someone."

"We both made it through following our own path." Oscar was clutching that pendant around his neck. "There's no shame in that. I've changed. You've changed. And I'm glad for both of us."

Had Finn changed?

Maybe it was fatherhood. But maybe it was Kendall. Maybe he was wrong, the way he'd been wrong about Oscar. Maybe he should try the impossible—win the heart of a city slicker, trust she'd fit into the ranch life and agree with him when it came to putting a pause on more treatment.

That was a lot of impossible hurdles to pass.

And he felt like he'd blown it with her already.

RAINDROPS SPLATTERED ON the windshield at midnight, softer than the thunder rolling across the valley. Both were a counterbalance to Oscar's snores.

There was a storm brewing, and it was only going to get worse. But it wasn't until one o'clock that lights bounced through the woods above them.

Finn didn't wake the old man. Not yet.

He waited for the lights to grow in brilliance, for headlights to become distinct and for a trailer's yellow running lights to appear. The rig stopped at the fire-road gate.

Finn shook Oscar's shoulder. "Wake up. They're here."

Oscar choked on a snore, coughing himself awake. If the rain hadn't been coming down in a steady drizzle, or if the windows had been open, the sound might have traveled across the pasture.

The old man wiped the condensation from his window, peering out. "What now?"

"You're going to call the sheriff." Finn opened his door, pelted by rain almost immediately. He'd removed the interior light bulbs before their venture tonight to avoid alerting anyone to their presence. The night was as dark inside the truck as it was outside. "Tell Sheriff Tate to wait on the highway at the fire-road outlet."

"You're gonna let them steal more cattle?" Oscar sounded incredulous, but he searched his jacket pockets, presumably for his phone.

"What better way to prove their guilt than to catch them red-handed?" Finn started to close the door.

"Wait." Oscar pulled his phone out of a pocket, quickly covering the light on the screen with his palm. "If the sheriff's going to catch them red-handed, why are you going out there?"

"To video their actions and record their license plates." Just in case the sheriff wasn't waiting for them when they left.

CHAPTER EIGHTEEN

LIZZIE'S SPARE MATTRESS was hard as a rock.

And since Kendall had been sleeping on a lumpy bunk in the barn, that was saying something. No wonder Julie slept in a different room when she visited.

Kendall silenced her phone alarm and sat up.

From Lizzie's bed, Peanut thumped his tail. Lizzie didn't stir.

Kendall missed Boo, her own personal misfit.

But she also missed her bed in Philadelphia with its fluffy pillows and frilly comforter. She missed walking from her downtown apartment to the corner coffee shop for a cup of hot tea. She missed wearing dainty shoes that fit and defined who she was. She missed skirts, unruffled hair and flawless makeup. She missed all the things that defined who she was—a capable woman with a ton of self-respect who was in charge of her destiny.

Capable women with self-respect didn't let

attractive men just kiss them and walk away
without explanation. Especially when said
woman had been harboring feelings for said
skittish man. She'd made all kinds of excuses
for Finn during the night. He had a lot on his
plate, including a medical challenge. And she
was a bit much by anyone's standards. Perhaps
he hadn't completely recovered from the loss
of his wife. It had devolved from there. None
of the excuses made her heart feel hopeful.
She was as bruised inside as she was outside.

And now, a new day was dawning.

The house was quiet. Finn hadn't returned.
She would have heard him. She'd left Lizzie's
bedroom door open, and the stairs creaked. So
where was he…?

Fear crawled into her belly and made her
shiver. Was he okay?

She stood and padded to the window. His
truck was still gone.

She checked her phone for messages. The
first was from Franny. Shane was being released from the hospital today. They were
going to have an open house at the Bucking
Bull after dinner so the family could visit.
But she cautioned everyone that visits had to
be brief.

Kendall drew a deep breath, relieved.

The second message was from Laurel asking her to dinner in a few days, telling her how much their night out had positively impacted her motherly energy.

The third message was from Finn. He'd left for Boise, following the sheriff who'd arrested the cattle rustlers. He wouldn't be back until later that day. The herd is fine where it is. You know what to do with everything else.

She did. And it all started with coffee.

Kendall drew another deep, relieved breath. She could smell the coffee brewing downstairs. Trust Finn to remember to set the coffee to brew. It was normal, almost as if that kiss and his reaction had never happened.

A few minutes later, Kendall was downstairs in the kitchen, preparing to cook herself an egg. It required a review of Finn's verbal instructions from a few days ago. Low heat. Pat of butter melted in the pan. She cracked an egg and gently opened it over the frying pan. In no time, she had herself an unburned breakfast—even the toast was a light brown color.

"All without witnesses." She took a picture of her plate before sitting down to eat. The rope burn on her hand throbbed enough to be noticed but not enough to ruin her morning.

Last night, when she'd been emotionally bruised, Kendall hadn't been in the mood to create new social-media posts for her Second Chance Ranch account. But she did today.

Not perfect, but just right, she posted beneath a picture of the peacock strutting in front of the farmhouse and its askew cupola.

Photobombing llama, she posted of the selfie she'd taken with Romeo before the lunging accident.

A little bit country and a little bit comfy, Kendall posted with the picture of her fuzzy pink slippers next to Lizzie's fancy cowboy hat.

Single female seeking nonexclusive single dude, she posted with a picture of a heifer staring at her with a herd behind her. That was a subtle advertisement for cattle business. She'd gained a few followers with the hashtags she'd included on her posts—cowboys and ranchers by the looks of their profiles. If someone did want to do business with Finn…

They couldn't get in touch with him because she hadn't used the McAfee Ranch anywhere, nor had she included his contact information in the page set-ups.

Kendall frowned at her cracked phone screen. She'd won their little race yesterday. Yes, by cheating. But he'd capitulated and told her she could create a social-media presence for him.

She opened her social-media settings and edited the contact information, changing her phone number to his. And then she glanced through her history of posts, few though they were.

"Do you know what I like about those posts?" Kendall glanced around. There was no one in the room, not even an animal she could use as an excuse for talking to herself. Kendall sighed. "Just a single girl in her thirties, keeping it real."

Kendall glanced at Lizzie's artwork on the refrigerator. Would she be single much longer if she agreed with Finn's health-care decisions? Was that why he'd broken off the kiss? Could she agree to them after losing Elizabeth?

Her gut instinct said no. Her gut instinct said she didn't belong here. Sometimes a flower didn't thrive in a different climate. Kendall needed to be true to who she was inside. But she also wanted to be true to her feelings.

Her heart ached, wondering where Finn was and if he was well. He was the king of understatement and might have been injured when the thieves were captured.

Her phone pinged with a new text message.

She practically pounced on it, bringing the text to her main screen. It was Carol.

Daddy's ready to meet you. Just name the date.

Kendall frowned.
If I leave Finn now, I won't come back.
Or more precisely, Finn wouldn't give her another opportunity like this. He'd wrap his heart back up in its protective cocoon.

Who was she kidding? He already had.

"You're in trouble, Ken." And not just because she talked to herself. Because she'd run out of time. It was the Connelly account or Finn that she'd be fighting for, not both.

Kendall finished eating, loaded her dishes in the dishwasher and went to the front door to put on her groovy, hot pink boots. The best thing about those boots were comfort. Finally, Kendall's toes and ankles were getting the treatment they deserved.

Boo didn't bat an eye when Kendall opened the bunk-room door. She stayed curled on her pillow.

"I know you missed me," Kendall told the kitten, checking that she still had food and water.

Kendall fed the horses and made sure to

give them love. No one was going out for a ride today and with the rope burn on her hand, she wasn't going to attempt exercising them. They nickered and whinnied and otherwise greeted her with a return of affection.

Don't get attached.

She made a mental note to make a dinner reservation at her favorite sushi restaurant.

The misfits were next. She loaded the wheelbarrow with their food and headed out back. "Good morning, guys." For a second day in a row, Kendall fed them by herself.

Gary trotted over with his awkward gait. She'd have to check the splint on his broken leg later. Doug extended his nose for a brief scratch before diving into his food. Larry blinked those thick lashes at her, posing like a supermodel llama before starting his breakfast.

Don't get attached.

She made a mental note to call a friend in Philadelphia and offer to meet her for a glass of pinot noir.

Kendall climbed the fence and leaned over to drop Evie's bucket of food in place. The emu walked past it and extended her feathered neck forward.

Kendall watched her warily as she climbed down, but the emu wasn't making the same excited noises she'd made yesterday or the day before, nor was she making eyes at Kendall's boot fringe. Could it be…? "You want a little affection?" She extended a hand and gave Evie a neck rub. "Maybe those leather fringes didn't taste as good as your bird food. Is this my apology?"

The emu made a grumbly noise and turned toward her bucket of food, missing Kendall's too-late smile.

Don't get attached.

She made a mental note to check the release schedule of her favorite designer's spring fashion collection.

It was on to the chicken coop.

Kendall pushed the wheelbarrow around the back. Once inside the coop, the chickens and ducklings surrounded her.

"I'm feeling all the feels this morning." Kendall tossed out her bucket of feed and corn. While the birds ate, she collected their eggs. There were fewer than usual, which she blamed on the unsettling cries of… "Where's Charles?"

She hadn't heard any peacock shrieks since before bed last night. What if the coyotes got him? What was she going to tell Lizzie if Charles was gone?

A familiar, agonizing screech filled the air.

"Charles?" Kendall followed the squawking sound until she found the bird.

Charles strutted through the misfits' pasture, fully plumed.

Evie wasn't happy. Or maybe she thought Charles wanted some of her bird seed. She charged the peacock and drove him out of the pasture.

"Way to move, Evie." Kendall turned back toward the barn. Since they weren't moving the herd, she had little to do this morning.

I'll have to dip into my feed supply sooner than I thought.

That's what Finn had said when they'd brought the herds closer to the ranch yesterday.

But they'd caught the rustlers. What was to stop them from moving the herd back a pasture or two?

Other than the fact that it was only Kendall and Lizzie.

WHEN FINN RETURNED to the ranch that afternoon, he was spent.

He'd dropped off Oscar on his way to Boise last night so his father-in-law could drive home and get some sleep before he started his shift this afternoon.

"Thank you for riding shotgun," Finn had said as he'd pulled into the ranch yard.

"Anytime. I mean it." Oscar yawned. "In fact, I'd like to return to work here, if you'll have me. Lizzie looks so much like my Jenny and…" He dug his truck keys out of his pocket. "I wouldn't mind giving up that old house as long as I had a place here."

Finn nodded, knowing it would be awkward at first, but feeling that Jenny would have wanted them to do more than reconcile. She'd have wanted them to be a true family. "You have a timeline in mind?"

"I'll give them my notice today and start tomorrow. They have plenty of drivers and were giving me the hard routes." Oscar rubbed a hand over his head as if trying to keep himself awake. "Quite an adventure you took me on last night. Those pictures you got… I've seen that fella around town."

"Me, too." The cowboy he'd bumped into at the diner and then later at the general store, the one with the green-check shirt and bent straw hat. "Sheriff Tate is going to search his place. Maybe I'll get my stolen stock back."

"You deserve some good fortune, son. I'll report for work tomorrow."

And just like that, Finn had an experienced ranch hand coming on board, which meant he'd no longer have room for Kendall. He'd stewed about that all the way down to Boise, where he turned over his video of the theft and made his statement to the police. He'd stopped by his sister's house to visit his parents.

"I found a hot prospect," Mom had said, grabbing his arm when he came in. "She's interested in coming up with me this weekend and staying the night. That is… Unless something's changed between you and Ken."

"Nothing's changed." Kendall was still leaving for Texas eventually, plans for a career on her mind. He had responsibilities that collided with her dreams.

He made the turn down his driveway, taking in the things he loved—the view of the valley, the bright white of the farm house, the traditional red of the barn, large herds of cattle in the distance, and…

Cattle. His cattle weren't in the pastures, where he'd left them.

He pulled into the ranch yard faster than usual.

Lizzie was in her bathing suit, splashing in the plastic swimming pool he'd bought her last summer. Only she was splashing clouds of bubbles.

Kendall sat in a nearby lawn chair, feet propped on a milk crate, petting Peanut.

"Daddy!" Lizzie leaped out of the pool and ran to him, an imp covered in bubble-bath bubbles. She wrapped herself around his legs, soaking the denim. "We moved the herd, and I didn't nap on my horse."

He caught on to the specific words. "What do you mean 'your horse'?"

His phone rang.

Assuming it was Sheriff Tate, Finn picked it up without checking the number. "Make it quick, Sheriff. I'm drowning in bubble-bath bubbles and horse malarkey."

Lizzie ran back to the pool, giggling.

"Hello?" A man's startled voice. A man who wasn't Sheriff Tate. "I was trying to reach Findlay McAfee at the McAfee Ranch."

Finn allowed himself a moment of silent groaning. "I'm Finn."

"I'm Martin Hancock from the Horseshoe Ranch out in Missouri. I'm calling about a stock trade or sale. Is now a bad time?"

Yes. He glanced at Kendall, who was speaking to Lizzie in a low voice he couldn't hear. "No. I'm just…" He blew out a breath. "I just heard my daughter confess something and was about to move to interrogate."

"Teenager?"

"Toddler."

"It won't be the first confession. I've got

three girls. Folks always say boys are more trouble. That's not true. Girls are a different kind of trouble, especially to their dads."

"Agreed." Finn shook a finger at Lizzie and then Kendall, moving from under the shade of the tree into the afternoon sunshine. "What are you looking to trade? I've got some young bulls and some heifers."

They talked shop for a few minutes and agreed to email their proposed animal-trade records.

Finn walked slowly back toward the tree. "Just out of curiosity, Martin, how did you find me?"

"I thought you knew. I—I saw your social-media posts. Second Chance Ranch? It's how I find a lot of new blood lately for my herd. But I've gotta tell you, you were hard to track down. You didn't answer the private message I sent you until a few minutes ago, when you gave me access to your phone number."

A few minutes ago, when he'd pulled up. Finn's gaze found Kendall's. "Oh. Great. I'm a newbie when it comes to this stuff and… I'm glad that worked."

"You have an amusing social-media presence, Finn. Wish I had the talent for it, but I don't."

"Thanks. We'll talk soon." Finn hung up the

phone and went to see Kendall. He wanted to talk about social media. But first things first. "You moved my herd."

"We backtracked each herd a little to give them a new grazing pasture." Kendall flashed him that enduring smile. She had her legs crossed now and her booted foot swung, giving life to her sparkly fringe. "It's not hard once you remember to turn off the electricity."

She'd moved the cattle by herself? Kendall Monroe? City girl? A quick perusal revealed no new bandages or bruises. Finn rubbed a hand over his cheek, needing to feel the scars. "And you let Lizzie ride a horse?"

"I put her on Rebel, and I rode Romeo. I left Rebel's halter on beneath her hackamore and that's what I attached her lead rope to. I didn't want to risk Lizzie losing control."

"But I didn't lose control, Daddy." Lizzie held a giant ball of bubbles in her cradled hands. "I rode a big horse. When I'm five, I want Rebel to be my horse."

"We'll talk about that when you're five." Finn drew a deep breath and addressed Kendall. "Maybe you want to show me your work on social media? What did you call this place? Second Chance Ranch?" The name would have to go. The Hollisters had been ranching under that brand for nearly as long as the

McAfees had been in the valley. "Apparently, thanks and apologies are in order from this dinosaur. Your work just got me a stock trade."

"Sometimes the new methods are good methods." Kendall smiled the same the way she had the night they'd met and she'd tossed the hefty bag of dog food in his truck. There was triumph, but there was also distance. "I created the account as practice for the C-Bar-C in Texas. It feels...not exactly ranchy. But it feels like me."

"Show me." He moved closer, reminded of their kiss and all the reasons he was wrong for her.

While Lizzie continued to splash about, Kendall produced her damaged phone and her work. Her pictures of the ranch were stunning, better than any photo he'd ever taken on his phone. And her captions were short and sweet. She was right. They expressed who she was—a woman with a naive fondness for this place and a sense of humor. She saw the ranch through the lens of an outsider without capturing the hard reality it could be.

Finn stepped back.

That didn't make what he had to do next any easier.

"You're talented." Finn drew a breath, preparing to tell Kendall that he was going to need her to leave.

"Thanks, Finn." She blushed a little, smile faltering. "Would you like to come with me to the Bucking Bull tonight after dinner? Shane came home today, and I thought Lizzie would like the chance to play with some other kids."

"Kids, Daddy!" Lizzie stopped splashing. "Oh, can we go? Please, please, please."

Options darted through Finn's mind like the black birds that flitted through his pastures after a light rain.

If he told Kendall about Oscar moving in tomorrow and the need for Kendall to move out, she'd most likely rescind her invitation to the Bucking Bull. That would crush Lizzie for the rest of the day.

If he told Kendall that Oscar was moving in tomorrow and offered Kendall a bedroom in the house, she'd get the impression that they had a future. When the truth came out, that would crush Kendall for who knew how long.

And what his decision came down to was his heart. And his heart didn't have the courage to put an end to things with Kendall.

CHAPTER NINETEEN

CARS AND TRUCKS were double-parked at the Bucking Bull Ranch when Kendall, Finn and Lizzie arrived.

"Quite a gathering." Since Finn had taken over the ranch, he wasn't much for socializing and wasn't fond of crowds.

Kendall didn't answer.

Which was no more than he deserved.

Finn parked behind what looked like Holden's truck. "We'll wait in the truck, Kendall. I know Franny but not Shane or any of the rest of these people." He gestured toward the cluster of kids and adults milling about in front of the two-story farmhouse.

Lizzie kicked her boots against his seat back. "I see kids, Daddy. Lots and lots of kids."

Sure enough, several boys and a little girl were running around the barn.

"Those are the Clark boys, plus Tanner's kids, Quinn and Mia." Kendall got out. She was dressed for life outside a ranch, wearing a pretty red blouse, black slacks and white polka-dot flats. Already, she was drifting away from him. "It'll be good for Lizzie to run around with kids her age."

"Please, Daddy!" Lizzie squirmed in her car seat.

"All right." Finn got out and soon Lizzie was running toward the barn and shouting, "Wait for me!"

"Quite a gathering," Finn said again. He accompanied Kendall up the gravel driveway, careful not to touch her, although he wanted to hold on to her hand or drape his arm around her waist, anything to ground him in this sea of Monroes. He angled his hat brim down on the left side instead. "Take as long as you need. Visiting with family is important."

"Thanks." Kendall disappeared inside the house.

Almost immediately, Dr. Carlisle came outside with Holden and greeted Finn. "How are you feeling?"

"Same as always, Doc. Just fine." He hoped she took him at his word and laid off the follow-up-treatment lecture.

Holden cocked his head. "I think the children are in the chicken coop." He marched off without another word.

Dr. Carlisle chuckled. "A man of action. That's my Holden."

"He's probably worried about his kid." Finn was. He couldn't see Lizzie anywhere.

Dr. Carlisle shook her head, rubbing a palm over her prominent baby bump. "This is Holden's kid. This, and his oldest, who just started college." She hooked her elbow through Finn's. "Walk with me."

It wasn't a request.

She led him toward the trees, tall pines growing on the slope above the house.

"You've got help at the ranch now," she said matter-of-factly.

"Yes." How had she heard about Oscar so quickly?

"Wouldn't it be great if Kendall stayed with you for four weeks?"

So she hadn't heard about Oscar. He chose not to correct her.

Dr. Carlisle glanced up at Finn through those thick glasses of hers. The breeze lifted her short blond hair. "With Kendall around to help, you could get through your IV therapy. After that, you could administer the thrice-weekly shots yourself."

If Dr. Carlisle suggested this to Kendall, it would only make his asking her to leave that much worse. "Please don't mention this to Kendall. She isn't staying. She's already learned all she needs to know."

"She'd stay if you asked her. In fact, you need her." Dr. Carlisle had a slow and steady pace, but she also had a one-track mind where Finn was concerned. "Kendall's a Monroe. They're responsible like that."

Finn pressed his lips together and dug in his boot heels, not wanting to walk any farther from the ranch proper.

Dr. Carlisle released his arm and gave him a slight frown. "You have insurance, don't you?"

"Insurance?" Suddenly, Finn doubted the entire trajectory of his life. Fear landed firmly in his gut and made as if to stay. "Life insurance?"

"Car insurance. Property insurance." She waved a hand. "Insurance of any kind."

He nodded numbly. What in the world was his doctor getting at?

"Then you'll understand," she said simply. "This follow-up treatment is like insurance. It'll control the growth and spread of any melanomas in your body, the ones we haven't identified yet, the ones not attached to the mole we removed. The treatment will stimulate your immune system to destroy any remaining cancerous cells."

"Insurance." Jeez, he'd gone a whole different direction with her metaphor.

"Yes," she said gently. No one would fault her bedside manner. "Isn't that worth a little bit of lost hours not spent ranching?"

The depth of her meaning struck him, agitating the fear in his gut, making him want to turn around, get in his truck and head home. But he couldn't. Lizzie was around here somewhere enjoying life. And Kendall was inside that farmhouse celebrating life. "We've never really talked about this before. I've done some research about it online." He looked around, lowering his voice. "My hesitation has been... My concern is...permanent infertility. I want to have more kids."

"Hey, how goes the master's degree in ranching?" Shane's smile was as weak as his joke.

Kendall took his hand and gave it a squeeze, bringing forth her tried-and-true smile, the one that said everything was fine despite black eyes, hollow cheeks and bandages. "I found a good teacher, no thanks to you."

"Yeah, Holden told me." Shane's voice was a cracked shell of what it used to be. He squeezed Kendall's hand, and she was heartened that it was a strong grip. "Be proactive with the Connellys. Call tomorrow. Set a date."

Kendall didn't want to. She promised anyway. "And don't you meddle. I'll know if you contact them behind my back. Let me do this on my own."

He smirked. "Franny took my cell phone away from me."

"He wasn't getting any sleep." From the other side of the bed, Franny smoothed Shane's hair from his eyes. "The doctor said he needs rest. I figure boredom will have him closing his eyes."

"I already caught him outside once today." Gertie stood in the doorway, leaning on a cane and looking fondly at Shane. She was Franny's grandmother and a survivor the way Kendall hoped Shane was.

Shane smiled, looking like his old self. "If I slack off, Holden will be running Second Chance in no time."

They all laughed. Holden and Shane would vie with each other over anything, including the last cookie on a tray.

"You know, Grandpa Harlan once told me that coyotes yip to make their prey panic." Shane's eyes, ringed in shades of puffy purple, had a faraway look to them.

Franny and Gertie came forward, seemingly intent upon distracting Shane.

But Kendall squeezed his hand. "I understand."

Shane sighed, closing his eyes.

"You do?" Franny whispered.

Kendall nodded. But she didn't explain. It was the kind of cryptic advice Grandpa Harlan would impart while trying to hold the attention of his twelve grandchildren. Now Shane's take on it—stay the course in the midst of uncertainty—made sense.

More people were clustering in the hallway. Kendall gave up her seat and went into the kitchen to get a glass of water and one of Gertie's famously good chocolate chip cookies.

Her cousin Jonah was standing at the sink drinking a tall glass of water. The rays from the setting sun glinted off his bright red hair and goatee. He glanced at Kendall. "What's this I hear about the McAfee Ranch being a home for misfit animals? That sounds like there's a story to be found there." Jonah wrote screenplays for a living. "And another story behind your new boss's scar. I could have had more than a few dates back in Hollywood with a scar like that. I'd love to interview him."

"Do you want to date Hollywood starlets?"

Emily, Jonah's fiancée, came up beside him. She was a former rodeo cowgirl and had a tolerance for Jonah's jokes.

"The brightest star in my life is you, babe." Jonah fought for a quick recovery, abetted by his impish grin.

"And you caught this star without the benefit of a scar." Emily tsked, wrapping her arms around his waist. "Leave Finn alone. He's sensitive about his appearance. I've never heard him say much about it."

"I could ease into the topic." Jonah wasn't ready to give up. "I'm a sensitive guy."

Emily made a noise of disbelief. "Come on, Mr. Sensitive. The garbage in the kitchen needs to be taken out." She handed him a bag and led him toward the back door.

"You don't look good, Ken." Bo entered the kitchen, opened the refrigerator with the familiarity of someone who lived there—he did not—and got himself a cold beer. "The mountain air doesn't suit you. That's your grin-and-bear-it smile."

He knew about that, too? Kendall shook her head, dropping the facade. "You're the only person here who noticed."

"I'm your brother. That means I have insight into your soul." He sipped his beer, gaze searching her face. "Fell for the rancher, did you?"

Kendall crossed her arms over her chest, bracing for the punch line.

"I'm available if you need a hug." And without waiting to hear if she needed one, he gave her a side-arm hug. "If he doesn't love you, Ken, he doesn't deserve you."

"Jeez, you sound so adult." And his gentle teasing didn't set her teeth on edge.

"It's only taken me thirty-six years and a broken heart to get here." Bo grinned. "What's your excuse?"

THE KIDS WERE playing hide-and-seek.

Lizzie had been crouching in the chicken coop with another little girl for the last five minutes.

Finn wanted to go check on them, but that would only draw attention to the girls and then they'd be "it."

"It's tough, isn't it? Knowing where they are but not saying a thing?" A cowboy came to stand next to Finn. "I think your little girl is hiding with my Mia."

"In the chicken coop?" Finn asked, and at the man's nod, he added, "That's my Lizzie. She loves animals."

"I think Mia was in shock that another girl

showed up." The cowboy extended his hand. "I'm Tanner." He had a strong grip.

"Are you a Monroe or do you work on the Bucking Bull?" Finn couldn't remember seeing him before.

"I'm sort of a Monroe. I mean, I'm a Monroe." He tipped his black cowboy hat back. "A recently acknowledged branch. It takes some getting used to, mostly because they take some getting used to."

Finn nodded as if he understood, when in truth he didn't. "I run the McAfee Ranch north of town." Another opening for the cowboy to say what he did.

"I've got a little place to the north. Past the Bar D." Tanner chewed on his bottom lip. "I haven't decided if I'm staying."

"Are you looking for work?" Finn tried to play it cool. It was always good to have extra hands on a ranch, or on call for branding and such.

"I'm set for now. I put on a rodeo school for kids a few weeks back. And I'm trying to decide where to go from here. I'm a widower. Got two kids."

"Same." Finn nodded curtly. "But it's just me and Lizzie."

And Kendall, a voice whispered in his head.

A group of boys ran past.

"The skinny cowboy with the brown felt hat is Quinn. Also mine." He smiled fondly at his son. "You and I should get together. Mia would love to have a friend in town."

Screams erupted from the henhouse as the girls were discovered. It sent the hens into a tizzy.

"Frankly, I'm actively cultivating friendships with non-Monroes." Tanner chuckled. "They can be a bit much."

Finn nodded.

Tanner cleared his throat. "Of course, I say that but you're the one who took Kendall in, right?"

"Is it written on my face?"

"No. It's what everyone was talking about before you came." He cleared his throat again, as if he'd said too much. "I've met her a few times. To be honest, I'm a little surprised she'd opt for living on a ranch—she doesn't seem suited. But then appearances can be deceiving."

Finn thought about how Kendall had never said no to anything he'd asked her to do. And then he played back Tanner's words about her family talking about her being on the ranch, adding that to her fear that she'd be laughed at. She hid her sensitivity well. "You know, she surprised me. She's come a long way in a short amount of time with respect to ranching. She's going to impress the socks off those people in Texas." He let that statement settle before adding another. "You know they're breeding Gelbviehs." It was a test of Tanner's ranching knowledge.

"No." Tanner chuckled. "The rich man's cattle? Kendall will fit right in."

It didn't matter that Finn was prepared to say goodbye to Kendall. Kendall fitting in in Texas was exactly what Finn was afraid of.

CHAPTER TWENTY

LIZZIE FELL ASLEEP in the back seat before Finn reached the end of the Bucking Bull's winding driveway. Her head was tilted in her car seat.

"She's precious, Finn." Kendall glanced back at his daughter. "Your wife would be proud of the job you're doing raising her alone."

"Thanks."

"You still love her," Kendall said softly. She stared at Finn with those big gray eyes that often said more than she did. "Is that why you look at me with such pained regret? It was just a kiss, Finn."

"You and I both know it wasn't just a kiss," he said thickly.

"Yes, but…"

"There's something between us. There has been from the moment we laid eyes on each other." He drove slowly, partly for safety and partly because he knew he had to tell Kendall she had to leave before they reached the ranch. If he didn't, he might not be able to say it at all. "Let's not lie about that."

She fell silent, lacing her hands together in her lap.

"Can we get to the gist of this conversation? Why can't you just say that I'm the city mouse and you're the country mouse in this relationship? That we can be friends, maybe date a little when I'm in town, but we're just too different to ever be a couple in the long run."

There was a lie he couldn't bring himself to accept.

"I need you to vacate the bunk room." Finn hadn't meant to say it so bluntly. But the alternative was to bring up his feelings and to bring up hers and to make this even worse than it was.

"Well, that's adult of you, country mouse." Kendall crossed her arms over her chest. "One kiss and a bit of honesty and you've got to remove me from the premises. You can't see beyond what I'm wearing to recognize me as one of your misfits."

"You? A misfit?" Finn scoffed, so upset that he pulled over to the side of the road with the lights from Second Chance proper just ahead. "Let's be clear. You aren't a misfit. You don't fit in on a ranch—on any ranch. And I'm the misfit. I'm the broken one. Just look at my face."

"I have been." Kendall laid a cool hand over his left cheek, tracing his scars, brushing her fingers over his whiskers. "I see the symmetry. And the badge earned by a hard life lived, a duty carried out, a—"

"Don't." He took her wrist and lowered her hand. "Jenny's love… I understood that. She knew me before. She loved me before. But she also loved the animals no one else could. Maybe I was like that, too, in some way before. Maybe that's why she chose me."

"You're not broken, not now and not before you were scarred. And those animals you take in aren't broken either. They have personality. They give love." There was fire in her tone, mirrored in her gray eyes. But then that fire banked and turned into a plea. "Anything that gives love is worthwhile, don't you think?"

"You're wrong." He wanted to agree, to kiss her, and promise her the moon. But she wasn't destined to be his. Instead, he set her hand away from him.

"It's just how you look. Your appearance doesn't speak for who you are inside," Kendall said, louder and clearer, her voice filling the truck, risking waking Lizzie. "And inside you may feel like me—like you're a misfit—but that doesn't mean you're ruined." She released her seat belt, leaned over the center console and kissed him.

Finn foolishly deepened the kiss—how could he not?—letting her combination of warmth and indignation seep into him. He was going to cherish this moment. Because it wouldn't last.

She'd said so herself yesterday morning, when she'd stolen a look at his discharge papers. She was the kind of woman that shied away from the unknown. She'd never give her heart to a man who didn't do everything in his power to ensure his good health and longevity.

He'd stared down death. He knew it could come at any time. No follow-up treatment could give her the guarantee she was looking for.

Finn broke off the kiss. "I'm sorry." It sounded odd to apologize to Kendall, since she'd been serial apologizing to him from the start. "But you're going to have to move out of the bunk room soon. I'm bringing on a full-time ranch hand and he starts tomorrow."

"I don't understand." Kendall ran a hand through her hair. "We just… I know what you feel for me. It's all there when we kiss. I can cover the cost of an additional ranch hand so you can take that treatment. I have a good feeling about the Connellys. And if that were to fall through, I can ask someone for a loan to help us get by."

Finn stared at Kendall with a gaze that held no hope. "You've been very clear about your goals. Let me be clear about mine. I want to be with you, Kendall, but I need to be with a woman who wants kids right away. There might be aftereffects of the follow-up treatment that could make that impossible for me." Dr. Carlisle had confirmed that tonight. "That's why I can't let the spark between us turn to flame. You can't be an important person and do all the important things you're destined to do on the McAfee Ranch."

"Excuse me?" Kendall's hand went to her throat. "There's a lot to unpack here, starting with you deciding what I need to make me happy and ending with you wanting a wife this second just to have more children."

"Family is everything to me. It always has been." He should have left it at that, but he couldn't. "I had that family in the service and—"

"A family not made of blood ties."

"—it only proved to me what I want. Here. In Second Chance. Didn't you feel the love in the circle of family that gathered tonight for Shane? I don't have that in town, a short drive away. And I'm worried Lizzie won't have that either."

A truck slowed as it passed them. It looked like Holden's truck but it didn't stop.

"It's why you want to delay the treatment," Kendall said slowly. "It all makes sense now."

"It's my future I'm thinking of. My dream. Nothing in my bloodwork says there's active cancer inside of me." He had to believe that or he couldn't delay treatment. He reached for her hands gingerly, because she had that rope burn on one, tentatively because he should be letting her go. "You and me... Yes, there's attraction. And, yes, there are feelings. But I need to find attraction and feelings with a woman who wants to stay in these mountains and—"

"Get pregnant right away." Kendall stared at their hands. "Like someone who doesn't have dreams that might get in the way of saving your life."

It sounded awful when she said it out loud. "Yes."

"So you're dumping me instead of looking at other ways to create family?" Her mouth worked as if she was trying to put that defensive smile in place. "Is your next ranch hand the woman who checks all the boxes?"

"No. It's Oscar, Lizzie's grandfather." Finn

couldn't help himself. He reached for her again.

"I… I'm getting out of here." She snatched up her purse and reached for the door.

"Hang on…all your things are at home."

"Home?" She made a derisive sound. "That isn't my home." Kendall hopped out, slammed the door and ran across the deserted highway, walking toward the Bent Nickel and the Lodgepole Inn.

And he followed her until she reached the inn safely with everything but her heart intact.

Because if she felt anything like him, her heart was surely broken.

CHAPTER TWENTY-ONE

KENDALL ENTERED THE Lodgepole Inn on a sob, startling Mitch, who was reading a book in front of the lobby fireplace.

"What's wrong?" he whispered, getting to his feet. "Laurel's asleep and I don't want to wake her unless it's an emergency." He ran a hand through his dark hair. "Is it Shane? Please don't let it be Shane."

"It's not Shane," Kendall whispered, moving closer to him, mindful of Laurel's rest. "I need to borrow your SUV. And then I need a room."

"Do you also need a friendly ear? I'm a good listener." Mitch smiled gently, brushing away a tear she hadn't known was on her cheek.

"Thanks, but no." That sounded harsh. "Maybe tomorrow?" When she'd had the chance to cry a little and purge this feeling that the deck had been stacked against her the entire time, even though she'd had no idea what game was being played.

Regardless, Kendall took Mitch's keys and hit the road.

When she arrived at the McAfee Ranch, Finn must have been busy putting Lizzie to bed. She hurried into the barn and glanced around, blinking back tears as various horses poked their heads out and greeted her with a chuff of breath or a nicker. She went over to Rebel and scratched her behind the ears. "I don't care what Finn says or Tucker thinks. You're the ruler of the roost."

Rebel nudged her with her velvety nose, obviously in agreement.

"Whoever Finn chooses to marry...you be good to her." Kendall spoke quietly, half expecting Finn to show up and slip into the barn to apologize about the way things had ended.

She paused, listening. But all she heard were the soft movements of horses and the shifting of straw in stalls. Not even Charles shrieked.

Kendall went into the bathroom, gathering her things and packing them into the travel case she'd hung off a hook on the back of the door.

She stared at the red boots she'd sprayed off that were still drying under the sink. The white piping would never be white again. Nor would she have any use for them since they were a horrendous fit. She left them for Finn to deal with.

Since she'd done laundry the day before, there wasn't much to pack into her suitcase. She dumped Boo's litter in the barn trash and put her into her carrier, an action for which she received very vocal complaints. Kendall was going to leave her hot pink, fringed boots, but at the last minute, she decided to take them. And then she loaded everything up in the back seat of Mitch's SUV and left.

All without seeing Finn again.

"FEEL BETTER, LOVE?" Finn tucked Lizzie into bed.

She'd had a stomachache since their return from the Bucking Bull, having eaten something there that didn't agree with her. Or maybe one of the other kids had a stomach bug she'd caught.

He'd heard someone drive up as he was consoling Lizzie. And he'd heard someone pull away now, as he tucked her into bed.

"Where's Ken?" Lizzie said in a weak voice. "I want to say good-night."

"It's late, love. You need to get your rest." He'd break it to her tomorrow that Kendall was gone. And if she made a fuss, he might drive into town for groceries and casually check on her at the Lodgepole Inn.

"I had fun with the kids." Lizzie's eyes were closed. "Mia is my best friend."

"We'll set up a playdate, love." He'd add it to his long list of things to do every week to make sure she was happy. "Grandpa Oscar is moving back in tomorrow so you can play checkers. I'll have more time to set up playdates and take you to see Grandma and Grandpa in Boise." He didn't add anything about the woman his mother planned to bring this weekend, the one she felt was a perfect match for Finn.

Lizzie snuggled deeper under the covers. "Do you think Ken would like to marry us, Daddy? I like Ken."

Finn didn't know how to answer that question. And so, he didn't.

And perhaps because he didn't, Lizzie finally drifted off to sleep.

But her question remained, and it followed him about as he went around making sure everything was shut tight for the night.

Do you think Ken would like to marry us, Daddy?

The answer would have to be no.

CHAPTER TWENTY-TWO

BO DROVE KENDALL to the airport first thing in the morning.

It was a silent ride. Bo wasn't a morning person and Kendall wasn't good at hiding her broken heart.

The closer they got to the Boise airport, the more Kendall's heart ached. But she couldn't go back to a hardheaded cowboy. Why couldn't he see that families came in all forms and from all places?

Kendall caught herself again. She was not the woman of his dreams.

When Bo pulled up to the passenger-drop-off area, she latched on to his arm. "Promise me you'll take good care of Boo." Kendall had left the kitten in his room at the Lodgepole Inn rather than having to leave her alone at a hotel in Dallas.

"I promised already. Twice," Bo said patiently.

"And you'll help Laurel with the babies?" She gathered her purse.

"I promised already. Twice." Bo no longer tried to hide his exasperation. "There are other people trying to drop off here, Ken."

She didn't care. And to prove it, she set her purse back down. "And if Finn shows up—"

"I promised not to have it out with him. Twice." But the vehemence in his tone wasn't believable.

"Did you make that promise when you had your fingers crossed or something?"

He shook his head slowly. "That'd be Shane or Jonah. Are you sure you want to go to Texas? Because we could head back. Sometimes when you fall fast and hard and it doesn't work out, you need to stop and think, rather than run." He spoke from recent experience. A playboy who had finally fallen in love, only to fall for the wrong woman.

"I appreciate the advice, but there's nothing more to say." She'd booked a flight the night before and texted Carol, scheduling time to visit in two days. Kendall gathered her purse straps.

"I don't know about that. What little you said on this trip was all about Finn." Bo rolled what looked like weary eyes. "Maybe you should patch it up with this Finn and—"

"I'm over him, Bo." Or she would be. Someday. "I need a job, remember? Oh man, don't you talk to Holden?"

"Well, in that case, knock their socks off, sis." He bumped his fist against her arm.

"As a woman with blisters on her feet and ankles, I take offense to your rallying cry." Not that she'd prefer him to call her princess.

"Then how about this?" Bo leaned over the center console and hugged her. "I hope you find what you're looking for."

It was the perfect thing to say. And Kendall almost started crying again, because what she was looking for was back in Second Chance and not looking for her. "When did you become so nice?"

He sat back in his seat. "I've always been nice. Maybe you've just been too sensitive to notice."

Maybe she had.

When Kendall touched down in Dallas, she checked into a hotel at the Galleria and arranged for a spa day.

And then she called Carol to let her know everything was on schedule. She needed to drive east to their ranch, which required the renting of a car or, better yet, a truck. After which, Kendall spent a few minutes scrolling through the social-media posts of Burger by the Layer and wondered what all the fuss was about. They were just another burger joint.

And then Kendall headed out the hotel doors and into the Galleria mall because she needed to look the part of a proper Texas cowgirl, one who hadn't been dragged down by heartache.

"WHERE'S KEN, DADDY?"

Finn fumbled to release Lizzie's car-seat latch, which only reminded him of the night he and Kendall met.

He'd driven into town this morning to buy drinks with electrolytes for Lizzie, whose stomach seemed fine this morning. But she'd had relapses of stomach bugs before.

"Is Ken in the store, Daddy?"

"I don't know, love. She's probably at the Lodgepole Inn. But I bet she sees our truck and comes over to find us." Oh, that felt like a whopper of a lie. She'd realize someday that he was right. She didn't belong in Second Chance. But he was fairly certain that someday wasn't today.

Lizzie wiggled happily in her seat. "Let's buy Ken another pair of boots, Daddy."

He finally released the catch. "She might like flowers better." And a nice card with a heartfelt apology full of well-wishes for the future.

"Okay." Lizzie skipped to the general store.

Once they were inside, Lizzie ran to the checkout counter, and jumped up and down. "Mack, we need flowers!"

Mackenzie slumped. "I don't have any, honey. Sorry."

"What?" Finn glanced around. "You stock everything from air filters to cowboy boots and you don't have any flowers?"

"You have complaints?" Mack looked perplexed. "It's not like it's Valentine's Day."

"We need flowers," Lizzie said staunchly. "Ken left us, and we want her back."

That probably sent the wrong message. Finn attempted damage control. "We had to make room for Oscar to move in. Kendall moved back to the Lodgepole Inn, but Lizzie misses her."

"Okay." Mack shrugged. "Um… I don't have flowers, but I do have some boxes of chocolates. If you don't mind them being for Halloween."

Finn shook his head.

Despite that, Lizzie knew where the candy section was. She ran to find the chocolates.

"I don't think Halloween candy is what

we're looking for, love." Nor would candy solve the issues he and Kendall faced.

Didn't matter. A few minutes later, Finn and Lizzie entered the Lodgepole Inn with a box of chocolates shaped like a ghost.

"Boo!" Lizzie hurried over to the kitten, plopping on the floor to play with her.

Finn had never been so glad to see a cat as he was to see Boo. It meant Kendall hadn't taken off first thing for Texas or Philadelphia. "We're looking for Kendall," he told young Gabby, who sat behind the check-in counter.

"She isn't here." Gabby packed up her laptop. "And I'm late for school."

"Do you know when she'll be back?" Finn glanced around the lobby, evaluating potential places to hunker down and wait, if only to appease Lizzie.

And your broken heart, a voice in his head murmured.

He could live with a broken heart. He'd proven it many times before.

"She left." Laurel, Kendall's cousin, came out of the apartment behind the check-in desk, carrying a baby in each arm.

It was like getting a one-two punch. Kendall was gone and now Finn was staring at babies, and he knew with a sudden certainty that he'd never hold a baby of his own in his arms again—either one made of love or one found with love. Because with crystal clarity, he realized what Kendall and the world had been trying to tell him. Families were made by love and generosity, not genes and DNA. He'd had his band of brothers and sisters in the service. He'd considered Oscar to be part of the family before the drinking got bad. He could make a family with Kendall at a pace she was comfortable with in a way she was comfortable with.

Except he'd realized the truth of it all too late. She was gone.

As if reading his mind and taking pity on him, Laurel approached him and slid a baby into his arms. Wrapped in a pink blanket, the redheaded baby slept peacefully.

"She went to Texas," Laurel told him, which seemed highly unfair since his first reaction was to exit the building and howl.

Kendall was gone.

Boo attacked his feet, gnawing on his boot leather. Lizzie scooted across the floor to pet the kitten.

Finn stared down at the floor, where Boo and his broken heart rested.

Boo...

"When is Kendall coming back?" Because

she was going to return for her kitten. She loved Boo.

But does she love me?

Finn swallowed thickly, trying not to swallow hope.

Gabby hurried out the door, carrying a backpack and a disapproving look, which she sent Finn's way before closing the door behind her.

"We expect Kendall back in a few days." Laurel stood a few feet away, jiggling a baby. "What are your intentions toward her, Finn?"

"My own." The baby in his arms gave a breathy sigh and stretched, sleepily adorable.

"She's my cousin." Laurel shifted back and forth.

"She's my ranch hand."

"We want to marry her." Lizzie picked up Boo and snuggled her chin against her fluffy white fur.

Laurel pressed her lips together.

"My daughter is jumping the gun," Finn said, backpedaling. Sure, he loved Kendall, but that didn't mean it was smooth sailing. "Sometimes you have to work out philosophical differences before you make a commitment."

"And Kendall's reason for leaving becomes

clearer," Laurel murmured. "I'll take that baby back now." She extended one arm.

Finn hesitated, staring down into the sleeping face of a cherub. "I love her." And he didn't mean Laurel's little girl.

"You…" Laurel peered at him, leaning closer. "You love Kendall…or babies?"

"Both. I…" He couldn't seem to take his eyes off the little tyke's face.

"You…" Laurel hadn't stopped staring. "You want a baby."

"Daddy wants lots of babies," Lizzie said. "I heard him say so."

"Lizzie, time to go." Finn was shaken that Laurel could read him so well. He handed over the baby he'd borrowed. "Babies are… Babies are a maybe." He hoped Laurel understood. He wanted Kendall back on whatever terms she'd agree to. "Family is important to me, but so is Kendall's happiness."

"We're leaving? But… Boo…" Lizzie had the kitten cradled under her chin the way Kendall used to hold her.

"Put Boo down, love." Finn moved toward the door.

"You should take your chocolates," Laurel said, not unkindly. "Kendall prefers roses. And heartfelt apologies, something I imagine you'll need a lot of if she's even to consider making a go of it with you."

"Thank you for the advice." Finn grabbed the ghost-shaped box of chocolates on the floor, opened the door and ushered Lizzie through.

But through to what? He'd never been so unsure of his future in his life.

CHAPTER TWENTY-THREE

KENDALL DROVE HER rented truck through the grand arch that marked the entry to the C-Bar-C Ranch.

The road wasn't dirt or gravel. It was paved. There were no weeds growing like hedges on either side of the drive. Every fence post was rust-free and vertical. Even the cows in the fields looked cleaner.

At the end of the drive, there would be no hundred-year-old barn that looked like it might not make it another hundred years, no pasture behind the barn filled with misfit animals, no crooked cupola on top of an ancient farmhouse.

She had to face it. The worst shame of it all was that there would be no Finn when she got out.

There was a knoll ahead covered in scruffy-looking trees. There was just the right amount of trees for a romantic interlude and...

Kendall caught herself. *Today is about me, not Finn.*

The driveway wound around it and eased down into a small valley with a very large house, two very large barns and a series of paddocks and smaller pastures. It might have impressed someone else. She was used to the look, it being similar to her family's ranch.

She parked in front of the house and hopped out, leaving her purse on the floorboard, taking only her keys and phone. The Texas heat was oppressive more for the humidity than the actual heat itself. She left her keys on her windshield wiper in case anyone needed to move her truck, and tucked her phone in her back pocket.

"Kendall?" Carol stepped out on the front porch. She was a middle-aged woman with soft brown hair. She wore a blue plaid dress with a fitted waist and bright blue cowboy boots with stiletto heels.

"Carol." Kendall felt an instant affinity with the woman, more than she had during their other interactions. "Impressive spread you have here. I love your boots."

"Impressive statement of your own you're makin'." Carol gestured toward Kendall's feet.

A week ago, Kendall would have been embarrassed by her footwear. She put one hot pink forward, sending the fringe swinging and beaded sequins sparkling. "I've got a soft spot in my heart for these boots." And the man who'd bought them for her.

Carol led the way inside. "Those boots say a lot about you, darlin'."

Kendall resolved herself to the fact that they did, more so than the soft brown Stetson she'd purchased, or her purple fitted button-down with the pearly snaps.

The house was air-conditioned and decorated in old-school Texas tradition. Wood furniture with cowhide-covered cushions. A ten-foot-wide rack of longhorns above the stone fireplace.

"Daddy is in the library." Carol kept leading her deeper into the house. "The doctor released him to ride today, but only on the condition that he walk his horse."

"I'll do as I please." The gravelly voice belonged to a too-slender man with a white grizzled chin and sharp gaze that had lost nothing over the years. He assessed Kendall. "Your boots got more wear-and-tear on 'em than you do."

Carol chuckled, opening a closet and digging around inside.

Kendall turned her right boot out and pointed at the missing fringe. "Goat." She turned her left boot out, exposing another patch of missing fringe. "Emu." She pointed to the tops and the scratches. "Kitten."

The old man chuckled. "You can call me Harold." He gestured to the chair next to him. He had one foot propped on an ottoman. It was covered in a sock and looked like a bandage was underneath. "Tell me about your ranch operation."

Kendall settled in the chair. "The Monroe Ranch? I thought you'd been there."

"No, ma'am. I meant your ranch." He pointed at Kendall's boots. "The place you earned your stripes."

"Found them." Carol held up a pair of ostrich boots. "These are the ones you wanted, Daddy? The ones you wore when your gout flared up?"

"Those are them." Harold reached for them. "A full size too big. They ought to fit over this bandage of mine." He nodded to Kendall. "Don't mind me. Go on."

"I suppose some would say it's a ranch located in an inhospitable location." With an inhospitable rancher. "But you know that every ranch location has its challenges—water, fertile pasture, isolation from cattle rustlers."

Having succeeded in putting one boot on, Harold blinked. And then laughed. "I never thought about it that way. Tell me more."

"Do you need help, Daddy?" Carol didn't wait for his answer. She held up his boot, shaft opening wide.

The old man extended his foot tentatively. Together, the Connellys got his boot on.

"You were saying," Harold said with a sigh.

"About this ranch?" Kendall hadn't been saying much. She'd been waiting to see how this boot scenario played out. "Well, it always feels like disaster is one bad stock trade or sale away." At least, that was the impression Finn had given her. "And yet, there's always room to take in another misfit or unwanted animal."

Harold nodded, setting his boot soles on the hardwood and shifting his feet around. "Like your emu?"

Kendall nodded.

"You all are gonna make me cry." Carol sniffed, then whispered, "That poor unwanted emu."

Kendall chuckled. "Don't feel sorry for Evie."

They exchanged small talk a bit more before Harold suggested they go for a ride. "Before it gets too hot."

Since it had been hotter than blazes when Kendall had arrived, she wasn't enthusiastic about a ride, but she knew better than to turn down an invitation from a potential client. Besides, he was limited to walking his horse. It wasn't like they were going to be galloping across the plains.

Carol demurred accompanying them, claiming there was a sweet tea with ice in the kitchen calling her name.

"What kind of mount are you looking for, Kendall?" Harold moved at a slow pace as they crossed the ranch yard. "We have some high-spirited horseflesh in our stable."

"I'm rather fond of a smooth-gaited horse with a tender mouth," she said, thinking fondly of Rebel.

"Soft-handed rider, are you?" Harold chuckled. "I'll tell Andy to saddle Spitfire."

Spitfire?

Kendall felt a tremor of trepidation, one she quelled by telling herself there was only one speed on their ride today—slow.

They entered the smaller of the two barns. Harold barked his instructions to Andy, a young man who saddled their mounts with an efficiency Kendall envied. Soon, they were headed out on their horses, riding, Harold said, through the heart of the C-Bar-C.

"I've got a secret, Kendall." Harold's chuckle rumbled in his chest like a wheezy car engine.

"What's that?" The sun was beating down

on them. Kendall was sweating into her hat brim.

"We're going to defy the doctor's orders and air out our mounts." Before Kendall could make an excuse or protest, the old man gave a shout and heeled his horse into a trot and then a gallop.

Without any urging, Spitfire lurched into action, nearly unseating Kendall in the mare's haste to catch up.

Only she didn't just catch up—the mare galloped past Harold. It was all Kendall could do to hang on.

"Stop!" Harold shouted, and again: "Stop!"

Kendall pulled back on the reins and bounced in the saddle as Spitfire came to a stop. "Is everything okay? Does your foot hurt?"

"What in the world are you doing?" The old man had the fine art of scowling down pat. He lowered his hat brim. "Are you trying to put something over on me. You look like a bobble head on a horse."

Kendall considered making an excuse. But the reality was… "I'm not a good rider. Never have been. My seat has been criticized as dangerous. The fact is that my shock absorbers   "
she pointed at her hips "—aren't in good working order. And honestly, I don't think they ever will be."

Harold's face was a red and his scowl might have been more of a grimace. Kendall was willing to bet that he was going to send her packing.

"And quite frankly, Harold, if you shouldn't be riding, you shouldn't be riding to try and impress me. I'm the last person who's impressed by a cowboy's riding skill." Other than Finn's. Kendall glanced around the ranch, perhaps for the last time. "Now, we can either head back and call it a day. Or we can walk on, and you can tell me more about Gelbvieh. That is, as long as you think your foot can handle it."

"You…" Harold shook a finger at her, scowl breaking into a smile. "You remind me of Carol."

"I take it that's a good thing?" Because she didn't know the Connellys enough to be sure.

"It's a good thing," he said with a nod. "When we get back, she'll want to talk about everything you can do on the internet to help us win Burger by the Layer's business."

"I look forward to that." Along with a glass of ice-cold sweet tea.

"I DON'T UNDERSTAND YOU, Finn." His mother stood in the middle of the kitchen looking as if someone had just told her Christmas had been cancelled. "Where is Ken?"

"She left." Lizzie was coloring at the table, using the back of his medical papers. "I told Daddy to get her back."

"She went to Texas," Finn said, drawing his mother over to the kitchen table to sit down. "And we need to talk about it."

"Texas." His mother sat down slowly. "You shouldn't have told me to disinvite Dawn."

"Mom, we need to talk." Finn tapped Lizzie's artwork. "Hey, love. Can you go find Grandpa Oscar? He should be done exercising the horses, which means he's free to play checkers."

Lizzie gasped and slid out of her seat. "Come on, Peanut. Let's go." And off she went.

Finn waited until she'd slammed the front door behind them. "Mom, I need to talk to you about me and the ranch. We need to conference in Dad."

His mother paled but got his father on speakerphone.

"I wanted both of you to hear the details of my medical plans moving forward." He'd talked in more depth to Dr. Carlisle on the phone earlier in the morning.

Mom began to cry.

"No tears, Mom." Finn held onto her hand. "Families are created in all sorts of ways."

"But you've already been through so much." Mom sniffed.

"You want to sell?" his father said gruffly. It was, after all, his legacy, too.

"I don't," Finn reassured him in a voice just as choked with emotion. "I also don't want to lose Kendall."

"I'm so happy for you." Mom blew her nose and swiped at more tears. "Is there enough money to go to Texas and bring Ken back?"

Finn felt as if the air had been punched out of his body. Finally, he said, "She might not want to come back. We argued and… I was clinging to the wrong ideals. If we hadn't met, I'd never have changed my mind."

"She's my hero, that Ken." Mom sniffed.

Finn stared at his mother, eyebrows raised.

His mother straightened in her chair. "You know, I'm on your side, Finn."

"We're both on your side, son," Dad said through the speaker. "The ranch means something, but so does your happiness."

"Thanks, Dad."

Mom said goodbye to Dad and hung up, looking at Finn for a good long time before she spoke. "How badly did you two part? Is there any way you can patch things up? Ken's a keeper. And I don't say that lightly just to make alliteration."

"I'm not going to sugarcoat it, Mom." He shook his head. "No matter what I say or do, Kendall may never forgive me."

"In that case, it's her loss." Mom gave him a watery smile. "But life on this ranch is hard. And it's trained you to find solutions where others would give up. I have complete and total faith that you'll win her back."

"Good, because I'm going to need it."

CHAPTER TWENTY-FOUR

"WHY DIDN'T YOU BRING BOO WITH YOU?" Bo demanded of Kendall a day after her meeting with the Connellys. He'd picked her up at the airport and they were headed down the last hill into Second Chance.

"I miss her." Along with Rebel and Lizzie. Evie and Peanut. And yes, even Finn.

"You won the account that quickly?" Bo took a hand off the wheel and pointed to her hot pink fringed boots. "Those won't go over well when you get back home to Philadelphia or wherever it is that you're going to be working from." Because she'd told him media managers can work anywhere.

"Not everything in life should be about appearances." Kendall pushed her brother's hand back toward the wheel. "Besides, the boots give me character. They say I've been down the road." To quote Harold. The Connellys had been impressed.

Instead of putting his hand back on the wheel, Bo slapped his palm over his heart.

"Who are you and what have you done with my sister?"

"These bad jokes are why you're still single."

That shut him up.

Kendall almost laughed. Almost, because Bo seemed so serious. "Get out. You have a girlfriend? A steady girlfriend who's stolen your heart after it was so ruthlessly broken?"

There's hope for me yet.

"I didn't say that." Bo grimaced. "But maybe my bachelor days are behind me. Me, the last single Monroe of our generation."

"What? Hello. I'm sitting right here. A Monroe of your generation. And I'm still single."

"You don't count."

Kendall rolled her eyes. "Older brothers are the most annoying thing on the planet. Of course, I count. Ha! You are so lucky you're driving right now. I just saw a slug bug back there and I pretended not to notice." Meaning she'd seen a Volkswagen Beetle, which in childhood-car-trip terms meant she had the right to slug Bo in the arm. Not that she did.

"We haven't played 'slug bug' since we used to travel with Grandpa Harlan in his motorhome."

"Don't think nostalgia will save you." The

Lodgepole Inn came into view at the bottom of the hill. She planned on staying one night, maybe two. But her goal was to return to Philadelphia without seeing Finn again since her detached smile was still on the fritz.

"Nostalgia seems like all I have left." He came to a stop at the bottom of the hill.

It wasn't fair how the Sawtooth Mountains rose up in the distance and reminded her of days on the McAfee Ranch, of heated glances and heart-pumping kisses.

Kendall caught herself. What was in the past was in the past.

"Don't go spreading the word that I'm ready to settle down," Bo said, still not having driven through the town's only intersection. "You never know. I might not be ready for all that." Instead of eyes sparkling with a tease, he looked serious. "I haven't had much practice."

Kendall promised not to divulge his state of mind. And as she did so, she realized that the brothers who had picked on her as a child had grown up and changed in so many ways.

Bo parked in front of the inn and offered to carry her suitcase inside.

Kendall hadn't even shut the door to the inn when Boo pounced on her boots. And she didn't have time to pick her up before a small, warm body slammed into her legs.

"Ken!"

"Lizzie?" Kendall ran her hand through the girl's soft, blond curls. "What are you...?" The question died on her lips.

Finn was standing in the middle of the hotel lobby with a bouquet of flowers in his hand and an apology in his eyes. "Howdy, honey."

His unexpected appearance... His cowboy charm and sincerity... Kendall had the impulse to run into his arms. If only that would solve anything between them.

This was followed by the brief urge to turn around and leave. But there was a kitten clinging to her foot and a kidlet wrapped around her leg. Running would cause some upset. And then she remembered Shane's words about the coyote and staying the course. And then she recalled her grandfather's long-ago advice about forgiveness and not letting pride get in the way when things weren't hunky dory. There was an emotional risk to hearing him out, but how much risk when her heart had already been broken?

"I've been a fool," Finn said in a clear voice, one that carried across the room to her, as well as to their audience. His mother. Mitch, Laurel, Gabby and the twin babies.

And Bo, who'd come in behind Kendall with her suitcase. "This is why you don't count," he told her, proceeding past them all and up the stairs.

Bo knew?

Kendall made a mental note to dish out his slug bug later.

Finn was walking toward her, as mesmerizing now as he'd been nearly a week ago. Broad shoulders. Strong, unique features. Intense blue eyes. And that cowboy swagger.

No one swaggered quite the way Finn did.

Kendall swallowed a sigh. He had yet to prove why he'd been a fool. Until then, she'd hold her head high and keep her silence.

"I shouldn't have been willing to gamble with my health. For any reason." Finn was off to a good start. "I shouldn't have been clinging to only one definition of family." He presented Kendall with the bouquet of red roses. "I shouldn't have imagined a perfect spouse and partner as being a small-town cowgirl. Although…" He glanced toward her feet. "I like your boots."

Kendall drank in the sweet smell of the roses, and the sweet words about her footwear.

"You challenged my thinking. Love doesn't come with requirements. Dreams can and should change as people grow and change."

His words, and the way he was looking at her, with his heart in his eyes, was smoothing over the pain of the last few days. "Did you pass the cowboy test in Texas?"

"I failed the test." Kendall laughed a little. "But I think it was my honesty that won the account."

"And your talent," Finn added. "Your intelligence. Your big heart. Your stick-to-itiveness. I could go on."

"Please do." Kendall hid her blush in the soft fragrant rose petals.

"But the point is…" He grinned at her. "I have family now, I always have," Finn said quickly, gesturing to those assembled, arm sweeping to include the rest of Second Chance. "I just didn't see it."

Lizzie grinned up at Kendall. "We all missed you."

"Even Evie?" Kendall asked, unable to resist.

"Especially Evie," Lizzie said solemnly. "She's been so sad that she's been running Charles out of the misfit pasture."

Kendall bit back a chuckle.

"I have so much to tell you." Finn took Kendall's hand, the one with the healing rope burn on her palm. "Starting with I'm sorry and ending with I think I love you."

That elicited a chorus of gasps and sighs, including from Kendall. She blinked back sudden tears.

"My business is starting to take off." Kendall felt that needed to be said. Her chin came up a bit. "I'm still not ready for children. Not yet, which means—"

"Family will come when we're both ready, princess," Finn said in a voice raspy with emotion. "I've scheduled my follow-up treatment. And the family we make may not look like a traditional one, but it'll be our family."

Oh, he earned points there.

"What do you say?" Finn lifted her hand and kissed her knuckles. "Will you give me… us…a second chance?"

Who knew he had such a romantic streak?
Who knew I'd enjoy romance this much?

"Finn…" Kendall sighed in capitulation. "When our eyes first met, I didn't understand what was happening. It only took days for me to get the picture. The big picture. Which is that I could love you—"

"And me?" Lizzie asked, piping up.

"—and Lizzie—"

"And the misfits?" Lizzie was on a roll.

"—and the misfits…" Kendall checked in with the little girl to see if there were any other additions to her statement. When there weren't, she continued, heart swelling with love. "The big picture is that I could love you and Lizzie and the misfits and your ranch and live happily ever after. That's what I saw in your eyes that first day. And when you kissed me… When you kissed me there was no doubt in my mind that I did love you, all of you. And I would be honored if you'd open your heart to me."

"Done." Finn inched closer, drawing her hand over his heart. "You have my heart. Forever and always."

"Love…" Kendall wound one arm around his neck thinking about everything loving Finn entailed. "That's all I need."

EPILOGUE

LIFE HAD A FUNNY WAY of repeating itself.

Kendall was walking back to the McAfee Ranch after Rebel had taken off toward the barn.

The day was as clear and sunny as it had been three Septembers ago, when Kendall had worked her first day as a ranch hand. She ambled along, the sparse fringe on her worn, hot pink boots sparkling in the sunlight.

"That's probably what spooked the coyote." The one that had surprised Rebel and made her run before she'd had a chance to tie her reins properly to a post.

Thundering hooves approached. Finn was astride a galloping Tucker. Lizzie was behind him, riding a dapple gray with more balance and control on horseback than Kendall would ever have. Peanut trotted behind them, tongue hanging out of his graying muzzle.

Finn threw himself out of the saddle almost before he'd brought Tucker to a sliding stop in front of Kendall. And then his arms were around her, strong and comforting. "Are you all right? What happened? Rebel showed up without you."

"Did you forget to tie her before you started snapping pictures?" Lizzie was seven and still thought she knew everything about the world. Or at least, the McAfee Ranch. She leaned on her saddle horn like the competent cowgirl she was becoming. "You know, when it comes to horses, there's a process." She grinned.

"I didn't have the chance." Kendall explained about the coyote, giving Peanut a reassuring pat.

"Are you all right, love?" Concern rimmed Finn's eyes. His wedding ring caught the sun's rays and glowed the way Kendall glowed whenever she thought about the path their love had taken.

Shortly after their wedding two years ago, they'd begun fostering a three-year-old boy. Michael was still with them, a quiet child with a curiosity that rivaled Lizzie's. Michael filled their hearts, but the family at the ranch had grown in other ways. Julie and Dale had built a small bungalow not far from the original ranch house. Dale had recovered from his stroke enough to watch the kids and ride the horses.

There was still the possibility of expanding their family the more traditional way. Before Finn took his cancer treatments, Dr. Carlisle had connected them with a charity organization that funded sperm banks for male cancer patients. That avenue would be available to them if and when they wanted to pursue it.

"Love?" Finn prompted when Kendall still hadn't answered him.

"I'm fine. I had both feet on the ground when it happened." It felt as if she'd had both feet on the ground since the day she'd met Finn.

"Come on." Finn drew her toward Tucker. "I'll give you a ride back."

"No." She dug in her heels. "I'd rather walk. It's days like today that make me feel grateful for so many things."

"Like dirt and bumblebees?" Lizzie turned her horse around, whistling for Peanut. "Someone dropped a beehive off in the ranch yard. Grandpa Oscar shut all the barn doors and called in the experts." With a mighty whoop, she sent her horse into a gallop.

Peanut chuffed before running after her.

"Who are the experts?" Kendall wondered.

Finn regarded her with a tender gaze. "Beekeepers from Boise. Are you sure you don't want to ride back?"

Kendall placed her palm over his left cheek, over the beard and scars that so dearly defined him as a man who could triumph over adversity. "I'm fine." And she smiled to prove it.

Finn drew her close and kissed her thoroughly. He would have kept on kissing her, except Tucker nudged his arm, impatient to get back home.

Finn slung his arm over Kendall's shoulder, and they set off for the barn with Tucker plodding along behind them.

"Are bees misfits?" Kendall asked. "And can a hive survive an Idaho mountain winter?"

"Anything and anyone dropped off here is welcome, but we'll let the experts decide if the bees stay." He pressed a soft kiss to her temple.

"I bet Laurel would like to sell honey at the mercantile."

"I bet Mack would call first dibs for it in the general store." Finn moved his hand back and forth across her back in a gentle caress. "You've become quite the cowgirl, princess. I've half a mind to buy you a pair of expensive boots for Christmas."

"Don't you dare." Kendall nudged his ribs with her elbow. "Boo and Evie would be upset." Boo was still an indoor cat who couldn't resist dangly, sparkly things. And Evie enjoyed looking at Kendall's boots, mesmerized by their shine. "Besides, if I showed up at the C-Bar-C without them, I think Carol would send out a search party to locate the real me." Carol was her first and largest client. She was now also one of Kendall's closest friends and Burger by the Layer's largest beef supplier. "Do you know what I'd like for Christmas?" Kendall leaned her head on Finn's sturdy shoulder.

"If you say a straightened cupola, I may have to recommend Santa bring you a lump of coal." Finn chuckled, clearly teasing. The cupola had become a symbol of their ranch. It wasn't straight or perfect, and neither were they. "Actually, if we're talking about Christmas presents, the county called. There's a little girl just north of here. About two, they say, and in need of a long-term situation because—"

"We'll take her."

"Love." Finn stopped walking and turned to face her. "We've got Michael and Lizzie, three grandparents, a ranch full of stock and misfits, not to mention you have your business to run and someday we may want to try for our own—"

"We'll take her," Kendall said, louder this time and with a smile. "I'm excited about adding to our family. Ten years from now when our house is full of love and children, we'll look back and marvel on all the ways our family has grown."

Finn took in that smile for a moment or two. And then the corners of his mouth tipped up. "I rather missed that grin of yours."

She raised her nose in the air. "I smile at you all the time."

"That you do." He nodded. "Thankful smiles. Joyful smiles. Loving smiles." He brought his nose close to hers. "But it was the secretly stubborn—"

"Challenging."

"—smile of yours that won my heart." He pressed a quick kiss on her lips. "Are you sure?"

"I am. We have a dining-room table that seats twelve."

"And a kitchen table that can sit four more." He returned his arm to her shoulders and sauntered ahead.

"Don't forget the TV trays in the hall closet."

He chuckled. "There's room for everyone at the McAfee Ranch."

"Forever and always, love. Forever and always."

* * * * *

For more romances in
The Mountain Monroes miniseries from
acclaimed author Melinda Curtis,
visit www.Harlequin.com today!

Get 4 FREE REWARDS!

We'll send you 2 FREE Books plus 2 FREE Mystery Gifts.

FREE
Value Over
$20

Both the **Love Inspired**® and **Love Inspired**® **Suspense** series feature compelling novels filled with inspirational romance, faith, forgiveness, and hope.

YES! Please send me 2 FREE novels from the Love Inspired or Love Inspired Suspense series and my 2 FREE gifts (gifts are worth about $10 retail). After receiving them, if I don't wish to receive any more books, I can return the shipping statement marked "cancel." If I don't cancel, I will receive 6 brand-new Love Inspired Larger-Print books or Love Inspired Suspense Larger-Print books every month and be billed just $5.99 each in the U.S. or $6.24 each in Canada. That is a savings of at least 17% off the cover price. It's quite a bargain! Shipping and handling is just 50¢ per book in the U.S. and $1.25 per book in Canada.* I understand that accepting the 2 free books and gifts places me under no obligation to buy anything. I can always return a shipment and cancel at any time. The free books and gifts are mine to keep no matter what I decide.

Choose one: ☐ **Love Inspired**
Larger-Print
(122/322 IDN GNWC)

☐ **Love Inspired Suspense**
Larger-Print
(107/307 IDN GNWN)

Name (please print)

Address   Apt. #

City   State/Province   Zip/Postal Code

Email: Please check this box ☐ if you would like to receive newsletters and promotional emails from Harlequin Enterprises ULC and its affiliates. You can unsubscribe anytime.

Mail to the Harlequin Reader Service:
IN U.S.A.: P.O. Box 1341, Buffalo, NY 14240-8531
IN CANADA: P.O. Box 603, Fort Erie, Ontario L2A 5X3

Want to try 2 free books from another series? Call 1-800-873-8635 or visit www.ReaderService.com.

*Terms and prices subject to change without notice. Prices do not include sales taxes, which will be charged (if applicable) based on your state or country of residence. Canadian residents will be charged applicable taxes. Offer not valid in Quebec. This offer is limited to one order per household. Books received may not be as shown. Not valid for current subscribers to the Love Inspired or Love Inspired Suspense series. All orders subject to approval. Credit or debit balances in a customer's account(s) may be offset by any other outstanding balance owed by or to the customer. Please allow 4 to 6 weeks for delivery. Offer available while quantities last.

Your Privacy—Your information is being collected by Harlequin Enterprises ULC, operating as Harlequin Reader Service. For a complete summary of the information we collect, how we use this information and to whom it is disclosed, please visit our privacy notice located at corporate.harlequin.com/privacy-notice. From time to time we may also exchange your personal information with reputable third parties. If you wish to opt out of this sharing of your personal information, please visit readerservice.com/consumerschoice or call 1-800-873-8635. **Notice to California Residents**—Under California law, you have specific rights to control and access your data. For more information on these rights and how to exercise them, visit corporate.harlequin.com/california-privacy.

LIRLIS22

Get 4 FREE REWARDS!

We'll send you 2 FREE Books plus 2 FREE Mystery Gifts.

The Charming Checklist
HEATHERLY BELL

A Rancher's Touch
ALLISON LEIGH

The Wrong Cowboy

A Cowgirl's Secret
Melinda Curtis

FREE Value Over **$20**

Both the **Harlequin® Special Edition** and **Harlequin® Heartwarming™** series series feature compelling novels filled with stories of love and strength where the bonds of friendship, family and community unite.

YES! Please send me 2 FREE novels from the Harlequin Special Edition or Harlequin Heartwarming series and my 2 FREE gifts (gifts are worth about $10 retail). After receiving them, if I don't wish to receive any more books, I can return the shipping statement marked "cancel." If I don't cancel, I will receive 6 brand-new Harlequin Special Edition books every month and be billed just $4.99 each in the U.S or $5.74 each in Canada, a savings of at least 17% off the cover price or 4 brand-new Harlequin Heartwarming Larger-Print books every month and be billed just $5.74 each in the U.S. or $6.24 each in Canada, a savings of at least 21% off the cover price. It's quite a bargain! Shipping and handling is just 50¢ per book in the U.S. and $1.25 per book in Canada.* I understand that accepting the 2 free books and gifts places me under no obligation to buy anything. I can always return a shipment and cancel at any time. The free books and gifts are mine to keep no matter what I decide.

Choose one: ☐ **Harlequin Special Edition**
(235/335 HDN GNMP)
☐ **Harlequin Heartwarming Larger-Print**
(161/361 HDN GNPZ)

Name (please print)

Address   Apt. #

City   State/Province   Zip/Postal Code

Email: Please check this box ☐ if you would like to receive newsletters and promotional emails from Harlequin Enterprises ULC and its affiliates. You can unsubscribe anytime.

Mail to the **Harlequin Reader Service:**
IN U.S.A.: P.O. Box 1341, Buffalo, NY 14240-8531
IN CANADA: P.O. Box 603, Fort Erie, Ontario L2A 5X3

Want to try 2 free books from another series! Call 1-800-873-8635 or visit www.ReaderService.com.

*Terms and prices subject to change without notice. Prices do not include sales taxes, which will be charged (if applicable) based on your state or country of residence. Canadian residents will be charged applicable taxes. Offer not valid in Quebec. This offer is limited to one order per household. Books received may not be as shown. Not valid for current subscribers to the Harlequin Special Edition or Harlequin Heartwarming series. All orders subject to approval. Credit or debit balances in a customer's account(s) may be offset by any other outstanding balance owed by or to the customer. Please allow 4 to 6 weeks for delivery. Offer available while quantities last.

Your Privacy—Your information is being collected by Harlequin Enterprises ULC, operating as Harlequin Reader Service. For a complete summary of the information we collect, how we use this information and to whom it is disclosed, please visit our privacy notice located at corporate.harlequin.com/privacy-notice. From time to time we may also exchange your personal information with reputable third parties. If you wish to opt out of this sharing of your personal information, please visit readerservice.com/consumerschoice or call 1-800-873-8635. **Notice to California Residents**—Under California law, you have specific rights to control and access your data. For more information on these rights and how to exercise them, visit corporate.harlequin.com/california-privacy.

HSEHW22

COUNTRY LEGACY COLLECTION

19 FREE BOOKS IN ALL!

EMMETT
Diana Palmer

COURTED BY THE COWBOY

THE RANCHER AND THE BABY

Cowboys, adventure and romance await you in this new collection! Enjoy superb reading all year long with books by bestselling authors like Diana Palmer, Sasha Summers and Marie Ferrarella!

YES! Please send me the **Country Legacy Collection**! This collection begins with 3 FREE books and 2 FREE gifts in the first shipment. Along with my 3 free books, I'll also get 3 more books from the **Country Legacy Collection**, which I may either return and owe nothing or keep for the low price of $24.60 U.S./$28.12 CDN each plus $2.99 U.S./$7.49 CDN for shipping and handling per shipment*. If I decide to continue, about once a month for 8 months, I will get 6 or 7 more books but will only pay for 4. That means 2 or 3 books in every shipment will be FREE! If I decide to keep the entire collection, I'll have paid for only 32 books because 19 are FREE! I understand that accepting the 3 free books and gifts places me under no obligation to buy anything. I can always return a shipment and cancel at any time. My free books and gifts are mine to keep no matter what I decide.

☐ 275 HCK 1939   ☐ 475 HCK 1939

Name (please print)

Address   Apt. #

City   State/Province   Zip/Postal Code

Mail to the **Harlequin Reader Service:**
IN U.S.A.: P.O. Box 1341, Buffalo, NY 14240-8571
IN CANADA: P.O. Box 603, Fort Erie, Ontario L2A 5X3

*Terms and prices subject to change without notice. Prices do not include sales taxes, which will be charged (if applicable) based on your state or country of residence. Canadian residents will be charged applicable taxes. Offer not valid in Quebec. All orders subject to approval. Credit or debit balances in a customer's account(s) may be offset by any other outstanding balance owed by or to the customer. Please allow 3 to 4 weeks for delivery. Offer available while quantities last. © 2021 Harlequin Enterprises ULC. ® and ™ are trademarks owned by Harlequin Enterprises ULC.

Your Privacy—Your information is being collected by Harlequin Enterprises ULC, operating as Harlequin Reader Service. To see how we collect and use this information visit https://corporate.harlequin.com/privacy-notice. From time to time we may also exchange your personal information with reputable third parties. If you wish to opt out of this sharing of your personal information, please visit www.readerservice.com/consumerchoice or call 1-800-873-8635. Notice to California Residents—Under California law, you have specific rights to control and access your data. For more information visit https://corporate.harlequin.com/california-privacy.

50BOOKCL22

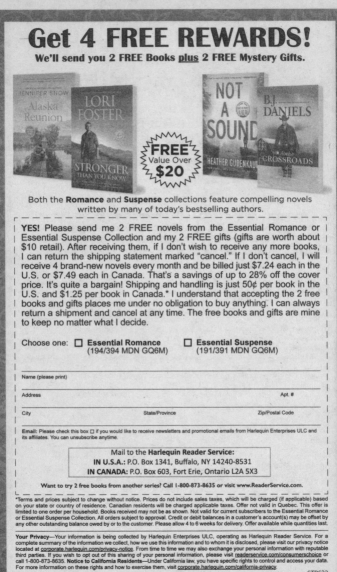

Get 4 FREE REWARDS!

We'll send you 2 FREE Books plus 2 FREE Mystery Gifts.

FREE Value Over $20

Both the **Romance** and **Suspense** collections feature compelling novels written by many of today's bestselling authors.

YES! Please send me 2 FREE novels from the Essential Romance or Essential Suspense Collection and my 2 FREE gifts (gifts are worth about $10 retail). After receiving them, if I don't wish to receive any more books, I can return the shipping statement marked "cancel." If I don't cancel, I will receive 4 brand-new novels every month and be billed just $7.24 each in the U.S. or $7.49 each in Canada. That's a savings of up to 28% off the cover price. It's quite a bargain! Shipping and handling is just 50¢ per book in the U.S. and $1.25 per book in Canada.* I understand that accepting the 2 free books and gifts places me under no obligation to buy anything. I can always return a shipment and cancel at any time. The free books and gifts are mine to keep no matter what I decide.

Choose one: ☐ **Essential Romance**
(194/394 MDN GQ6M)

☐ **Essential Suspense**
(191/391 MDN GQ6M)

Name (please print)

Address   Apt. #

City   State/Province   Zip/Postal Code

Email: Please check this box ☐ if you would like to receive newsletters and promotional emails from Harlequin Enterprises ULC and its affiliates. You can unsubscribe anytime.

Mail to the Harlequin Reader Service:
IN U.S.A.: P.O. Box 1341, Buffalo, NY 14240-8531
IN CANADA: P.O. Box 603, Fort Erie, Ontario L2A 5X3

Want to try 2 free books from another series! Call 1-800-873-8635 or visit www.ReaderService.com.

*Terms and prices subject to change without notice. Prices do not include sales taxes, which will be charged (if applicable) based on your state or country of residence. Canadian residents will be charged applicable taxes. Offer not valid in Quebec. This offer is limited to one order per household. Books received may not be as shown. Not valid for current subscribers to the Essential Romance or Essential Suspense Collection. All orders subject to approval. Credit or debit balances in a customer's account(s) may be offset by any other outstanding balance owed by or to the customer. Please allow 4 to 6 weeks for delivery. Offer available while quantities last.

Your Privacy—Your information is being collected by Harlequin Enterprises ULC, operating as Harlequin Reader Service. For a complete summary of the information we collect, how we use this information and to whom it is disclosed, please visit our privacy notice located at corporate.harlequin.com/privacy-notice. From time to time we may also exchange your personal information with reputable third parties. If you wish to opt out of this sharing of your personal information, please visit readerservice.com/consumerschoice or call 1-800-873-8635. **Notice to California Residents**—Under California law, you have specific rights to control and access your data. For more information on these rights and how to exercise them, visit corporate.harlequin.com/california-privacy.

STRS22